THE LAND

BOOK ONE

THE LAND

BOOK ONE

Come away, O human child

James A Lloyd

Matador
Unit E2 Airfield Business Park
Harrison Road, Market Harborough
Leicestershire LE16 7UL
Tel: 0116 279 2299
Email: books@troubador.co.uk
Web: www.troubador.co.uk/matador
Twitter: @matadorbooks

ISBN 978 1 80514 070 2

British Library Cataloguing in Publication Data.
A catalogue record for this book is available from the British Library.

Printed and bound in Great Britain by 4edge Limited
Typeset in 11pt Baskerville by Troubador Publishing Ltd, Leicester, UK

Matador is an imprint of Troubador Publishing Ltd

For Vikki, Emma, Sian and Kate.

Prologue

Tall cliffs hugged the parched Great Bay, reflecting the intense heat rising from the sun-baked seabed. Far in the distance, stretching from headland to headland, a long, high wall of hard sand denied entrance to the glittering ocean. Gull, soaring on the roasting thermals, skirted the huge, desolate sandcastle, its turrets challenging the dominance of the cliffs. Shortly after, he glided towards the half-buried wrecks of the little fleet, his keen eyes drawn to rags flapping weakly on a rack of bleached, short timber ribs. Impaled on one of the sharp spars was a rapidly desiccating child's body, lifeless eyes staring from its sad, shrunken face, torn nightdress fluttering around its contorted torso. Dark tracks betrayed the passage of fluids down the cruel timber. Nearby, other small corpses hung: shrivelled, ghoulish puppets. Little heaps of bleached bones between the spars were all that remained of less recent victims.

Gull's undulating cry paid its respects as he wheeled away, knowing that with each small sacrifice, the wall pushed the ocean away and the demise of the nesting colonies continued.

1

Maia, a tiny, barely discernible figure sitting high in a large tree facing the threshold, took multiple universes for granted. Throughout her long life she had come to this spot in the Great Forest, at this exact time each year. She sat waiting, drawn by instinct. Her mother had kept the same vigil long before villages, towns and cities replaced the forests that once covered the other land she would see through the portal.

Just before midnight, it shimmered into life and the field appeared, as it had in one form or another each midsummer's night over the hundreds of years she had briefly observed it. As she gazed at the familiar scene, remembering how it had slowly changed, a shadow flitted through the trees below her, swiftly passing into the other land and out of view. Although this disturbed her, her natural curiosity was suppressed by the compulsion to continue watching the field. A little later, she was disturbed again as the shadow crossed back, barely a blur, but with a natural ability to function at great speed she saw that it now carried something it hadn't taken through. Filing this away to tell the Great One, she returned to her lonely vigil. The portal wouldn't stay open long; it never did, little more than an hour, and she always stayed until the last glimmer of the other land faded…

*

Anja woke, rubbed her sore eyes and looked blearily around. She'd fallen asleep awkwardly, sprawled across the sofa. A slither of moonlight sliced her throat; another, wider, highlighted toys and cushions jumbled about the silent room. She was still wearing her thin summer dress. Beside her, Alfie was huddled on the floor near the empty fireplace, his face pressed into the thin pile of the carpet, soft features hardened in the grey light. Anxiety forced a sigh from her and she squeezed her eyes, trying to focus, remember what had happened. Immediately, this switched to concern for Toby; her younger brother, barely two. Before their parents had gone out, he'd been changed into pyjamas. She should have put a night nappy on him long ago. He was mischievous and inquisitive. A glance around the room failed to detect him.

Her eyes and brain began to function. The clock on the mantelpiece told her it was just past midnight. When had she fallen asleep? She couldn't remember what they'd been doing, only that it had been such fun, but that must have been hours ago. Her parents had reluctantly gone to the midsummer dance, giving her strict instructions. Easing her cramped body over to the open window, she

2

could just hear dull music and laughter coming from the village hall down the lane. She still had time. As she shook her brother roughly with her foot, his unfocused eyes looked up at her for an age before he sat up and yawned.

'Where's Toby?'

Alfie shrugged.

They began to search. She desperately needed them all in bed before their parents returned. When the most obvious places had been checked, her heart began to flutter. After every room, cupboard and cranny had been searched, they stopped. Alfie, barely eight, showed concern on his serious little face. Anja, four years older, was frantic with worry. She couldn't remember falling asleep, or exactly when she'd last seen Toby. The novelty of being left alone for the evening and the time passing so quickly had somehow made her forget the promises she had so solemnly given; the game had been such fun. Now, the enormity of her predicament was overwhelming.

Chewing her lip, she stared hopelessly out of the window. Her gaze sharpened and she gasped. In the strong moonlight, she could see that the gate was open; the garden gate that was never left open. Running into the hall, she knew even before she got there that the front door would also be open. How had they missed it?

'No, no, he's gone out,' she shouted, and went running up the path with Alfie close behind her. She knew instinctively where Toby would have gone, they both knew; to the field beside the wood, their favourite place to play. He'd gone there with them only that morning, running on ahead in his funny toddler gait, sure of the way. Turning

3

left through the open gate, they ran on up the stony lane. In her panic, she didn't notice that the distant music had stopped. Just a few faint voices exchanging goodbyes reached the house staring mutely after them, its door gaping wide.

They raced past a small row of cottages on their right, disturbing young Constable Hemmersley reading late in his room with the slip, slap of their bare feet on the narrow pavement, loud in the still, warm night. Reaching the vicarage, the old church clock sped them on as it struck the first half-hour of morning. They turned left around the graveyard wall, crossed the ditch and continued up the footpath between the cemetery and the fallow field.

Hardly pausing for breath, they reached the corner of the small ancient wood that nestled against the back of the churchyard. Here, the path angled right, weaving briefly between the gnarled trunks of the old trees before emerging into the grassy, flowered pasture where they idled their summer days away. They expected to find him there, highlighted in the short shadows of the moon, crouched over an interesting stone or twig, absorbed in some unfathomable game, to run up, hug and kiss him, hear his little voice and happy laughter.

As they emerged, there was nothing; not a blade of grass stirred, not a breath of air broke the silence. Calling out, their small voices were swallowed by the little wood at the edge of the field. He wasn't there. Anja flapped her arms; she'd been so sure he would be that her mind reeled with shock. Grabbing Alfie's hand, she turned back. He was still in the house. She couldn't remember shutting the door. Was there somewhere obvious they hadn't looked? This was beyond anything she had ever experienced, and her ability to cope shattered. Her parents must have returned by now. She was in so much trouble; they had to go back.

Nearby, the church clock struck the last quarter of the first hour, urging them back to the narrow path through the wood. Above, the moon shimmered and paled as the first wisps of cloud passed over it. As the moonlight faded, the trees closed their leafy canopy over the woodland floor and the path became indistinct. Sharp brambles that shouldn't have been there tore at the children's legs, and hard tree roots tripped them up.

Dragging Alfie with her, Anja blundered on, knowing they must be heading in the right direction, that the wood was small and they'd soon be through it. On they went, tripping and falling in the tangled undergrowth. They began to push through bushy thickets, retracing their steps when they could go no further. At last, in the sanctuary of a small clearing, Anja stopped. Alfie peered up at her through the gloom. 'Are we lost, Anja?' She nodded, tears trickling down her cheeks.

The little oak wood was just not this big; they'd often explored its entire area. It was old and wild, but they couldn't get lost in it, even in the dark. She realised how long they'd been running through it and that they should have heard the church clock strike again; the clock that always called them home. Trying not to show him she was crying, wracked with anguish deeper than she'd ever known in her short life, she choked back a sob and sank down to the soft, leafy ground. Alfie put his arms around her neck to console her. The enormity of her predicament was too great for him to understand, but she was the centre of his life and he loved her so much. The Land, the sentient entity into which they had blundered, felt their presence, examined Anja's mind and intervened. Consciousness faded.

Long before the brown-clad monks and their grim lords had arrived and built a small church nearby, the beautiful little oak grove on the outskirts of the wild forest had been venerated. They hadn't questioned, in their arrogant piety, the knowing smiles on the faces of the peaceful, compliant peasants they'd inherited. Nor did they wonder why they couldn't bring themselves to cut down the ancient trees. Generations worshipped in the small church, and although the rest of the forest shrank, no one laid an axe to the little wood. There was always a reason to leave it undisturbed. Locked within was the small portal, the gateway to the Land's Great Forest.

The Great Forest encompassed innumerable hills and valleys, ran with the melodies of myriad rivers and streams that fed spectacular waterfalls and boomed in hidden galleries beneath deep, gnarled roots. It soared to towering heights where the sun warmed its topmost leaves and plunged to gloomy depths where stars were but a pale rumour, sagely passed from elder to kit. Anything unusual disturbing the forest's harmony spread ripples of tension, at first locally, then wider depending on the strength of the disturbance.

From Anja and Alfie there radiated such a strangeness

and vulnerability that this vast forest held its breath. Napes bristled, ears sharpened, and eyes narrowed. Slumbering forms became restless and whined, trembling and wary as the Land responded to their arrival, disturbing the dreams of its servant, the Great One; Lord of the Forest. Instantly, his eyes snapped open and he was aware, extracting from the warm night the whole wordless story. Something had strayed into his realm, something he must protect. He rose and sprang away towards the children. The Great Forest relaxed and sighed, continuing its eternal life.

In the bite of the morning, as the sun rose slowly through the forest, mist carpeted the glade. Although it lay gently around and over the children, its warm, damp breath was not what woke Anja; a light quilt of dry leaves and moss covered them as they snuggled together. What woke her was the music; liquid notes to soothe fretful dreams, softly rousing her reluctant mind. She tried to remember, but the music wove patterns that drew apart the strands of her memory and compelled her to move. Desire overwhelming her, she crawled free of the warm blanket, rising through the thin mist to answer the beguiling call, leaves and tendrils of moss still clinging to her hair. She began a slow, graceful dance. Smiling, radiant and beautiful, she lost herself to the forest rhapsody.

Alfie stirred. The sun had risen sufficiently to evaporate the last wisps of mist. He screwed his eyes against the light that speared through the tracery of a leaf. A piece of moss tickled his nose; he snorted and heard the music. Struggling to sit up, he rubbed his eyes and saw his sister. He felt no desire to copy her example, and watched. He'd

7

never seen her so graceful, but then she'd never danced like this before. He loved her. She was his big sister, his constant friend and mentor. Where she led, he followed. She bossed him around and he mostly accepted it with explicit trust. Now he was confused and, remembering what had happened, wondered why Anja was behaving so strangely. It unsettled and upset him.

He gasped with astonishment as his attention was caught by a movement at the edge of his vision. He had found the source of the music: a large creature sitting on a rock nestling amongst a few low bushes. Alfie instantly felt afraid and hostile, not sensing malice but because it was causing his sister's strange behaviour. He studied it, his brows beetled, small mouth set with resentment.

It was larger than a man, even his father, who was tall and strong, and in part resembled one, with deep, golden brown skin glistening with a faint oily sheen. Its body swayed imperceptibly to the rhythm of the music; naked, broad-shouldered torso ripping with muscle. Alfie's keen sight examined every detail of its face: a small wispy beard, broad turned-up nose and arching eyebrows that gave it a sardonic expression. However, the similarity ended abruptly when he saw the two small twisting horns growing from the tight, curly hairline each side of its forehead. The difference became even more marked where, from the creature's hips and groin, a thick pelt of russet fur grew down massive thighs to reveal slender goat-like legs and neat pointed hooves, softly ringing out the beat of the music against the rock. Alfie's eyes were drawn back to the face, to full lips darting across a row of small bound pipes,

8

scarcely drawing breath. His resentment turned to blazing anger when he saw its eyes; pupils dancing with the music, mirroring every ecstatic movement his sister made.

He rose, crossed the glade to where it sat, and stood in front of it, glaring indignantly. The creature ignored him. Clenching his small fists, he drew in a deep breath and shouted, 'Stop doing that!' The creature stopped playing and looked down. Anja panted up and stood beside him, her eyes unfocused. Fear, anger, confusion were overshadowed by awe of the impossible creature staring down at them, exuding power and intelligence.

2

Maia's ears sharpened; voices, children's voices. A girl and a younger boy came into view and began running around the field, shouting urgently. She watched with unemotional detachment as they became more upset and was mildly astonished when they ran into the portal, passing below her into the Land. Unmoved, she kept her watch, ignoring their agitated voices as they blundered deeper into the Great Forest. She sighed; soon the portal would close, and she would resume her role in the Land until drawn back to relive her brief vigil next year, but it was another incident to tell the Great One.

Just as the children's voices faded, she heard another that made her senses sharpen with an intensity that she'd never experienced before. Another human, a young man, entered the field. She rose from the branch, her translucent wings carrying her gently to the ground, and began to walk towards the portal, unaware of her actions. A small, latent part of her essence had awakened and she was intuitively following its direction.

The young man came closer. 'Anja! Alfie! It's Constable Hemmersley. I know you're here somewhere. You're not in any trouble, but it's a bit late for playing.'

As Maia crossed the threshold of the portal and began to grow, the flimsy scrap of material she was wearing tore and dropped away as she slowly drifted towards the man, her feet skimming the cool grass. He watched her, unable to tear his eyes from the beautiful, small figure gliding towards him. She stopped just a few feet away, her face level with his chest. He stuttered something about her lack of clothing, but Maia was incapable of coherent thought, let alone speech. Drawing in a long, deep breath, after a pause, she opened her mouth. A thick, milky film stretched across her lips. She released the breath and the film bulged, expanding into a large shimmering bubble that detached with a slight wobble. She gently blew it towards him. He watched, mesmerised, as it approached, and involuntarily drew in a sharp breath as it reached his lips and burst.

Maia awoke the following morning back in the Great Forest in a leafy nest near the top of a tall tree, overlooking a small pond far below. She was back to her normal size. Next to her, gently snoring, was the young man, also tiny and naked. He was strong, virile; their coupling in the field had been successful, her body already signalling that she should go to the nursery to prepare. He stirred and she gently kissed him, lulling him back to sleep. One of the Great Ones was summoning her, which was timely; she needed to tell them that she would be away for a short time. Glancing again at the young man, she wrinkled her nose, wondering why she'd brought him back to the Land. It was unfortunate, but the call was urgent. He'd have to fend for himself. Likely he wouldn't survive. Lifting from the branch, she sped away, a blur of shimmering wings.

Rob eventually woke but, refusing to acknowledge he had, didn't open his eyes until blissful contentment was disturbed by a persistent roaring that swelled and ebbed around him. Strong rays pierced the great leaves, intermittently blinding him as he tried to guess the cause of the noise. When a huge bee, almost half his size, rose into sight a few yards away, he leapt to his feet in confused panic, ran along the branch, realised how high above the ground he was, stumbled, lost his footing and fell.

He plummeted, but his eyes denied this and told him he was only drifting past huge clumps of leaves. Seeing one coming up at him, he realised it was unavoidable and braced himself for the fatal impact. Instead, he landed lightly, tried to stay on but, finding no purchase for his fingers, slowly slid off, continuing his fall until he met the next leaf. This repeated itself, supporting the belief that he must be dreaming, until there were no more leaves and he tumbled through the air, splashing gently into the pond. Barely submerged, he easily swam to the edge on top of the still water. After some difficulty clambering up a steep, wet bank, huge vegetation providing slippery handholds, he collapsed on his back and peered through large blades of grass at the gigantic scenery surrounding him…

*

'**Y**ou danced beautifully,' the man-like being said, his face displaying no emotion to accompany the compliment.

Anja blushed. She was beginning to recover her composure and glanced up at him for the first time.

'My name is Pan,' he announced.

If he'd expected some sort of reaction, he didn't show any disappointment at the lack of it, although Anja realised she was now staring at his hooves and quickly looked back to his face.

'My name's Anja,' she whispered. 'This is my brother Alfie. We've another little brother, Toby. We were looking for him. Am I dreaming?' With this, she stopped, the events of the previous night gnawing back into her memory.

Pan was shaking his head.

She swallowed and stammered on. 'T-T-Toby disappeared last night. We came looking for him but got lost as we crossed the little wood by the churchyard.' She looked around in confusion. 'This isn't the little wood, though, is it?' Her voice was tight with concern, and scarcely audible. Pan slowly shook his head again.

'Have *you* seen him?' Alfie asked, suspicion narrowing his eyes. He then added accusingly, 'I've seen something like you in a book.'

'I've been sitting here since the small hours wondering about you and what happened to bring you here. You must have been drawn here, and so it follows that this brother of yours must also be here, somewhere.' Pan seemed content with this assumption.

Anja was desperately trying to keep up with a situation

13

way beyond her comprehension. She tried to pull herself together, collect her thoughts and reason sensibly. But in the back of her mind, always threatening to swamp her ability to do this, were the warnings and lectures that pleaded with her to grab Alfie and run as fast as their legs could carry them. But where to? Where were they? What was happening? Fear clenched, and then threatened to liquefy her stomach. She blanched. Looking directly into Pan's eyes, and breathing slowly and deeply, she asked in a voice as normal as she could manage, 'Well, could you help us find him, so that we can take him home?' Her voice began to quaver. 'We've been gone all night and Mummy and Daddy will be worried out of…' Her voice trailed off. She couldn't ignore the slow, serious way he continued shaking his head. Darkness began to grow at the edge of her vision; her breathing became shallow and laboured. Words that echoed around her head died in her throat and her legs began to buckle. As Anja's voice failed, Alfie saw her face turning a sickly grey and realised that something was very wrong. He called her name and wrapped his arms around her waist to support her.

Pan slid from the rock, caught her, then gently placed her on the thick grass. A small flask appeared in his hands which he unstopped. Supporting her head, he brushed a few drops against her lips and within seconds, Anja's eyes fluttered, opened and then slowly focused. His face still showed little concern as she weakly sat up, colour blotchily returning to her face, too shocked even to cry. He had to help her; the Land had sent him to do so. He also remembered how gracefully she danced. He would

14

protect them, but first he had to gain her trust. Folding his strange legs beneath him, he sat down, held Anja's hand and spoke quietly.

'I didn't take your brother, Anja, nor did I bring you here. However, this is my domain, and what happens within it *is* my concern. Since you're here, I must consider your protection. If I could send you back, I would, but I can't,' he lied.

As Pan gauged Anja's reaction, Alfie turned to her. 'We're really in trouble now, aren't we, Anja?' She sniffed glumly and nodded.

Pan sighed; they had at least begun to accept the situation as it was. 'I'll find out what has happened to your brother and why. Meanwhile, you shall stay with me.'

'No! No, we can't,' Anja said sharply. 'What about Mummy and Daddy? We should go home and get Daddy.'

Pan realised it was still going to be difficult. He squeezed her hand gently. 'I know it's hard to understand, but you're now a long way from your home. This is not your world. What's happened has happened, I can't change it, but it's now my duty to ensure that no harm comes to either of you. I can only help you as things are now, you must understand that. I can't leave you here alone, you will both die. Who else can help you?'

He was telling them a version of the truth. He didn't himself understand the issues involved, but he needed to take control from the girl. The resigned way she shrugged convinced him he'd said enough. They had some way to travel and it was time to move. 'Come on, we'll go to a place where you'll be comfortable and safe, then I'll find out what has happened and what can be done.' With no other course of action left open to her, Anja reluctantly nodded.

The Land was pleased; Pan had done well. It delved subtly into the essence of the girl's mind and began to introduce imperceptible changes.

As they found themselves led deeper into the forest by their strange companion, Anja burned with guilt but found it difficult to dislike or mistrust him. He was all she had. Alfie held her hand, often looking up at her for encouragement, but she steadfastly looked ahead, avoiding his eyes.

She was a little taller than average for her age, with dark shoulder-length hair framing a pretty face, large perceptive eyes and a mouth usually quick to smile but now set with worry. She brushed a strand of hair back from her eyes. Like her brother's, her skin had an olive complexion glowing with health. They were both naturally athletic, although Alfie had a careless clumsiness that caused her endless amusement. The only thing that he feared from her was her wit; she never failed to detect the slightest weaknesses, and one gentle, barbed comment could cut him to the quick. Her teasing could be protracted and funny, but never cruel. He loved her unconditionally and knew that she felt the same for him. They both adored Toby.

Their surroundings were so vibrant and magical that Anja found it difficult to dwell on her problems, which seemed to fade as she walked through the scented air past wonderfully blossomed bushes and trees. Now and again, familiar woodland creatures peeped out, ran across the paths ahead or chattered noisily at them as they passed. Who could resist such wonder?

Alfie was content to let Anja worry about whether they were doing the right thing, and although she seemed to be a bit better, he still kept close and watched her carefully. Thicker woodland gave way to tall, musty trees, but Alfie's mood didn't lighten towards Pan. He didn't share his sister's apparent trust in him.

The cool shade of the large trees was very welcome. The sun, directly above, had baked their tender necks as it filtered through the birches and azalea groves they'd left behind. Sweat streaked their dirty faces, and as the afternoon set in, a growing weariness dulled their senses. Their legs began tiring as they plodded up and down the forested hills. Pan allowed them brief rests but generally urged them on. As the trees grew increasingly massive and the deep loam became softer beneath their bare feet, the sun, shafting its way through the lofty foliage, dappled the forest with swathes of light that creased their eyes as they passed through them.

By the middle of the afternoon, the ground had gradually begun to slope steadily downwards, deep rivulets bisecting the path, slowing their pace as they negotiated them. The route became more defined as they followed one of the larger streams; the path steepened and the water began to gurgle and leap as it descended beside them. Ferns and waterside foliage tangled open roots, and moisture seeped from everything they passed and touched, dampening their clothes. Lower and lower they descended beside the cascading stream, each step becoming slipperier and more torturous.

Pan led the way, a few yards ahead of Anja, who nimbly kept herself upright. Alfie lagged further behind, looking decidedly bedraggled and using every bad word his vocabulary possessed to accompany his increasingly uncontrolled descent. After one unexpected, painful slip and stubbed toe, his fortitude finally ran out. He sat in a muddy puddle, glowering and rubbing his aching ankles, making no effort to continue. Pan ambled back and sat beside him.

'There's just a bit more of this and then the path becomes easier. We'll be there before the sun goes down.'

Alfie didn't even make the effort to reply. He blew out a long breath of indignation, hauled himself up and half scrambled, half fell to the bottom of the treacherous slope where Anja was waiting. He'd asked for no help, nor would he have accepted any had it been offered. Pan snorted as he followed the stubborn boy down. Anja thought that her brother looked so fed up and sweet that she gave him a kiss, which he brushed off in embarrassment but secretly loved. He stomped off, feeling a bit better.

The stream joined a large brook which they followed along a trail of round river- worn stones. Wet and uneven, the path was no longer steep but often merged with the water as it tumbled deeply between boulders. Pan helped each of them in turn to clamber over the slippery rocks, leaping nimbly over any obstacle, more animal than man. As the light waned, the water began to deepen and churn, crashing through the rocks.

Pan now kept a close eye on the children, and even Alfie reluctantly clasped his hand. Rocky banks rose either side as the surging river threatened to wash them off the slim ledge they stumbled along. Narrower and narrower, the small gorge squeezed the ledge and gushing water until a veil of mist obliterated any way forward. It now roared and crashed chaotically beyond the barrier created by the misty spray, the slender ledge disappearing into this unwelcoming cleft.

'Stay here,' Pan mouthed to Anja and, before she could reply, he plunged into the tumult with Alfie. Soaked by the spray, she flattened herself away from the water in terror. After a few seconds that seemed like an age, he reappeared, dripping from head to hoof. Before she could ask where Alfie was, his hand closed around her wrist and her scream was smothered by the wet fury they entered. The cold, hammering water swirling around her thighs threatened to sweep her from her feet. She gasped for air as the spray filled her mouth until, when she thought that she could take no more, he pulled her out of the spume into the beauty of a stunning sunset.

Anja stepped back against Pan, her heart racing, the wet, musky smell of his fur strangely comforting as she took in the panorama from the frighteningly exposed position where they'd emerged. The stream they had followed, constantly fed and swollen by a legion of small tributaries, gouged through the narrow defile to emerge as a sparkling waterfall that cascaded down a tall cliff face.

From their dizzying, narrow vantage point beside it, a beautiful valley spread before them. Immediately below, a deep, clear basin collected the water plunging through the air in a rainbow of sunset colours. This opened into a large pool which fed a narrow river meandering its way through lush, grassy banks that climbed to endless swathes of forest either side. Pan let them gaze at the enchanting scene for a moment before drawing their attention to an area of grass that snuggled between the pool and a thick canopy of oaks flanking the steep right-hand side of the valley. 'Our camp is down there,' he said.

After she'd recovered from the enchantment of the valley, and relieved that they had reached their destination, Anja's concern grew at how they were going to climb down. Heights bothered her and she kept well back from the edge, scolding Alfie for not being so wary. Pan walked to the side of the ledge away from the gushing water, gesturing them to follow. Alfie did, and Anja gingerly made her way after them. From there, a steep, narrow path descended towards the trees below.

Her head and shaking legs held her back, but with Alfie already jumping down from rock to rock, she had little choice. Luckily, an abundance of hardy trees and shrubs growing out of the steep rocks supplied enough handholds to provide an illusion of safety. As they neared the bottom and came level with the top of the oak trees, the path cut back across the gradient to bring them down to a narrow strip of verdant grass between the trees and the pool, permanently dampened by mist from the waterfall. Further around, it widened to a broad lawn between the grove and where the pool fed the river.

Pan let them flop down onto the warm grass beside

the pool, which was a lot larger than it looked from the heights above. He walked with his peculiar gait into the oak grove. The trees had grown in a bizarre fashion; broad-trunked, no branches grew near the ground but were densely intertwined higher up to form an impenetrable canopy over the whole area. Within this great bower, roughly hewn furniture was randomly placed between the shadowed trunks. Deeper within, recessed against rocks in the valley wall and just visible between the trunks, a flickering fire was crackling into life, revealing the black outline of a large cauldron. Smoke curled and wound its way up through trees, rocks and vegetation. Only the most sensitive nose would have detected its presence on the ridge far above. Over the cauldron, highlighted by the glowing fire, Pan, a saturnine shadow-box figure, bent, busily attending to it. Neither of the children saw this; both were lying exhausted on the grass, hands behind their heads, recovering from the trek as their thin clothes dried on them in the warm evening sun.

When Pan eventually emerged from the trees, his face, whilst certainly saturnine, radiated only strength; an air of devilment could be detected, but not deviltry. He seemed more relaxed and friendly, trying to carry three large wooden bowls, one balanced precariously on the others. Each halting step he took threatened to spill the steaming contents of one or other of them, but he managed to reach the children without serious mishap. Handing them a bowl each, he began to drink the contents of his own. It was a broth, thick with wild vegetables and aromatic herbs. As he emptied his, the delicious aroma and their own hunger incited them to follow his example. They sipped greedily. Soon, two tired pairs of eyes tentatively signalled that if more was available, it wouldn't be wasted.

Their first day in the Land coming to a close, Pan led them into the bower where he prepared a place for them to sleep. Then, after explaining a few domestic niceties that left Anja cringing but grateful, he went back out and sat beside the pool. Glancing into the bower, his fingers ran across the pipes, but he decided not to lift them to his lips that evening. A tiny niggle momentarily distracted him; something close to where he'd found the children, near the portal. Probably some creatures upset with what had occurred. It could wait.

*

Rob hit his forehead repeatedly with his hand. What was the last thing he remembered? He was losing his mind. Something on the edge of his memory… something? Yes, children, he had been following those children. They'd brought him to this nightmare. Was he even awake? What was that behind him?

The Land watched. This one was strong; insanity would make him stronger. He would be ready when the time came. His meeting Maia had been fortuitous.

3

The next morning, Pan showed the children around the valley and said it was safe to explore the surrounding forest, but that the small river flowed faster than it looked. He explained that they were within the western part of the Great Forest, less than a day's walk from its southern border with the North Downs, that to the north and north-east, the Great Forest rose slowly and spread for hundreds of miles until it reached the huge grass pastures that led to the feet of the northern mountain ranges, and that lower to the east, it bordered the rapids down which the Great River descended through a mighty canyon on its journey to the ocean, almost a thousand miles to the south.

'While you slept, I sent for news of your brother. While we wait for a reply, you will stay here. Unlike your world, we live here by the grace of the Land, and although many things look familiar, they may not be. You must learn to survive. You are young and your minds will quickly open to new ways.' They listened intently but understood little of what he was saying. 'It's also warmer here than in your world. Again, you'll get used to it. I'll teach you how to live here and look after your stomachs, there's plenty to eat if you know how to find it.'

'How long?' Anja asked. 'Mummy and Daddy will be so worried.'

Pan was relieved when Alfie butted in with an unusually sensible question: 'How do you know about our world, if this is a different one?'

'We don't use the word world, that's a human word. This is the Land. It is aware, intelligent, and our role is to help it maintain its balance. I know your world, Alfie, because I've lived there. It was thousands of years ago. I'm different, as you will have noticed.' They laughed, but his face didn't quite share their humour. 'Not everyone took to me; not in the same way they did the others.' He shook his head. 'Your land was similar to this once but now it's different.' Anja detected regret and even anger in Pan's voice.

'Why were you in that book?' Alfie asked, still probing in his innocent, direct way.

'I haven't seen it, but I suppose the memory of me has lasted.'

Alfie nodded; that he could believe. Anja suspected that there was more to it than their host's strange appearance. She wished she knew the stories that went with the pictures; she was intrigued by their host.

'It's been a very, very long time since I returned from your land. Humans regard difference as a threat; competition to be destroyed.' He shrugged.

'Could they destroy you?' Alfie liked the word destroy.

'No,' Pan replied abruptly.

Aspects of the conversation worried Anja; she picked up where she had been interrupted. 'Why do we need to learn to survive? And what about Mummy and Daddy? We need to let them know.'

'Anja, you are in the Land, it is not yours. So is your lost brother. Do you want to find him or not?' The question was direct, cold. Anja stared bleakly back, her mind still struggling with the issues she was facing.

Later, towards evening, she became fretful again, unable to accept what had happened, or that it wasn't a terrible nightmare she couldn't wake from. Alfie tried consoling her, but she became irrational and his anxiety fed her anguish. Pan knew he had to act quickly to ensure her survival, because the Land wished it. Her adjustment was beginning. He didn't know how extreme the change would be or how long it would take. Besides, he was drawn to her, more so each day. Usually, he played a sweet, soft melody that floated over the trees to lull the evening into night. However, as the sun began to set, he played a special, slow, delicate air, his mind focused on the unhappy girl.

Anja's eyes lifted and she smiled, listening, mesmerised. After a while, her head swayed to the music. She rose and started to dance. Alfie watched at first, spellbound with love for his big sister, but gradually a profound sadness filled his heart. He couldn't understand why he felt that way, and when a tear trickled down his cheek he crept away and went to bed. He was soon asleep and didn't feel her snuggle up to him later.

Pan sat outside, staring up into the sparkling night sky. The girl's response had been incredible. His music would always charm, but seldom had its recipient charmed him in response, not like this. She danced as part of the forest; beautiful, slow, graceful and innocent, but also with a seductive power that could only be gifted by the Land.

From that day, each morning and evening, the same ritual was enacted. Pan would play the pipes and as the first notes drifted through the air, Anja would rise or stop whatever she was doing, walk dreamily to an area of grass between the pool and the trees and dance. Over the days, she became distant, enmeshed in the haunting moods of the forest, deep and a part of something that Alfie wasn't. They had always been close, and he looked to her for leadership. Now her behaviour distressed him. As the days turned to weeks, she grew less and less like her old self, distracted and gentle, often smiling but seldom laughing. She still talked and played with him, but not as enthusiastically as she had in the past. He blamed Pan and couldn't bear to watch the serene oblivion that overcame her as his music wove patterns, bonding her to him, easing the changes happening to her mind.

His resentment smouldered. Except during their survival lessons, Pan almost disregarded him, paying little attention to his younger charge. His pride dented, Alfie took to walking alone in the forest, bored and brooding. He regularly put off getting up until after the sun had risen and Anja had finished dancing, resenting the loss of her close warmth as she slipped away at the first chorus of daybreak. Often, he didn't return until after dark.

One morning, at the beginning of their third week in the valley, Alfie was climbing one of the steep paths into the forest when a feeling that he was being followed came over him. Each day, the sensation returned as soon as he entered the forest. He decided not to mention it. Pan had taken great pains to assure them that nothing could harm them whilst they were under his protection. Besides, Alfie was sure that his shadow was not dangerous, but couldn't detect any tangible evidence of its existence.

A few mornings after this new occurrence, he tumbled sulkily out of the bower as the last strains of the music died, went to the poolside and splashed his face with water to freshen himself up. After a few minutes, Anja joined him with a bowl of broth for each of them and sat silently beside him. Pan had gone about some business of his own.

'Heard anything about Toby?' he asked.

She shrugged in a non-committal way, bit her lower lip, and looked away.

'Well, has he said anything, Anja? It's been ages now.' Alfie stared hard to force some reaction.

'We've got to have patience,' she replied, obviously repeating Pan's words. 'As soon as he knows anything, he'll tell us. He sent away for news; he's waiting. It's all right.' Then she smiled a very silly smile and ran her fingers through his hair. Alfie pulled away. It was always "all right", and she used that silly, secret smile whenever he mentioned Toby and took no notice whatsoever of his nagging worries. *It's not "all right", it's "all wrong"*, he thought bitterly. He left her and stomped off towards the forest.

Alfie was so wrapped in his bad mood that it was some time before he realised his shy companion was with him. When he stopped to listen and make sure, for the first time, he heard a sound, a distinct rustling somewhere behind him in the undergrowth. A game developed; he would walk for a few hundred yards, suddenly stop and turn around. Each time, a scampering sound came from nearby. As abruptly as the game started, it stopped. He tried to restart it, but there was nothing, and yet he was positive it was still there.

Dark thoughts began to surface again, and he sat down trying to settle his mind but could not get a grip on his problems, so he plodded on until another intangible feeling disturbed this murky daydreaming. He stopped to listen but shook his head. As he stepped forward again, he realised what it was; somewhere behind him he could faintly hear lightly pattering feet, not human feet but something on four legs. He span around. About twenty feet away sat a fox, grinning widely as only a fox can.

They studied each other for a few seconds and then it trotted up, turned to one side and without any change of pace, glided off into the trees. Alfie followed. He almost lost it before reaching a small clearing where it stood waiting for him. Not wanting to frighten it, he sat down without getting too close, but without a hint of fear it came and plonked itself down by his side, still grinning idiotically.

Alfie was grinning nearly as widely. Tentatively, he tickled its long nose. 'Well, I didn't think you'd be a fox,' he whispered half to himself. He was just about to add something about its rather strong smell, when it gave a small grunt of pleasure, pressed its nose harder against his finger and closed its eyes, obviously enjoying every second of Alfie's attention.

'Hmm, just a little higher up.'

Alfie pulled his hand away as if he'd been bitten. The fox made a low, wheezy sound that passed for a laugh. Then, giving Alfie a distinct look of intelligence, it added, 'And harder.'

Alfie was so shocked that he automatically did as requested. When he'd recovered a little, he realised the fox was still talking to him. He was fascinated by the way it managed to speak. The words were understandable, yet its mouth was not made for the job and it resorted to facial tricks to make the necessary sounds. As the conversation blossomed, he noticed one particularly comical trick: whenever the fox wanted to say 'yes,' it threw its head sharply up and down, the word expelled like a sneeze on the downward movement. Alfie was not so rude as to laugh but couldn't suppress the occasional giggle. Before long, it seemed as natural as wiping his nose to be talking to a fox, especially one that listened so patiently to a small boy's problems.

'Pan is a Great One,' Fox said. 'He is the Lord of the Great Forest and everything within it. He's wise and should be treated with respect.'

'I know that,' Alfie replied, 'but he's not really helping us, I'm sure he isn't, and he's making Anja behave strangely. She isn't how she should be.' Fox made no comment but was not grinning so widely.

From that day, Alfie's happiness depended on the time

he spent in the company of this new friend. A week passed during which Alfie poured out his heart and history to this strangest of mentors. Fox wanted to know everything, but Alfie also asked questions of his own.

'Pan says that he knows everything that goes on in the Great Forest, but I'm sure he doesn't know that you're my friend. Does he know you?'

Fox nodded his head seriously. 'Oh, he knows me, Alfie. The Land gifts the Great Ones power and responsibility to maintain its balance. Most creatures are also under their protection, but a few are different, not quite as we should be. There have always been beings like us, and our lives are a bit adventurous. The Land tolerates us and we go where we like and do what we want, so long as we respect the balance. Life can be a bit exciting.' He wheezed for a while, his spare body shaking with mirth. Obviously, this understatement was lost on Alfie.

'Pan won't harm me. In fact, he's very friendly and there are others I'm quite friendly with, but we should always be respectful of them. They've different priorities and reasons for the decisions they make. They serve the Land but also have free will. Pan ignores my presence in his kingdom. He can't be bothered with either of us at the moment.' Alfie nodded earnestly. He wasn't sure what Fox meant, but it sounded very convincing.

For his part, Fox knew it was time for the children to leave the Great Forest and find their brother. The longer they stayed, the more difficult it would be for Anja to leave Pan. He urged Alfie to take his advice, that there was a reason why Pan was reluctant to let them go, not a bad

30

reason but one that had to be challenged. Alfie replied that he had tried to talk to Anja, but she wouldn't listen to him. Fox finally announced that he was going away for a while. He told Alfie that he wouldn't be gone long and promised to return.

Alfie went to their usual meeting place the following morning, half hoping Fox hadn't meant what he had said, but the clearing echoed back his sad calls. For the next few days, he aimlessly wandered the forest, but without the company of Fox the familiar trails had lost their appeal. He sat miserably in the bower away from the sun and, as it rose and sank, would peer from the shadows and sullenly watch his sister dance. Anja saw how unhappy he was, and on occasion hugged and talked to him, but her words were empty echoes of Pan's thin promises. The roots of the forest were tunnelling deep into her mind and tangling her thoughts. Instead of comforting him, she was feeding his bitterness.

When Alfie thought that a week had passed, he began to venture back into the forest, anxiously expecting Fox's return. On the third morning, his perseverance was rewarded; in the clearing, his friend lay curled up, sunning himself. Alfie ran up and fell beside him, wrapping his arms tightly around Fox's neck.

'Steady on, you'll strangle me,' Fox said, making no effort to disentangle Alfie, and followed this with a very uncharacteristic and sloppy lick. They both laughed as Alfie wiped it off. 'Where did you go?' Alfie asked.

'I went to find help and more information about your brother, and I've been successful. I know what happened and roughly where he is. However, he's a great distance away and to have any hope of rescuing him, you must leave soon. Alfie, you *must* persuade your sister that the time has come to leave. Someone is coming who has agreed to help.' He placed one paw gently over Alfie's hand. 'It's time to leave the Great Forest.'

Alfie made a face. 'Anja keeps promising she'll ask Pan about leaving or if he's got any news. Then, when I ask her what he said, she says she forgot to ask or didn't get the chance.' He pulled a blade of grass fiercely out of the ground. 'He plays those silly pipes and she dances, every morning and every night, and when I say, "What about Toby?" she looks away and says that she'll ask the next day, and the same thing happens.' His eyes were rimmed with tears.

'It's not her fault, and neither is it Pan's. He is torn between protecting her and letting her go. His music is seductive and Anja finds it irresistible. She has developed an affinity with the Great Forest, and a bond with Pan. He can't help it and she finds his power and protection compelling. You must leave him and find your brother, both of you. It's as simple as that.'

'I'll tell her not to dance anymore, and that we must leave,' Alfie declared decisively, his face fired with determination.

'Not good enough. You must take the pipes to stop Pan playing.'

Alfie had never stolen anything. To break the conditioning drummed into him during his short life was daunting. Fox made clear they wouldn't be keeping the pipes. They would be returned when Pan agreed to help them leave immediately.

'I've put a lot of thought into it. Pan must understand that you're not betraying his friendship. It will be difficult, but it's the only way.' Fox then explained exactly how it had to be done, who should do what and when. 'It must be tonight,' Fox insisted. 'If you wait any longer, he'll sense something's wrong. Go and talk to you sister. Persuade her. Now, do you remember all the instructions, exactly as I told you?' Alfie nodded, but just to make sure, Fox patiently repeated the most important points to his little co-conspirator. Alfie went over them as he made his way back...

*

Ignoring the gore splattered on his feet from the huge insect he'd killed, Rob giggled. Were they also sniggering; the children? Every long, terrifying night he first imagined then heard them, laughing at him. He consoled himself by conceiving unspeakable horrors to inflict on their soft bodies. He gagged on his disgusting meal, vomited, wiped his mouth and giggled again.

She will do well to survive this one, let alone the other, the Land mused. We'll see if she is the right choice.

4

That evening, Alfie didn't creep into the bower but stayed by the pool. As the sun began to set, the sound of Pan's pipes rose, mingling with the sweet fragrance of dusk scents, stilling all but Anja. Had some stranger secretly found the valley and watched from the cover of the darkening forest above, it would have appeared a mystical, enthralling scene: the slow, abandoned grace of a girl dancing to the haunting music played by a legendary creature. But watched by Alfie, it only fuelled his resolve. As the final lingering notes faded, he furtively studied Pan's movements, peering through the dim light to see where he went and what he did.

Anja came over and sat a little way from him, by the edge of the pool. She still had a faraway look in her eyes and was trembling slightly. Alfie studied her intently, his mind working furiously. Then he walked to the cauldron in the bower, filled two bowls and made his way back, hoping that the dreamy look had gone. She acknowledged his return with a wistful, friendly smile and together they

34

sipped their food. Only when Anja had finished did he speak, his voice barely audible above the splashing of the waterfall.

'Anja, we've got to leave.'

She stared into the water. Alfie was just about to repeat his statement a little more forcibly when she sighed and sprawled back onto the grass. She looked up at him, chewing a strand of her hair.

'We've got to find Toby. We've got to make Pan keep his promise and help us.'

Sitting up again, she brushed her hair back with her hand, then looked keenly at him, as if she'd not seen him properly for a long time. Alfie thought that it was going to be the same as the other times, when she reached out and touched his face very gently with the back of her fingers. 'You're filthy.'

He looked at his hands and arms. Camouflaged by the rich tan, he supposed that he was a bit grubby. The nearest he had come to getting properly wet had been the two single days of gentle rain that had fallen since they had arrived and the cool drinks of sweet water from forest streams. He glowed happily with the scolding and looked at his sister. She too was deeply tanned, but her skin was unblemished by a single smudge of dirt. Indeed, she looked cleaner and healthier than he'd ever seen her. He almost cried at how beautiful she looked, and felt small, scruffy and overwhelmed. She smiled, leant forward and kissed him on the nose.

His confidence soared. 'What we've got to do is take his flute thing and hide it until he keeps his promise,' he blurted out. He waited for a reaction. She was more like his old Anja than she had been at any time lately, but he could also see by her eyes that she was humouring him. A smile hovered on her lips. Time to tell her about Fox. He had wondered how he was going to do it all afternoon and the thought of doing so now when she was in her "big sister" mood tapped his confidence, but he had her attention and she seemed to be normal. He took a deep breath.

'Anyway, I've met someone who will help us.' Her eyes grew sharp. 'Well, not exactly a someone. It's sort of an animal I met in the forest. He's my friend.'

Anja's face softened, the half-smile came back, and her eyes sparkled. Alfie recognised the signs from a wealth of embarrassing memories. He knew what was coming but couldn't give up now. He had to go on.

'He's a fox.'

She raised her eyebrows. Her mouth hardly moved but her eyes blazed mischievously. A blush exploded through the tan on his face. 'It's true!' he said, trying to make her take him seriously. 'He can talk.'

She sniggered. He desperately wanted to be serious, but her mood was infectious. He tore his gaze away and fought to smother a giggle.

It was so ridiculous. She began to snigger again. Looking away to control herself, she failed and collapsed into laughter. His defence melted; she caught his eye and he dissolved into a squealing heap. Tears that should have been shed weeks ago erupted. Pan listened from a distance, pleased to hear them happy.

The lovely moment passed, and Alfie realised that finally he had his old, wonderful sister back and might succeed. 'Seriously, Anja, we really do have to leave.'

'It's true then, about this fox? It isn't just pretend?' The night was closing in and he peered to see her reaction before he answered.

'Of course. You know it's different here.' He told her everything that had happened. Then what Fox wanted them to do.

'Please, Anja, please.'

Resting her chin on her knees, she rocked back and forth for what seemed like an eternity. 'And you're sure we'll give him the pipes back, that your Fox won't just run off with them. How can we trust him? After all, he *is* a fox, isn't he?'

Alfie was relieved that she had not simply dismissed the plan. 'You know it's right, Anja. You know you won't leave otherwise. He couldn't care less about me or Toby. He only likes you.'

Shards of half-truth in his words pierced her guilt. Alfie could sense her weakening.

'Only you can do it, Anja. Only you can talk to him. It's the most important part of it all. Only you can get him to help us.'

'I don't think that he will understand,' she said sadly. 'He doesn't mean any harm. He thinks that what he's doing is for the best.' The tone of her voice began to bother Alfie.

'Anja, we've got to, it's been weeks now. What about Toby?' His reproof stung her. 'We've got to do it, Anja.

37

Please, you're not going to tell him, are you?' He hovered between anger and desperation.

'No, of course I won't tell. I know we have to find Toby.'

Alfie stared hard at her through the evening gloom, trying to detect any sign of deceit but only saw sad resignation. He hid the immense relief he felt. It had been hard.

Whilst they had been talking, the moon had risen, so they retired into the dark cover of the bower. From the blackness, the steady breathing of their host reassured them that he was unaware of the real reason for their show of sibling affection earlier.

Since their first traumatic night in the forest, the children had slept snuggled together, partly for warmth, but mostly for the comfort and reassurance that Alfie needed. Of late, they hadn't talked much, Alfie retiring earlier than Anja, and he was either asleep or pretending to be because of his frame of mind when she joined him. Now, their silence was the hush of trepidation. Aware of Pan's acute senses, they strained to hear the continuing sound of his deep slumber, although they were sure he had no reason to suspect intrigue. After a couple of hours, nudging one another to make sure they'd not drifted to sleep, Alfie slowly raised his head. Anja drew a sharp breath as the bed softly rustled. He was gone.

Weeks of being alone in the forest had taught him the quality and skill of silence and he could now, even in the dark, move as quietly as any forest creature. Bent low, he felt his way slowly and carefully across the earthen floor, weaving between trunks and over roots towards the sound of gentle, resonant breathing. When he was past Pan's dark form, he rose gingerly and went to where he'd seen him go earlier. Groping from tree to tree, he eventually found what he was looking for: a hole between the roots of an oak. Feeling inside, he was rewarded when his fingers closed around a large bumpy object; he'd found the pipes. Gently lifting them out, he briefly began to tremble; he was stealing but there was no going back and nothing could excuse such behaviour if he was caught now. Only in the morning would the theft be justified.

Alfie tried to control his fear, but his heart was beating so loudly he thought that even Anja must be able to hear it. He pulled himself together and headed towards the moonlight. Outside the gloom of the bower, he felt the cool grass under his bare feet and crept towards the forest. Halfway there, he looked bravely back before racing to the safety of the first trees. He paused until he'd calmed down then, regaining his breath, melted into the dark undergrowth. On reaching the agreed place, he stopped and softly called.

Fox padded out of the shadows. 'Did you get them?' Alfie nodded and held the pipes out. By the moonlight illuminating the clearing, they inspected the object of their conspiracy. Polished by countless years of handling and use, they gleamed like carved amber. Fox turned and made a curious coughing sound. A shadowy figure appeared, blending so well with the gloomy surroundings that only when it was almost next to him did he realise it was a youth just a few years older than Anja.

'This is the friend that I went away to find,' Fox said. 'He'll guide you to where your brother is. There's no one better who could help you.' Alfie studied the face of the older boy for a reaction to this commendation, but detected little emotion except curiosity, which he also shared. He was wary but didn't feel instant dislike.

'My name is Quicksilver,' the boy offered, with firmness that indicated he approved of Alfie's wariness.

Alfie thought that it was a funny sort of name, not really a name at all. Then he remembered his manners. 'I'm Alfie.'

'We have to hurry,' Fox said anxiously. 'Give Quicksilver the pipes, go back to Anja, and don't get caught. If Pan is aware his pipes are missing before the morning, this will not go well.'

Alfie had a lot more questions but reluctantly gave the pipes to Quicksilver. They turned and walked away. As they quickly disappeared into the gloom, Fox called back to him.

'Don't forget, Anja must explain to Pan that the pipes will be returned when he guides you to the edge of the Great Forest. We'll be waiting by the southern path at the edge of the Downs all day tomorrow. He knows where it is.'

Alfie waited for a few moments, feeling very lonely. They had gone and so had the pipes, leaving him scared and apprehensive. Retracing his steps, he crawled silently into the bower and gingerly made his way back to Anja. Passing close to Pan, he was reassured by the even breathing he could hear. He carefully climbed back onto their bed and cuddled up to his warm sister. Feeling her face turn to him, he whispered, 'I did it.' They said no more, although both dearly wanted to, and lay pondering what the morning might bring. Eventually, weariness overcame them and both fell asleep.

As the first hint of light heralded the rising sun, the sweet smell of simmering herbs wafted through the bower, diffusing throughout the forest above on a gentle breeze.

Pan breakfasted alone, remembering the happy laughter of his two young charges the evening before. He wondered if perhaps it signalled a change in Alfie, final acceptance he was doing his best for them. He wiped his lips with his fingers and stretched. This morning, they would regale the forest with a beautiful melody to suit his mood.

As always, Anja woke first. Her eyes refused to stay open and she had difficulty escaping the vivid images her recent dream had left. All this vanished, however, as she remembered. She gasped, realising that filtering through the trees was not the fresh light of a new dawn but the full glory of a sun-drenched, ominously silent mid-morning. She nudged Alfie. He wriggled away from her insistent elbow, then sat up as his mind also cleared. They looked at each other, straining to hear the slightest sound. Rising, they gathered courage, held hands and walked apprehensively outside. Immediately, Anja saw Pan. He was sitting by the edge of the pool with his back to them. It was where they'd sat and laughed the evening before.

Now that the time had arrived, Alfie's enthusiasm for the enterprise faded. His legs were reluctant to walk the short distance to the pool. Within Anja, however, a deep sadness blossomed. She experienced no fear or guilt, only the need to explain, to pour out the feelings that she'd been repressing, tell him why she had joined the conspiracy and see him understand. She tugged Alfie forward. Pan rose, turned and faced them. There was suppressed emotion in his cold expression; hardly contained violence, which terrified Alfie. They stopped; Anja couldn't bear the tension.

'We have to go.'

She had practised all sorts of things to say at this point, but none seemed as right as that simple phrase. Pan still said nothing. Only the sound of the waterfall broke the oppressive silence. She couldn't break away from his stare. It transferred to Alfie and she pushed him behind her, holding him tightly against her back, then focused again on her. His eyes were icy. He stepped forward.

'Don't.' A surge of confidence filled Anja. Tiny flecks of gold blossomed in her eyes. The iciness melted in his. He looked up to the sky and sighed. When he looked back at her, it was with pride and deep, deep love. Kneeling down, he gently pulled her to him and held his forehead against hers for long seconds.

'So, my little princess, tell me.'

'We must go, today. Will you take us to the edge of the forest, to the beginning of the path from the Southern Downs? You did promise to help us and that's where we have to go, today. Please.'

Pan looked around her at Alfie, who stepped forward again to Anja's side, squirming with guilt.

'You took them.'

Alfie nodded imperceptibly.

'Give them back,' he growled, moving his face a fraction closer to Alfie's.

'We can't, not yet,' Anja answered, taking the initiative from her brother and pulling him closer. 'We haven't got them.'

Unexpectedly, Pan threw back his head and laughed. 'Ah! So, it's a conspiracy. And who has got them, someone I know? – Because I know *everyone!*'

'A friend,' Anja answered hesitantly, reflecting that she'd not even met this Fox.

'A friend?' he repeated. 'Well, we will see.' He rose and strode away on his strange legs towards the bower.

They remained where they were, not knowing quite what to do. They'd not even finished telling him everything. After a few minutes, he reappeared. A large bag was slung from his shoulder.

'Come on. The quicker we get this over, the better. Is that not right?' He was still smiling.

They didn't move; Alfie's hand was still clasped tightly in his sister's.

'Come on,' he barked, his narrowed eyes betraying the smile. 'Let's meet this "friend".'

'Don't be like that. You *have* been kind, really kind. But you're keeping us here and we don't understand why. You're confusing me. We only took the pipes because when you play them, I can't think. I promise you'll get them back today.'

'I *am* keeping you here, keeping you safe, Anja. You are

43

not ready to journey across the Land, and I can't take you myself. So tell me, *how can I let you go*?' His eyes bored into hers and revealed his soul. She plunged through his anger, then the savage power simmering beneath, revealing the love he was desperately trying to conceal.

'Someone's going to help us,' Alfie whispered, shattering the connection.

Pan laughed. 'Someone's going to help you. Of course someone is. The Land is full of friendly, kind people, isn't it?' His sarcasm was lost on Anja, still confused about the insight she'd felt. He dropped the bag and stomped into the bower. 'First breakfast, and then I will meet this someone,' he called back.

'That was weird.'

Alfie's remark made her realise that something profound had changed, in her and in Pan.

'What do you mean?'

'He got really angry and suddenly sort of friendly. I thought he was going to kill me.'

'He wouldn't hurt us, Alfie, and we did steal his pipes.'

'He wouldn't hurt *you*, Anja.'

They sat and ate whilst Anja somewhat shamefully spelt out the bargain, whilst Pan tutted at their disloyalty. He said little in return apart from giving a loud snort when Fox was mentioned, then quietly helped them get ready to travel and led them away from the bower. A sadness settled over the little group as they trooped away from the camp they had called home since their arrival.

The journey out of the forest was not as arduous as their descent into the valley had been all those weeks

44

ago. They went the same way that Alfie had gone during the night and then continued in that direction; south. By midday, they had reached a narrow well-defined track threading its way out of the great trees into pleasant woodland. Pan's mood was still confusingly bright, and they spent most of the journey reassuring him that they had learnt the lessons he'd taught them.

'Edible plants can be found throughout the Land, but you must know where to look, although I'm sure that this *someone* will be used to living off the Land without its permission.' Then he casually changed the subject and Anja's heart quickened as he began to tell them what, in all the long weeks they had been with him, they'd so dearly wanted to know.

'This is what I know about your brother. He's being held by a creature who, before your untimely arrival, I'd only vaguely heard of. I've little interest outside my own domain. It was different once, but now the Great Forest is my only concern. In the scale of time that I've lived, this creature appeared very recently and has been of no interest to me. It has made its home in a large bay where the Downs meet the Southern Ocean, west of the mouth of the Great River estuary. The small brook that runs from the pool beside which we sat this morning feeds a tributary of the Great River that flows far south and broadens into this estuary. This creature was created during a great suffering. Apparently it has your brother, but I don't know how or why. I *would* like to know how it used the portal in the Great Forest without my knowledge. I don't know what it is, but it's not humankind or any

45

other species I've heard of. I also don't know why the Land suffers its presence.'

Whilst Pan was nonchalantly telling them this astounding news, they stumbled along beside him, mouths gaping with attentive horror. He had been deliberate with his timing and words and was very satisfied with their reaction.

'Now you know as much as me,' he said breezily.

He was not entirely truthful. He was tempted to scare them so thoroughly that they would give up whatever plans they had, but realised that their destiny would be fulfilled whatever action he took. The fate of the three children would be decided together. He would have happily left them to their fate had the Land not obliged him to help the girl, but during their short time together, Anja had moved him.

He understood why the Land had taken such an interest in her; her potential was extraordinary, but did this mean that she was simply destined to become an extraordinary sacrifice? He knew she had bonded to him and yet now she was displaying incredible willpower in leaving without his support. He wondered if the Land understood just how extraordinary she was. He had discarded this type of affection long ago and was annoyed that the Land had caused it to awaken again. The boy had also shown resilience adapting in his own way. He'd let him fend for himself. Obviously, the way events had happened, he might have kept him closer. Was it all the will of the Land, even their imminent departure? He took their hands, looked down at Anja and smiled warmly. She smiled back, confused but happily accepting his affection.

The day was almost at an end when the path began to widen. It passed through a last belt of great oaks, the low sun revealing a vast panorama of rich downland that rolled across undulating hills away into the distance. A few bright stars began to pierce the deepening blue sky. A slight, shadowed figure leant against the last tree. Seeing them approach, it stood in the middle of the path, becoming distinct. Alfie recognised the youth he'd given the pipes to the night before.

'I'm Quicksilver,' the youth declared before anyone else had time to say anything. Anja knew that this had been directed at her, intuitively feeling that he and Pan knew each other.

'So you are,' Pan replied, confirming the strange introduction, 'which makes it even stranger that I didn't sense what went on last night.'

Without prompting, the boy handed Pan his pipes.

'This wasn't really necessary, you know,' Pan said.

The boy shrugged. 'Not my idea, but it's done now.'

Pan looked at his pipes and, as the last tinge of blue was disappearing from the westernmost sky, placed them to his lips. Alfie and Quicksilver both gasped in consternation. His eyes twinkled and he smiled wickedly but, sensing the sadness overwhelming Anja, regretted his little joke and placed them in his bag.

'You don't intend to start out tonight?' he asked seriously.

'No,' the youth answered. 'By your leave, we'll spend the night here and start at first light tomorrow.'

'Good, then I'll remain with you, if you will accept my company for one more night.'

Even Alfie was glad that Pan had decided to stay. They lit a small fire to prepare some food. Afterwards, Anja sat beside Pan for a while, then went to Alfie and they fell asleep together, exhausted by the previous night's adventure and subsequent trauma. Pan and Quicksilver talked long into the night in low serious voices before taking their rest. Pan did most of the talking and the boy often nodded his acquiescence. Anja woke briefly as their conversation was ending. Pan had raised his voice a little to emphasis what he was saying: 'Take them to her, Quicksilver, promise me you will.' The youth must have agreed because she heard no more and went back to sleep.

Dawn heralded a melancholy start to the next day. They all felt that this was not the way they would have preferred to part. Pan still had grave misgivings, Alfie hated goodbyes and now wanted to get on with it, and Anja wanted to go but wished that Pan was going with them. She asked him why he wouldn't.

He crouched low, his face inches from hers. Alfie, standing next to her, was looking closely at Pan's peculiar horns; the way they grew from his head with tight wiry curls framing them fascinated him. He wondered what it would be like to have horns.

Pan studied Anja, so beautiful and so vulnerable. 'I won't leave the Great Forest, but will follow your progress. You have a better guide anyway. I'm surprised but pleased that he agreed to help you. His own company is usually sufficient for his needs.'

Quicksilver was listening nearby but made no comment.

'Take these with you.' Pan reached into his bag and took out two small, heavy leather flasks. He suspended one over each of their shoulders, across their chests, so that they hung at their hips. 'Where you're going is hot, your thirst may become great. These flasks contain the purest forest water. My power is within it so don't use them except in the greatest need. Promise you will return to me, Anja,' he said, and she nodded. He waited.

'I promise.'

He turned to Alfie. 'Learn loyalty, Alfie, especially when someone helps you.' Alfie blushed, then mumbled something incomprehensible that might have been thank you, goodbye, or ruder. But those words burned into his mind and he never forgot them. Quicksilver said that it was time to go and Alfie ran to him. They began to walk away from the Great Forest. Anja hesitated, but Pan kissed her gently on the forehead and motioned her to follow. When she turned to wave a few minutes later, he had gone.

5

When the Great Forest was just a dark haze in the distance behind them, Anja stopped and turned, listening intently. After she had not moved for a minute or so, Quicksilver gently took her arm to lead her on. She shook his hand off and continued to gaze back at the forest, straining every sense.

Quicksilver walked in front of her, blocking her line of sight.

'It's only the wind and your imagination.'

She shook her head, took her brother's proffered hand and continued walking. Quicksilver stayed, staring back at the Great Forest, frowning and muttering to himself. By the time he had caught up with them, he showed no outward sign of concern.

Anja gradually perked up. Later, she drew Alfie to one side, glancing darkly at Quicksilver.

'I thought you said your friend was a fox.'

Alfie looked as if she'd bitten him. He'd totally forgotten about Fox. Without answering, he ran over to

Quicksilver. 'Where's Fox?' he asked anxiously, skipping sideways to keep up. 'I almost forgot about him.'

Quicksilver laughed. 'I wondered how long it would take you to notice. He's gone on ahead. He can travel faster overland than us and will go directly to the coast, to find exactly where your brother is and keep watch, so that when we arrive we can act quickly.'

'Aren't we going straight there then?' Anja had been listening.

'Sort of, but for us the direct way is not the quickest. Did Pan tell you how far it was to the coast?' They shook their heads.

'He just said it was a long way,' Alfie answered.

'Well, it's hundreds of miles away, you would never make it. I'll take you there the quickest way I know.'

Anja nodded; they had to trust him, there was no one else, and Pan had said that he was the best person to help them. She just felt that he was weird, then remembered Pan and laughed at herself.

So, they began their trek across the endless Downs. The low hills descended gradually away from the Great Forest. They were now both used to living out in the open, and apart from the boredom of walking for mile after mile across undulating grassland, broken only by occasional thin brushland and a few deep, lonely woods, did not find the exercise arduous. Even Alfie could cover a fair distance on his shorter, sturdy legs with only the minimum of whining when he was hungry.

There were no paths except those made by animals, which were no use to them, only pure unspoiled land.

Every now and again, they saw rabbits or a few deer in the distance, but nothing bothered them, and they disturbed nothing in turn. They gleaned their sparse meals from whatever they could forage, and the bits Quicksilver added from his bag. Being cold was now a memory; the days were warm and would become warmer as they travelled further south, and the nights were clear and balmy. They lay down each evening close to the nearest clump of trees or bushes, both for the small amount of privacy that it afforded and to find twigs for a cooking fire, and slept comfortably until dawn nudged them off again.

A week out from the forest, when it was time to think about finding somewhere to bed for the night, Quicksilver pointed out a large, dark patch nestling in a hollow between the low hills in front of them. It looked different to the scattered, small woods they had encountered so far. As they approached, it became a grove of huge broad-leafed trees. They had seen nothing like them in size or grandeur, even in the innermost depths of the Great Forest, and they felt out of place on the Downs.

As they passed between the first trees, Anja was reminded of the times they'd entered the old church along the lane at home; there was a similar air of timelessness, peace and tranquillity. The children talked in whispers, feeling like intruders, and they understood why Quicksilver had brought them there. He belonged; standing beside the smooth grey trunks, his tunic was the same hue, and his breeches and boots echoed the rich shades of the loam and leaves beneath his feet. In the gloom, his features became indistinct, no matter how close they were to him.

'From now, we'll spend our nights near the security of one of these groves,' he said.

'Why?' Anja asked.

'Because from here onwards, there could be danger.'

'What sort of danger?' they competed to ask.

'Between here and the coast, on the Downs, there's a problem. It's hard to explain. As we travel, I'll show you places to avoid and signs to watch for. One thing is certain. Inside these groves we're completely safe.'

Quicksilver did not elaborate, and neither of them felt the need to push him on the subject. However, for the first time since they had met him, he appeared relaxed. Normally, he was alert to the slightest sound and movement, and at night he never truly slept, but dozed, never for long and never deeply. Now, he quickly grew drowsy and fell into a deep sleep as soon as he'd eaten. Alfie and Anja followed his example.

Another unusual occurrence awaited them when they woke in the morning. The diversity of the food they had eaten at home was a dream. Their lives had taken on the pattern of the Land and how they had lived before seldom broke in upon it. It would be an understatement to say that Alfie often felt not quite as full as he wished after a long-awaited meal, but that morning they awoke to a mouth-watering smell permeating the grove. Quicksilver had prepared a thick, succulent stew. It was full of small pieces of meat, vegetables and herbs. It was even subtly seasoned. He didn't explain this sudden bounty. They ate ravenously.

'Do you know exactly where we're going?' Anja asked.

She felt unusually benign towards Quicksilver after such a feast. They were also so full of the rich food that they didn't feel like starting immediately.

'I know that the creature has a great home on the dry seabed in a bay along the coast west of the Great River estuary, but I haven't seen it myself. I have an interest of my own in this creature. I told Pan all that I knew and was about to go back down the Great River when Fox caught up with me. He told me about you, which Pan hadn't, and I agreed to help.'

'So, was it you that told him our brother was here?' Anja said.

'Oh no, he already knew. Don't forget that it was the Great Forest portal that you came through. If he hadn't been so far away that night, he may have been able to stop what happened. Pan can be dangerous. Great Ones don't do or behave as others. Their power is so great that they've learnt to harness it close and use it sparingly, only to maintain the balance for the Land. Anyway, I'm not the only one who travels the Land, but I usually travel further south, on the Southern Downs or along the Great River. I was told that Pan needed information, and I came. It was probably Maia who first told him.'

'Who's Maia?'

'She's a fairy, a small tree sprite who's the messenger of the Land, but she's away at the moment, so I brought news to him.'

Alfie looked bemused. 'A fairy?'

'Yes, she flies so fast you can't see her when she's moving.'

Anja looked puzzled. 'Can you travel fast then? To have brought the message such a long way would take you months.'

'Not that fast, but there are different ways to travel, some faster than others. I told you, I was already quite close.'

'So can we travel faster?'

'Yes, soon, but not this first part.'

'Pan must be a special friend,' Anja said, 'for you to travel such a long way to see him. He didn't say that he'd seen you recently, though, did he?'

Quicksilver snorted. 'I wouldn't describe Pan like that. He is what he is. I knew he'd be annoyed that it was me that had his pipes. If it hadn't been Fox who persuaded me, I wouldn't have got involved. Anja, when a Great One helps you, you should always wonder why. Nevertheless, if Pan or any Great One requests something, it's wise to do what you can. They never ask unless it's important. And the distances might seem great to you, but we are used to them, and usually there's no hurry.'

'Is this creature a Great One?' asked Alfie.

'No,' Quicksilver replied emphatically. 'I don't know what it is. It's a creature or an entity that up to now the Great Ones have tried to ignore, but it's becoming powerful.' He stopped; something painful had obviously stirred in his memory. He brusquely started to pack up and reminded them that they should start. Alfie never got the chance to ask what an entity was.

Days became weeks of endless trudging. Changes in their behaviour that had begun to appear during their time in the forest continued to develop. In Anja's case, they were subtle and disconcerting, but in Alfie, they tended to be anything but discreet. He was becoming independent and cheeky. Also, to Anja's annoyance, he started to copy Quicksilver's mannerisms. Only when he was especially tired, or when the night wind blew though the leaves of the great trees, did he have no scruples about holding an earlier scorned hand or accepting the warmth of his sister.

Now that she was away from Pan, Alfie didn't resent the changes in his sister so much. He'd always loved her unconditionally, but all this was affecting her profoundly. He often watched her adoringly as she walked so gracefully mile after mile, and simply being near her filled him with a deep feeling of warmth and contentment. Occasionally, he caught her squeezing her eyes tight, wincing to block out the guilt overwhelming her, and clumsily tried to comfort her. At other times, stranger and more distant moods took her, and when the secret smile smouldered in her eyes he kept away; those moods unfathomable, not to be shared. Quicksilver noticed them too and exchanged glances with Alfie. He wasn't puzzled by them, but they concerned him.

Alfie was often the catalyst of conversations that brightened their humdrum journey. One day, neither Quicksilver nor Anja had spoken for hours, the silence comfortable and natural. A question grew from a small thought Alfie had, until it became a niggle that refused to go away.

'We've been walking for weeks and weeks and it hasn't

rained once. Doesn't it rain here? It sometimes rained in the forest.'

Anja looked at Quicksilver with interest. It was true. Since they'd left the Great Forest, it hadn't rained. Not one drop of water had fallen; not one cloud had marred the azure sky.

'I know there are places where we come from that don't have rain, but those are deserts and places like that, aren't they, Anja? It's really warm here but it's not a desert, is it?'

His reasoning pricked Anja's curiosity.

'It's true, we've been travelling for weeks now and there hasn't even been a light shower. Doesn't it need to rain?' She answered her own question. 'I mean it must, it's so green and we've crossed lots of streams.'

'It does,' Quicksilver replied after some hesitation, 'but not like in the forest. The forest rain is beautiful, isn't it?' Alfie did not think that a whole day raining was beautiful, but he knew it wasn't the right answer and with a rare flash of tact, said nothing.

Quicksilver continued. 'On the Downs, the rain only comes when the Land cries out for it, then it comes swiftly.' His face implied that there was more to it than that. 'That's why we are keeping near the shelter of the groves. I would have expected some rain before now, though. This far north, when it comes, it's heavy but shouldn't be too bad. In the south, it'll be much hotter, and the call is far fiercer. It will storm and we must never be far from a grove.'

This explanation hadn't done much to clarify things but was obviously as much as they were going to get.

However, fate is tempted when something's discussed and invariably that something happens. Enlightenment was a frightening shock.

6

Everything went well and as usual until the afternoon. The morning had passed quickly due to a silly comment that Alfie made which Anja pounced on, and she teased him unmercifully until the surrounding hills echoed with their laughter. They were travelling through a valley that wound its way through a series of low hillocks carpeted with small blue fragrant flowers.

Midday passed and Anja noticed that she was perspiring, something that seldom happened and which she hated. Alfie also began to wipe the sweat from his forehead with his tattered sleeve. The fresh, sweet fragrance was now becoming heavy and cloying. Quicksilver stopped and looked all around. He said nothing but increased their pace. They became more uncomfortable and stickier as the atmosphere turned sultry and still. Quicksilver broke into a trot.

'Come on,' he said urgently. 'Faster, you're going to see what it means to have rain on the Downs, and I don't think it will be gentle.'

They trotted for some time along the valley floor. The sky turned a sickly yellow and darkened; huge clouds began to form.

'Run!' Quicksilver cried. 'The grove's about a quarter of a mile ahead. We must get there before it starts.'

They ran easily, Alfie's little legs pounding two steps to each of theirs. Without warning, a huge sheet of lightning split the air about them, immediately followed by the most tremendous crack of thunder that the children had ever heard. They both screamed. Quicksilver grabbed Alfie's arm.

'Take his other hand,' he yelled. Anja did so and they redoubled their efforts, Alfie's feet hardly touching the grass.

Needles and sheets of lightning flickered, illuminating the leaden sky, and constant deafening thunderclaps warned of the size of the massive storm breaking about them. Heavy drops of rain began to spatter.

'Not far now.' Quicksilver's voice was lost as another great crash stopped their hearts. A fierce wind whipped into their faces, accompanied by a fall of rain that lashed them with painful fury. At last, the grove loomed up and they raced inside.

'Keep going, it's hardly started. We must get to the safety of the shelter.' He dragged them deeper into the grove, weaving between the trees.

'Stop, it's this one,' he gasped, as they reached the broadest tree the children had ever seen.

The great tree towered over them. Fifteen feet from the ground, the massive trunk divided into five huge branches hung with heavy grey-green foliage. Anja stood drenched beneath its shelter, nervously listening to the frightful mayhem as the storm wound itself to greater and greater violence. She wondered, peering up through the rain thrashing the leaves and stinging her face, just how safe this haven was. Quicksilver ignored the tempest bending the mighty branches, walking slowly around the trunk and out of sight.

He quickly completed one circuit, concentrating so much that he didn't notice Alfie quietly following him, then started a second, this time feeling his way around. He climbed up and down over the roots, hands caressing the smooth bark, sliding them gently through the water cascading down. At last, he stopped, appearing to have found something, and, to Alfie's astonishment, pressed his fingers into the living wood as if it was putty. Flexing his hands as they slowly disappeared, he leant back, shuffled his feet to find good purchase, pushed and then pulled. Alfie guessed that his fingers were now hooked into the tree. After a couple of strenuous tugs, Quicksilver shook his head and muttered, 'It's grown together.' Then he gently withdrew his hands, and when the tips of his fingers emerged, that area of trunk was as whole and unblemished as it had been previously. He continued around the tree, so Alfie crept over and carefully examined where he'd performed the amazing act, looking for a crack or split of some kind, but could find nothing.

'Anja, Alfie, come quickly.' Quicksilver's urgent shout drove the mystery temporarily from his mind. Anja came around to her brother's side. The call had come from somewhere above them.

Quicksilver had climbed to where the trunk split into branches. They could barely make out his face as he shouted through the storm for them to join him. He pointed down to a line of deep indentations travelling up the trunk, easily deep enough for them to climb and join him. Alfie wondered how he'd missed seeing them before.

Conditions were now desperate. The wind roared through the grove, each gust threatening to blow them off their feet, and the rain was now a deluge, making the smooth bark dangerously slippery. Constant lightning and thunder added to their terror. Alfie began to climb. Anja waited until he had reached the top before following. As he did so, Quicksilver grabbed his shirt, heaved him onto the cleft between the branches and shoved him unceremoniously into a large hole just big enough for a man to squeeze into, where the two largest branches grew out of the trunk. As Alfie entered the darkness, Quicksilver shouted into his ear: 'Climb down, quickly. Keep going until you reach the bottom, we'll be right behind you.'

Alfie almost reached the bottom without having to climb down, letting out a small squeal that he cut off as his foot found purchase on the lumpy interior of the hollow trunk. Luckily, it was pitch black so he had no idea how far he would have dropped. Like a little fly, he gingerly felt for more holds and started down. As he grew accustomed to the blackness, it became easier and his confidence grew. Anja had no such luck.

'The wind won't blow the tree down, will it?' she yelled as she reached for his offered hand and he pulled her up.

'No, the groves will weather any storm, no matter how violent.' He turned her towards the hole Alfie had disappeared down. Her entry was not quite so rough; she had time to feel for hand and footholds, glad to escape the storm as she gingerly began to descend.

Then the darkness engulfed her and shut out the noise of the storm. She'd never had a problem with darkness in the past, but this was different. At first, she wondered how wide the hollow in the trunk was. There seemed to be plenty of room, but she could sometimes feel bumps and knobbles like the ones she was using to climb down scraping her back. Soon, Alfie's muffled progress below and Quicksilver's above was not as comforting as it should have been. She felt that the hollow was narrowing and strained her eyes in a futile attempt to see but couldn't make out her hands in front of her face. The feeling of being stifled grew.

'Is it much further?' she called, her voice betraying a tremor.

From somewhere above, Quicksilver answered, but it reached her as a muffled mumble and made matters worse. Her breathing became increasingly laboured, then she couldn't find the next foothold. Becoming more and more flustered, she gasped for air and began to panic. Quicksilver felt her stop below him, listened to her laboured breathing and, sensing her distress, slid down, his back melding with the tree until he'd squeezed tightly behind her, his face against the back of her neck. Normally, this would have mortified her but now she almost welcomed his presence.

'I don't know what's the matter,' she gasped. 'I can't breathe properly. I think I'm going to faint.'

'No, you're not,' he whispered calmly, 'keep going, just a few more minutes and we'll be at the bottom.'

'No, I've got to get out. I can't stand it.'

'Anja,' he said soothingly, 'there's not a great distance between you and the outside of the tree.' As he spoke, she felt his hands pass either side of her face. Suddenly a blinding flash of light forced her eyes shut and a cool rush of air filled her lungs. She felt drops of water wet her face. When she managed to open her eyes, she saw Quicksilver's arms and hands somehow wedged through the wall of the tree, his fingers entwined so that the outsides of each wrist was braced against the sides of a large crack in the trunk. The light, air and sound of the storm outside cleared her head. Quicksilver's cheek was now brushing hers. 'I'm going to let it close, just remember that we haven't got far to go. Look, you can see that we're almost below ground already.'

Anja could; her face was being splashed by rain bouncing off the roots and clumps of undergrowth framing the bottom of the crack. 'You've only the same distance to go down as you have already climbed. The area around you is larger below ground level, and there are foot and handholds. Feel them, here and here. At the bottom, there's a large tunnel that we can walk down where I can make light. Ready?'

He felt Anja nod. His palms brushed her face as he manoeuvred to withdraw his hands. The crack narrowed then the light and noise of the storm abruptly disappeared. They were in darkness again.

'Now, down you go,' he urged. As she brushed past his splayed feet, she felt alone again and struggled to control the dread that had almost overwhelmed her.

'Don't rush, and keep your eyes shut, gently, though, not squeezed tight.' His voice sounded muffled again. She found the hand and footholds and kept climbing down, taking his advice.

Alfie's voice reached up to her. 'What's happening up there? I reached the bottom ages ago. What was that light? I can hear you, Anja, you're nearly down. I think there's a big tunnel down here.'

His irrepressible chatter helped her down the last few feet.

'Careful! Let me get out of the way.' Then she felt his little hand fumble until he clasped hers.

'What was going on up there?' But before she had time to answer, they had to make room for Quicksilver to join them.

'Stay there until I find a torch,' he said.

They heard him scrabbling about near them in the passage. A few sparks exposed his silhouette briefly, followed by a crackle, and the tunnel danced with light. Anja breathed a sigh of relief. Quicksilver looked at her, deeply regretting the need to bring her underground.

'The worst's over now,' he said, trying to be reassuring. 'We couldn't stay up there. The storm was too fierce.'

'This is fun, Anja,' Alfie butted in, oblivious to the thread of the conversation. Anja was too drained to give him one of her stares.

Quicksilver led them down the steep, narrow tunnel.

It smelt earthy, but the air was cool and breathable. The walls and floor were made of polished, hard earth and the light of the torch flickered and threw strange shadows as they descended.

'We had to come down the air vent,' Quicksilver explained. 'There is a door, but it hasn't been opened for years and has grown back into the tree.'

Anja and Alfie both understood what he was trying to explain.

'Who made all this?' Alfie asked, unintentionally changing the direction of the conversation.

'I'm not sure. I think I should know, but I can't remember properly. I know that it was made for the Folk, for their protection, but it didn't help them in the end. They didn't make it,' he added.

'If it didn't do them any good, what's the point of bringing *us* down here?' Anja snapped, irritated at the weakness she'd shown and his part in exposing it.

Quicksilver sighed. 'I didn't mean it like that. These groves gave them protection from the storms. They just couldn't stay in the Land.'

'Are you one of them? You belong with the trees, don't you?' Alfie probed.

'Yes, I belong with the trees, Alfie, but no, I am not one of the Folk,' he answered, bewildered by Anja's sharpness. 'Come on, we should get inside, dry off and eat. I'm starving.'

The tunnel wasn't long and soon came to an abrupt end. In the floor was a large black hole. It looked very uninviting. They peered down and by the light of the burning torch could see the first few rungs of a ladder disappearing into the dark.

Anja's spirits sank. She'd regained some of her composure, but the memory of her reliance on Quicksilver in an environment of his choosing was still making her resentful. She gave him a look which he tried to ignore.

'Alfie first again, then Anja, and I'll follow with the torch,' he declared breezily, infuriating her even more by grinning at her. 'It's only about ten feet down.'

Her stare made him feel so uncomfortable that he was glad when she lowered herself in, following Alfie, who had shot down like a rabbit. This time, using a ladder made the descent easier, and she reached the bottom in seconds. As Quicksilver followed them down, the torch revealed that they'd entered through the ceiling into the corner of a large room. He found a small earthenware jug that stood nearby and walked slowly around the walls, filling and then kindling lamps set in niches, which caused the room to glow and cast shadows.

'We'll spend the night here. By morning, the storm will have finished. I'll make some food.' He began rummaging about in the wooden benches that lined the walls.

In the centre of the room stood a long, roughly hewn table and around this an assortment of dusty chairs and benches were arranged. Anja and Alfie sat down in their wet clothes. It wasn't that cold, but more than they were now used to. They shivered and watched their strange companion, who was becoming stranger with each turn of events. Anja still glowered at him.

The object of her indignation had found a sizable

pan and was lighting a fire in a large hearth in the wall opposite the one they had climbed down. The smoke trickled lazily up a chimney. Large clay urns stood near the fire and he delved from one to another, coming up each time with handfuls of dried food of different types, solving the mystery of the recent abundance of food. An ingenious pipe arrangement issued a healthy trickle of fresh water when unstopped, and with all the necessities at his disposal, Quicksilver began to cook.

Anja made sure that Quicksilver was busy, and then moved her stool close to Alfie, then leant even closer. 'He pulled the tree open up there,' she whispered. 'He pushed his hands right into the wood and pulled it open, right in front of me. I could see outside. How do you suppose he can do that?'

Alfie pulled a face. 'I don't know. I saw him do it as well, outside. Why don't you ask him?' Anja shook her head; it was the last thing she wanted to do.

'I'll ask him for you.'

'Don't you dare,' she hissed.

Alfie decided to leave it alone. He would ask when Anja wasn't around. He was sure Quicksilver wouldn't mind telling him.

Quicksilver called them over. 'Come, sit by the fire. We'll dry off, then eat. Oh! And if you need to relieve yourselves, there's a special place behind that curtain.' He nodded to direct their gaze, adding, 'It's specially made for it.'

Alfie giggled; he hadn't used any sort of real toilet for a long time and the idea seemed funny. However, Anja did not want to be reminded of the repeated instances of embarrassing anxiety she had endured since their arrival, and behind a curtain didn't exactly seem private. She raised her eyes and sighed.

They welcomed the meal when it was ready. Alfie could hardly keep his eyes open after the first couple of eager mouthfuls. He began to look pale and his usual chatter deserted him. Quicksilver led him to one of a number of padded benches placed around the edge of the room. He curled up and quickly fell into a fitful sleep.

After eating, Anja was dry, warm and feeling slightly more amicable towards Quicksilver. She sat quietly with him for a while before excusing herself and going to a bench near Alfie. There was no way she was going to use the "room". She could wait until they were back above and find somewhere private. The traumatic descent kept her awake for a while and she watched Quicksilver as he turned over the contents stored inside benches across the room. He was still poking around when she finally lost consciousness. Sometime later, after finding what he was searching for, Quicksilver flopped down where he was and also drifted contentedly into sleep.

Neither of them was aware of Alfie's restless slumbers becoming animated, nor did they hear his incoherent mutterings. He was dreaming, and it wasn't a normal dream. It started suddenly and did not develop out of another dream. It wasn't a hallucination, but it was vivid, made sense and was so real that he felt he was living it…

7

Alfie woke up, or rather thought he had, in the same room he'd fallen asleep in, but it was now full of strange people: Folk; they were the Folk, as was he. Most were huddled around the table and a couple of children of different ages sat, like him, on the benches around the walls. Fear cloyed the atmosphere. There was no shouting, just a low desperate murmur, rising and falling. One or two voices of authority seemed to be trying to speak with reason, calming the others. Their clothing was like Quicksilver's but in all other ways they were different. He looked around for him and then for Anja, but they weren't there and he was wondering what had happened to them when one of the louder voices at the table began to emphasis a point. The hubbub died down as the others listened, but before he could catch what was being said, his surroundings changed.

He was standing on the swaying deck of a large sailing ship. He felt that he'd been on the boat for some time, maybe weeks. Looking upwards, he saw many men lying across a single great crossbeam, hauling up the massive rectangular sail hanging beneath it, heaving and furling the heavy cloth, working and chanting in practised unison.

The deck was crowded with Folk, who were laughing, embracing each other, cheering and pressing him towards one side of the boat. All were pointing at the long coastline which, at the nearest point to them, about a mile away, reared into tall white cliffs. He knew that this was the first land they'd seen since the great storm, but everything was vague. He could almost remember what had happened, but didn't; only the memory of a great storm. The sea was calm, with only a hint of an offshore breeze.

Thousands of great white gulls had flown out to greet them, their raucous calls filling the purest blue sky. Alfie pushed his way onto the raised aft deck with some other children to get a better look and directed his gaze away from the coast to see the rest of the small fleet. Some of the boats were bigger than the one he stood on and others were smaller; a hodgepodge of craft that all bore signs of the terrible battering they had taken. There were about a dozen; there should have been more.

A hush fell over the boat. Someone was hailing them. One solitary voice floated across the waves, barely discernible above the noise of the gulls. A landing place had been spotted in this large bay, where there was a gap in the cliffs. Men scrambled to lower the sails again. Many hands seized the sheets, more than were necessary. In the excitement, Alfie was knocked over. When he managed to stand up again, there was sand and coarse grass beneath his feet.

He was near the centre of a sweeping arc of Folk. Facing them was a group of older adults, more men than women. Some distance behind them the boats had been drawn up above the tideline onto the shore, and beyond that the sea glistened away to the far horizon.

'Endurance has brought us here,' the elders declared. 'The way up through the cliffs leads to pastures. Spread out, for this seems an empty and bountiful land.'

The Folk cheered and rejoiced.

In rapid succession, Alfie relived other fleeting scenes, of small optimistic families trekking inland across the Southern Downs, venturing to find a new life. Coming across great stone circles, they explained them away as monuments of a long-departed race. Thereafter, they avoided the places where the stones sat, squat and forbidding on the crowns of the highest hills, or in bowl-shaped valleys where unsuspecting travellers stumbled upon them, feeling a chill of fear creep over them as they passed nearer to them than they would have wished.

Small settlements rose. Their few livestock multiplied, and a few children were born who would only know that land, yet Alfie sensed unease. This land did not belong to them. They lived upon it, from it, but it was a mystery; it was too big, the seas were different, as was the sky, especially at night. The frequent storms they came to accept, to endure, for they were the lifeblood of the Downs. However, nothing could diminish their fear and loathing of the great monoliths.

Another meeting: elders shaking their heads and issuing stern warnings to the Folk not to disturb the stones;

younger men and women loudly extolling the virtue of throwing them down, convincing many with eloquent talk of the shadows cast over their lives and the constant unease. 'This land will never be ours until the stones are destroyed, more children will be born,' they cried. As time went by, those voices became influential.

One lone voice remained, belonging to the one who lived in the groves that had appeared after they arrived. Who served no purpose other than to remind them of hollow promises of protection before the tragedy that had befallen them, a voice they once revered but now ignored.

Alfie relived this as a child of the Folk, but couldn't remember any details of his existence there, as if he were borrowing another identity. Each time he remembered where he lived, he would forget the way; a vague recollection of the path would fade, and his mind accepted this. However, the mood was changing, and anxiety began to mar his restless slumber.

He was now part of a gathering of Folk from the small settlements on the low hills surrounding the "Vale of the Great Stone Circle". It had been found not long after they'd arrived, was feared and avoided, but couldn't be ignored. It consisted of two concentric circles of massive rectangular stones with others lying across their tops. The largest formed gateways through these circles and in the middle sat one great flat slab. Filling the bottom of the bowl-like valley, it was the biggest circle they'd found. There were many others, but none radiated such enmity. No settlement had been built too close and its dark presence dominated all the other rings that blighted the Downs, even those scattered far to the north.

'Bring down these stones,' the voices said, 'and we will finally claim this land as our own.'

A grove of the mighty trees had risen nearby, just outside the valley. It was small but had quickly grown thick and strong, as if pitting its strength against the circle, but it was a small island of peace in a sea of fear. The Folk grew confident, determined to remove the symbol of their fear. Only that one lone voice now stood against them, but they would not listen and shunned the outsider who begged them not to touch the stones.

Around the top of one of the outer stones they tied great ropes; lines of Folk standing beside them as they snaked up the swell of the valley. Not a breath of breeze stroked the lush grass; not a grasshopper's chirrup broke the silence. By late morning, the heat was fierce as men bent to grasp the ropes, taking the strain as the cords stretched. Then, with the echoing encouragement of those watching, they lay back and heaved. The ropes creaked, stretched, and they stepped backwards as one. The ropes grew taut, the men's faces strained with effort, but the stone moved not an inch. Others ran forward with picks and shovels to hack around its base. For hours they dug, for hours they pulled until at last, as the afternoon waned, almost imperceptibly, it moved, and as it did it groaned: a deep shuddering groan that echoed far over the Downs beneath the setting sun. The Folk dropped their tools, released the ropes and fearfully backed away. The groan came again, this time growing as it echoed out over the hills.

Flocks of ravens, such as had never been seen before, appeared like wisps of smoke in the distance. They approached rapidly, wheeling and soaring on the hot thermals until as a great mass they blotted out the sky above the valley, adding their cries to the dreadful sound. The sky darkened and huge clouds billowed, buffeting the high atmosphere. Alfie ran with the Folk, hands over their ears, panic-stricken as they tried to escape the impending wrath building around them. Then came the first searing bolts of lightning, screams mingled with the roar of the thunder. The ensuing storm unleashed fury across the Downs, a maelstrom of destruction. The settlements were destroyed, many died, and their few livestock driven mad with fear. Only those who reached the safety of the groves survived, huddled together. The storm battered the land for days until, at last, it subsided.

Images came faster and faster. Alfie's mouth worked silently trying to scream, unable to escape the terrible nightmare, always so vivid, so very real. Then he was back in the chamber, knowing now that it was a sanctuary from the storms that wracked the land. One small chamber beneath each grove, the pitiful remnants of the Folk living a subterranean existence, emerging warily until the ravens appeared again and the storms once more descended. He saw images of black flapping wings, stone circles and bloody beaks, of more loved ones disappearing, never to be seen again. He heard angry words, recriminations, recollections of dire warnings, and messengers scurrying from one isolated group to another.

Then a final meeting; word had come to gather at

the coast. Group by group, the few survivors passed from grove to grove, sheltering in the chambers and making sure that they were stocked for the next visitors. The storms reduced to a few in number, which harried and kept them fearfully watching the deceptive skies.

Alfie was back on the shore of the bay as the last stragglers came in. Boats were rebuilt; fewer than when they had arrived, but more Folk had survived than was first thought, especially those farthest from the great circle. The storms held off. They were being allowed to leave as they had arrived, except that those intervening years of toil and hope had been wasted. The day of embarkation came with a mixture of relief to be away and apprehension for the future. As the sails cracked before the wind and the timbers creaked in the growing swell, there were no farewells, no cheers, only disbelief that this deceptively beautiful land held such horror.

Alfie was with the small remnant of the fleet as they began to tack westwards across the bay, back along the coast. As they drew away from the white cliffs, two lone birds flew out to watch them go; not graceful white gulls, but ragged black harbingers of evil. The ravens slowly circled the fleet, their cries mocking the stunned faces following their flight. Then the wind died, and the sky began to darken. The Folk fell to their knees. The terrible images that followed distressed Alfie to the limit of his young mind. The unnatural dream transmitted suffering beyond anything his tender years could imagine: the wallowing craft destroyed beneath his feet by mountainous seas, the deck sliding away as the churning water rose, the final desperate screams; then the blackness and cold as he was engulfed, gasping for breath as the water closed over him.

Anja's face.

Gulping desperately for air, the huge sea pulled him down, water filling his mouth and lungs.

Quicksilver.

Soundlessly, he tried to scream to them through the water.

Anja again.

Then both.

They were looking down and mouthing something to him. He was jerked sharply up and roughly shaken awake, still gulping for air.

'Alfie! Wake up. *Wake up now.* You're having a nightmare.' Anja's eyes were drilling into his, then she softened and stroked his brow soothingly.

'I was drowning,' he gasped, almost hysterical with fear. He wanted to tell them about it, but Anja hushed him and cuddled his thin sweat-soaked body tightly to hers. He slowly relaxed and the immediate terror began to fade.

'These places hold memories,' Quicksilver said regretfully. He was not looking at Alfie but questioningly at Anja. 'They were places of sanctuary. Perhaps you should only enter them if there is need.'

That will have to be some need, Anja thought, almost aloud. She felt Alfie's breathing subside. He gave a huge shuddering sigh and reluctantly disentangled himself from her sisterly embrace and began to tell them about the dream.

Quicksilver quickly interrupted. 'It will be morning soon. We must think about going soon.'

Anja wondered how he knew, since they were completely isolated from the outside.

'First,' he continued, 'I've got a surprise for both of you.' As he had intended, the statement interrupted their thoughts. 'I had a good look around last night and found some things for both of you.' He walked over to where he'd slept and picked up one of the bundles on the bench, then lit some more of the lamps to brighten the room up.

'You first, Alfie.'

Alfie brightened up a bit. Quicksilver theatrically looked him up and down. 'Bit of a mess!' he said. Alfie screwed up his nose, eyes glued to the bundle, and Anja giggled. She could see that the dream was already fading and for once was pleased at how Quicksilver was helping him forget the nightmare. The atmosphere lightened.

When they'd started their adventure on that fateful night, Alfie had been wearing an old school shirt, a pair of shorts and underpants. He had discarded the last item before they left the forest; its flimsiness, the lack of proper hygiene and washing soon made it unwearable. His shirt and shorts he still more or less wore, filthy and falling apart. None of his attire had been in any way suitable for the rigours of this life but, being a boy, he hadn't given this a moment's thought.

Quicksilver picked the first item from the neat bundle and handed it to Alfie. It was a shirt like the one he was wearing himself. Alfie failed to remember that it was also like the one he'd been wearing in the dream. He then passed him a pair of breeches, again like his own. Alfie beamed widely and without any propriety, pulled off what was left of his old clothes. He soon stood before them in his new clothes and a smile so wide that it threatened to split his face in two. A pair of soft buskins and a tooled leather belt that pulled the tunic in at his waist completed his wardrobe.

Anja giggled again, but for a different reason. All the recent traumas that had assailed them had created tension that had to snap. The sight of her brother bursting with pride in the outlandish garb stirred this mood and she couldn't help herself. Her eyes twinkled. Alfie caught her expression and began to colour, still smiling.

'What?'

She tried to control herself but failed miserably and snorted. 'You look like a little pixie,' she sniggered.

Alfie's cheeks blazed and he lifted his arm in a futile smacking gesture. Her eyes narrowed and she said, 'What you really need is a little pointy cap, just to make it perfect.'

For support, he turned to Quicksilver, who totally misread the situation. He had no idea what was developing and did what he thought he had been asked. He went over to one of the benches and produced a little leather cap for Alfie. It was perfect.

Anja dissolved into laughter. She took the hat and tried to put it on her brother, who was feebly punching her and laughing himself, so infectious was her mood. Then, Quicksilver, again not realising how his innocent well-intentioned actions could be misused, came to Alfie's rescue in the most stunning manner.

8

Whilst Anja was still mercilessly teasing her
brother, Quicksilver casually went back to the
bench and returned with another garment.
Wordlessly, he stood between them and held it up for
her inspection. It was a dress. Not just any dress, but the
loveliest dress she had ever seen. Her mouth fell open and
she gasped, knowing instinctively that it would fit her.
Even by the imperfect light of the lamps, she could see
that the luxurious material matched the deep green of the
forest and that the hems and bodice had been exquisitely
embroidered with silver thread. He held it up by the
shoulders, indicating that she should take it.

She didn't budge. She stared emptily at him for
a moment, looked back at the dress and then fixed her
gaze on the wall over his left shoulder. Her face was
expressionless.

There was a long silence. Quicksilver, confused,
turned to Alfie, who shrugged.

'It's beautiful, Anja,' Alfie said, genuinely trying to

understand and ease the situation. She darted a cold look at him, quickly returning her gaze to the wall.

Using a sense that all close siblings have, he suddenly realised what was the matter, and the enormity of the power it transferred to him filled his mischievous little mind, especially after the way she had teased him. 'Aren't you going to try it on?' he asked, as innocently as he could behind his glittering eyes. Anja darted another look of venom but could not control the flush beginning to prickle her cheeks. Alfie knew he had hit the bullseye.

She was trapped. Unlike her brother, she had taken great care to maintain her shabby clothing to some degree of cleanliness and decorum and, considering that her complete wardrobe consisted of a thin summer dress and flimsy underwear, this had demanded great care. In the almost constant company of her carefree little brother and strange older youth, this had also meant careful control of her privacy, which she had been able to manage extremely well, until now. She knew that Alfie, after she'd teased him so unmercifully, would not have the sense to restrain himself.

'What's the matter, Anja? That old dress is falling to bits. It'll look lovely on you, won't it, Quicksilver?' His eyes remained fixed on Anja, betraying his apparently innocent face. Quicksilver obliviously agreed. Her eyes snapped back to her brother, anger now matching her flaming cheeks, then focused on Quicksilver for being such an ignorant dolt. Quicksilver simply looked back at her uncomfortably, wondering what he had done. She couldn't believe that he could be so crass. Alfie could hardly restrain himself. He had never managed to embarrass his sister as well as this. Sensing victory, he pushed his luck further than sense dictated. 'Come on, it's lovely.'

Something inside Anja's mind welled up. The blush faded. Alfie suddenly smelt the warmth of the forest woodlands again and his expression changed. He remembered his walks in the forest, Fox was calling him, his mind began to unravel...

'Anja, Stop! Don't!' Quicksilver's shout snapped Alfie back. Anja looked bewildered. It took her a few moments to recover and then she remembered the correct way to handle her brother, the time-honoured way that big sisters punished their little brother's cheekiness. She flew at him.

All her carefully built decorum dissolved as she fell on him with a flurry of blows. They dropped to the floor. Alfie, helpless with laughter at this final acknowledgement of victory, was beyond defending himself. Anja was half laughing, half crying, but even her hardest punches could not suppress his laughter. Quicksilver, who moments before had briefly perceived a shocking revelation, was struggling to understand what was happening. Alfie, still trying to tease Anja, was not able to string two words together without exploding into giggles. Anja realised that her dignity was compromised and stood up. Quicksilver, without the slightest notion that his innocent actions were determining events, handed her the dress. 'I've found some other pretty things for you as well. They go with the dress, see if it fits.' She took the dress, chewed her lip and finally looked to Alfie for help.

'She won't put it on in front of us,' he said bluntly, 'she's a girl,' as if this was the only explanation necessary.

Quicksilver shook his head. 'Oh, I didn't realise. Use the room that I showed you, behind the curtain. Haven't either of you been there yet?' He motioned towards the hanging he had previously mentioned.

Anja sulkily walked over and pulled the hanging to one side. Behind it was a door. She opened it and went inside. A few seconds passed and she came back out, still holding the dress.

'We're not going anywhere yet, and you,' she said to Quicksilver, 'can heat the biggest pots of water you can find.'

Quicksilver sighed, his quick return to the outside fading, wondering if he would ever understand her. He nodded and went to do as he was told.

'It's a room, like a proper bathroom, and there's a sort of bathtub,' she told Alfie in her best big-sister voice, 'and when I've finished, it's your turn.'

Alfie grimaced. He *did* understand his sister and knew that one way or another, since he had nowhere to hide, he would be having a bath.

Anja supervised the filling of the tub whilst Quicksilver carted hot water. He then found pots of various substances that he said were sweet-smelling oils and creams that Folk ladies had used. 'And smelly boys,' she added. Quicksilver snorted. Anja hadn't meant him and coloured a little, because Quicksilver didn't smell like other boys. When he had pressed against her inside the tree trunk, she could still remember how he had smelt, like freshly cut wood;

sweet exotic wood, the sort they made boxes from that expensive gifts were packed in, as beautiful as the presents themselves. She wanted to apologise but didn't know how.

'I might as well make some food,' he said.

Anja nodded. 'Do I have to rush?' she asked wistfully.

'No, it won't harm to have one easy day.'

'But when we go back up, will it be the same way?'

'No, as soon as you're ready, there's another way out.'

Anja gave him a rare warm smile and he left her. The thought of a hot bath made the idea of staying underground just bearable; more so as she opened the pots and released the wonderful aromas within. She was definitely not going to hurry.

Quicksilver and Alfie sat quietly talking as they ate. They had sensibly decided not to wait for Anja. Alfie was confiding in his friend some of the details he could recall from his dream. Quicksilver sat and listened but didn't comment. The immediate horror having passed, Alfie asked Quicksilver what he thought the dream had been about.

'I don't know where it came from,' Alfie declared. 'I've never heard a story about anything like that.'

'It's not a story, it happened. It's the grove telling you about the people who came and lived here not long before you arrived, and the stone circles are real enough, we'll see some soon.'

Alfie looked at him. 'Do we have to go near them?'

'No, just be careful, but don't worry, I'm used to them.' In a way, he was almost glad that Alfie had had the nightmare. His natural curiosity would be controlled by the apprehension that the dream had instilled, and near the stone rings they would all have to be extremely cautious. He wondered why the grove had let Alfie experience the dream and felt that it had bound his little companion closer to him. In the back of his mind, he couldn't shake the possibility that Anja being there might have been part of the reason. Something serious was happening to her.

'Anja's been a long time,' Alfie said, as if he'd been listening to this thought.

'Why, are you in a hurry to have this bath?'

Alfie hadn't thought of that and looked darkly at the curtain hiding the door. At that moment, it was pushed aside, and his mouth gaped.

Anja looked so different, like another person. When she had gone in, she had been his lovely sister in very tatty clothes, but now…! She was wearing the "dress and other pretty things" that Quicksilver had found for her. It could have been made for her. Its fine, strong material clung to her and fell gracefully to just above her knees, and she had put on short, soft leather buskins. A fine belt of silver leaves hung about her hips. Her dark hair was brushed until it shone, and over it she wore a silver net cap studded with tiny pearls.

As she walked self-consciously towards them, the sweet scent of the oils wafted with her.

'You look like a princess of the forest,' Alfie said proudly.

More than that, Quicksilver thought. And although he could not help smiling at how beautiful she was, there was a tinge of sadness, because seeing her now and what he had glimpsed earlier convinced him of the importance of the promise he'd made to Pan.

Alfie stretched up and kissed her on the cheek. 'You're beautiful,' he whispered.

'And you're dirty and smelly,' she said, happily bathing in his love. She pointed to the door. He grinned sheepishly but was already pulling off his new tunic as he left the room.

She turned to Quicksilver. 'Who were these made for?'

He pointed to another bundle wrapped in strong cloth on the table. 'There are two, almost identical. I suppose you could say that they were made for you.'

Anja looked perplexed. 'I don't understand. How could they have been made for me?'

He sighed, not sure that he should have answered like that. He should have been more tactful. Now he had to try again. 'They are not clothes that the Folk wore. They were made for someone that did not really exist. I think young Folk girls mostly wear the same clothes as boys. I have found some for you to change into. Those are not really suitable for getting out of here and travelling in.'

She nodded, screwing up her nose. The thought of wearing the same as him and Alfie seemed wrong. 'Well, at least that will be the end of the forest princess thing.'

He continued, ignoring her prompt to drop the subject. 'Alfie was sort of right, what he said when you came in. They were made for someone the Folk thought at first might help them, I can't really remember, someone who might have in their own land. But this was not their own land and they drove away the only help they had.' He smiled at her. 'They probably would have driven you away as well. They would have been overwhelmed by you.' She shrugged, not wanting to continue this conversation; she didn't want to hear any more.

Whilst they waited for Alfie, she ate her food then examined the tunic and trousers that Quicksilver had found her. She was surprised at how small the bundle was that contained the other dress. She said it would be a shame to get them creased, that they should leave them. He shook his head.

'The material will never crease or tear, nor will it stay dirty. I still wouldn't keep it on today, but you should take them.'

She was preoccupied with her new clothes and could hear Alfie hopping about trying to dress behind the door, so didn't think to ask him why. When Alfie emerged, clean as a new pin, Anja disappeared again to change into her travel clothes. She was ready to leave.

They all laughed good-naturedly when she came back out. She was trying to stuff her hair into a cap like the one she had ribbed Alfie about. Her hair had always been shoulder-length and hadn't seemed to have grown since their arrival, but she had nothing to pin it up with. Prompted into a decision she had been considering for a while, she went back into the small side room and came out holding a small pair of shears.

'Cut my hair around the nape of my neck,' she told Quicksilver, 'and do it straight.'

Quicksilver looked questioningly at her for a second or two but saw that she was serious. He took the shears and snipped until the job was done. She gathered up the cut locks and put them in one of the bench lockers, then turned to Alfie and smiled in a "how do I look now?" sort of way. 'Wow!' was all he could manage. She laughed and this time her hair tucked neatly into the cap. That done, Quicksilver put all the bits and pieces into bags he had found for them, which they slung across their bodies with the flasks. It was time to leave.

'The way out,' he began with an apologetic glance to Anja, 'is a bit awkward.' He held his hand up to forestall her and continued. 'We came in down the ventilation shaft from high in the tree, but to get out we only have to get to ground level, and there's another way. It's a proper escape route. It involves a climb and is a bit dark.' He gave Anja another "wait until I've finished" look. 'But it isn't long and not as narrow.' He avoided any questions by going over to a large high-backed bench, and with some effort lifted one end away from the wall. Behind was a gaping black hole. Anja sighed miserably.

'Alfie, you first again.'

Alfie shrugged, proud of the responsibility.

'Can't we take a torch?' Anja asked hopefully.

'I'm afraid not, we would end up with someone getting singed or choking on the smoke.'

She nodded glumly. Quicksilver gave Alfie his instructions. 'After you've crawled in a few yards, you'll be able to stand up. You should feel the end of a thick rope hanging down. Climb up the rope. It can't rot so it's quite safe and is knotted all the way up. Only one of us can start at a time because there's not much room at the bottom.

When you get to the top, there'll be a layer of soil and matted, thin root covering the entrance. Don't look up, and scrape through with your hands. Have you got that?'

Alfie nodded enthusiastically and went to dive into the hole.

'Wait, I haven't finished,' Quicksilver laughed. 'When you feel the bottom of the rope, shout out and then, Anja, you can start. Wait at the bottom and relay any messages to me from Alfie. When Alfie gets to the top, duck back into the tunnel until he's cleared a way through, or you'll get covered in dirt. After that, there will be light for you to climb by. But don't forget to tell me when you've started to climb. Take the bags off. They'll get in the way.'

This time, Alfie waited for a second to make sure that he'd finished before vanishing into the hole. He scrambled into blackness, his body blocking the dim light of the chamber, forcing him to feel his way forward. After a few yards, as Quicksilver had promised, he sensed that he had space around him. Following the sides of the tunnel with his hands, he realised that he could go no further and tentatively stood up. His face brushed against something and he involuntarily jerked back. It took him a second or two to locate the rope again. 'I've found the rope,' he yelled.

'Good, start climbing,' came the muffled reply.

Alfie knew how to climb ropes. He had done it at school. Reaching up, he grasped the rope and pulled himself upwards, lifting his knees to feel for a knot with his feet. It was easy; the knots were quite big and had been spliced into the rope. He was light, very fit and strong. He scooted up, feeling his way in the darkness. He was just beginning to breathe heavily when his hands hit dirt as he slid them up above his head. A shower of loose material cascaded over and past him. It was then he realised Anja was waiting below.

'Alfie!' she shouted, as it poured down on her upturned face. He could hear her coughing and spluttering and, having received a face-full himself, wondered why they'd bothered to have a bath.

'You were supposed to tell me before you started digging,' she shouted furiously. 'Can you hear me?'

'I haven't started digging yet,' he shouted back, grinning as he pictured how she must look. 'My hand just hit the dirt. I got it as well.'

'Well, wait for me to get out of the way,' she yelled, backing into the tunnel. It was lucky for Quicksilver that she could not see him grinning. She hadn't needed to relay what was happening; her caustic shouting was enough.

Meanwhile, Alfie had decided how he was going to break through without getting too much soil in his face. He hoped it wouldn't take too long because his arms were getting tired. He positioned his feet on the highest knot that he could get purchase on and, tucking his head under the arm holding on to the rope, closed his mouth and eyes. With his free hand, he punched up as hard as he could. A couple of blows later, he felt the latticework of fine roots begin to weaken. He had a rest, breathing hard, and then got ready to attack it again. This time, the first blow broke the flimsy plug and a welter of earth, roots, stones, twigs and grass crashed down. This sudden success caught him unawares and he almost followed. Daylight streamed in, temporarily blinding him.

'You all right?' Anja's worried voice floated up a few seconds later.

'Yes, wait a minute.' He was struggling now and wanted to get out before his arms and legs gave out. He felt further up the rope and found that it went up and was secured somewhere out of the hole. He exerted himself one final time and pulled himself out. Luckily, there were no brambles in the undergrowth. He flopped down, half in a bush, exhausted.

Anja's insistent voice dragged him back to the rim of the hole. He shouted down to her. 'It's all right, I'm out.'

'I know, you idiot, I'm climbing. Get away from the top, you're knocking all sorts of mess onto me.'

She had to rest a couple of times during her ascent and was also exhausted when she finally emerged. She was even grateful for Alfie's help to get her legs over the edge, and collapsed in a dishevelled heap next to him. *So much for the forest princess*, she thought through the ache in her wrists. Not long afterwards, Quicksilver's grinning face emerged, and he effortlessly eased himself out of the hole that the other two had made larger with their struggles.

'That's why I suggested you change into those clothes,' he said cheerfully.

Anja shook her hair out of her cap and for the fourth or fifth time in a short while, murdered him with a glance. Ignoring it again, he turned back to the hole. They noticed he had a thin line tied to his belt. This line disappeared back down the shaft and he hauled it up, depositing the bags tied to it on the ground. Untying and picking them up, he led them away from the huge tree and out of the grove into open grassland.

9

Rob Hemmersley had been constantly terrified since he had fallen out of the tree into the pond. Tiny, naked and vulnerable, everything that swam, crawled, slithered or flew saw him as their next meal. His mind dissolved. In the depths of a thorny bush that gave him some protection, he sat or fitfully slept and forgot his lack of clothing in the sultry pond environment. He'd tried to remember what had happened, but his only fractured memory was of the two children passing his cottage, him rushing out after them down the lane, and turning off past the church into the fields. He had been lured to wherever this was by the children; they'd led him to this.

As weeks passed, Rob's constant fear became burning anger, then a fierce will to survive that descended into mania as he realised that there was no way out of his predicament. He fixated on the children. Driven by consuming hatred, he became feral, slaughtering anything that crossed his path. The inhabitants of the pond tried to avoid the strange little creature that crouched under the bush that supplied him with the long thorns with which he tormented and killed his victims. The monstrous insects and nightmare creatures he ambushed filled his dreams and he woke screaming night after night. Humanity and reason slipped away and, cursed, berating his fate, he turned to maniacally screaming the horrors he intended to inflict on those who had drawn him there. He killed everything, ate anything and since his body immediately expelled most of it, was oblivious to the filth that surrounded and coated him.

The final nail driven through his mind came by way of an unfortunate mole, as large as himself, crossing his path. Although it represented no danger and its meat was indigestible, he attacked it, unmoved by its desperate defence and screams of pain before it succumbed to his relentless assault. Using a small sliver of sharp flint, he crudely hacked through its thick pelt, skinning it over a period of days. He tried eating its raw flesh and suffered the consequences but returned every day, scraping away every stinking lump of fat until it was ready to be staked out to dry in the sun, the rotting carcass nearby drawing easier prey to slaughter. When the sun had finished its work, he wore the pelt like a great black cloak with its face for a hood. Convinced that he was now invincible, he spent long hours imagining horrific ways to inflict pain on the children. For two months, he languished in madness by the pool. Then his fate took another rude turn.

Shuffling down to the pond's edge to drink as the sun was going down, his eyes warily darting from side to side, without warning, a massive blow struck his back and he was whisked into the air. Before he could react, he was high above the trees, protected only by his thick cloak from the talons of the great raven that clutched him. His thorn was still in his hand, squashed against his side.

Rob realised he was in the air but the hood of the thick cape that had saved him from injury was pressed over his face, blinding him. He relaxed in his tight cocoon, sniggering, thinking only of the pain he would inflict on his captor. After many hours, the bird slowly descended, alighting on a large, flat stone ledge. He fell and struggled to his knees, aching as the blood began to circulate in the areas that had been compressed. His lack of fear drove him to stagger to his feet in time to see a large, dark face and hooked beak jabbing down at him. Instinctively, he stabbed back with his thorn spear. By good fortune, the sharp tip scraped along the hard beak and embedded itself in a glowing yellow eye. The bird's screech drowned out his own and he was knocked off the stone ledge as it flapped away in agony. He tumbled down onto the long, lush grass below, listening to its awful cries fading into the night.

Rob surveyed his surroundings as best he could in the bright moonlight from the midst of the thick, tall grass. He'd fallen from a lintel spanning two huge upright monoliths that towered high above him and could see more either side of these. Had he been his normal size he would have seen the jagged stone circle they were part of. He sat down abruptly with his back to the hard surface and pulled the moleskin tightly around him, not for warmth, but to shut out reality and ponder his continuing dismal luck. His warped mind focused again on the children, cursing them with venomous hatred and snarling to his spear the appalling vengeance he would inflict when he found them.

*

The lonely mew of the seagull echoed high amongst the towers and flying buttresses of the castle, soaring with the bird, tearing the harsh silence. On the crenelated roof of the highest tower a tiny figure stirred and raised a corner of his pyjama top with his free hand, the other had its thumb stuck firmly in his mouth. The pyjama top was draped carefully over his head, covering his face and narrow shoulders. He'd sat like that for most of the searing day, just as he had for almost as long as his short memory could remember. The gull had flown so close that it stirred him from his torpor, and he couldn't resist a peep at the rare sight of another living thing. The graceful bird swooped low, then caught a thermal and glided from sight. His little blue eye blinked and then disappeared once more behind the makeshift veil.

Roused from his hazy daydreams, the little boy got to his feet. His ludicrous headgear dangled down his back, and with his free hand, he again lifted the front just enough to see where he was going. Apart from this one practical concession to the sun, he was naked. His deep, almost unnatural brown tan denied the agonies his small body had suffered for the first month after his inexplicable arrival, pain that could still be detected on raw, sun-scarred areas of his body that he aimlessly scratched from time to time. In his young mind, that pain was a distant nightmare, but the experience had driven him

96

to spend most of his solitary days rocking gently inside the shaded doorway of the stairwell.

He toddled over to the low battlements with the weariness of having done so time and time again. He clambered up onto one of the embrasures and, sliding on his bare bottom over the hot, sandy top, swung his short legs over the edge to gaze at the distant cliffs from beneath his improvised sunshade. He was oblivious to the sheer dizzying drop to the top of a wall below and even further, to the parched seabed far beneath his swinging heels. His tower rose like an eagle's eyrie, higher than any other surmounting the castle walls.

Shuffling over to the centre of the embrasure, his position became precarious. He leant forward with his hands braced either side of his body. Every so often, he pushed down, lifting himself up slightly, swinging on his hands to find a more comfortable position. He balanced his bottom on the very edge over the long drop and put his hands in his lap. Looking down, he carefully swayed forward to achieve the exact point of balance. He wanted to be like the big white bird and fly down to the sand far beneath his perch. His pyjama jacket fell back over his face, but he was concentrating. He let his weight slowly pitch him forward until his body approached the maximum point of balance.

Behind him, the hard, sandy surface began to cave in. The rear of the embrasure collapsed and with a squeak of surprise, he tumbled back. Getting up, he grabbed his precious comforter and ran back to the doorway, where he sat in his favourite place, carefully arranged his pyjama top until it hung to his satisfaction and jammed his thumb back in his mouth.

The embrasure remade itself. After it was complete, the noise of gently pouring sand continued. A figure grew from the millions of grains of shifting sand. A tall, featureless parody of a man with

97

blank, soulless eyes dispassionately watched the small boy rocking gently in the doorway. *'Not yet, it is not time,'* the creature said in a soft, rasping voice. It had no memory, no plan or purpose other than to push the ocean back. By chance of fate, it had discovered how to fulfil this compulsion. As each child it brought back was torn open on the spars, as each drop of blood soaked into the baked seabed, so its rudimentary intelligence grew and the wall across the bay advanced. Soon there would be more blood, a lot more, powerful blood.

The figure disassembled, flowing back into the tower. Immediately, the silence was broken by the clamouring multitude of gulls on the distant cliffs. The little boy stopped sucking for a moment to listen but didn't look from under the barrier he had constructed between himself and a world he didn't wish to see. A memory flashed into his mind, filling him with unbearable desire.

'Anja?' Toby whispered.

10

In the late-afternoon sun, they sat on the grass a short way from the grove. Anja ran her hands over the lush turf. 'With all that rain, you'd expect it to be soaking wet.'

'The Land cried out for water and has drunk deeply,' Quicksilver replied. 'The sun is hot and has had all day to do its work. In the valleys, the streams will be tumbling with fresh water and the Great River swollen and angry. We'll camp here tonight and start out again in the morning.' They settled down to relax. Alfie gathered wood for a fire whilst Anja lay back and breathed the clean, fresh air, trying to erase the memory of the underground shelter from her mind.

Quicksilver was busy tipping out the contents of the bags, rearranging them for the journey ahead. He was also thinking about the night they had experienced. He wondered about the unusual severity of the storm, which was worrying. However, what he had observed within Alfie, and more so Anja, was more disturbing. Both, in different ways, were showing indications of the Land influencing them. Alfie, he could manage, the growing affinity he felt for his little companion heightened by the grove giving him the dream. However, with Anja he was out of his depth; she needed help, and very soon. What had happened when she'd been angry was especially worrying. Again, he thought how glad he was he'd taken Pan's advice to take this route to the coast, because along the way she would get that help.

He watched Alfie and Anja building the fire as he had shown them, and soon stew was cooking. 'At the last minute, I decided to bring along some more stuff,' he told them when they'd finished. 'It's the largest shelter this far north and well stocked. The further south we travel, the more provisions will have been used by the Folk retreating to the coast.' Anja and Alfie hardly heard him. Snuggled together, they were already dozing. He smiled and shook his head. His thoughts strayed to his friend, Fox, who had got him involved in all this, and he wondered how he was faring. On reflection, taking all into consideration, he had coped well so far. He had taken on a serious challenge. Initially, he had thought that the chance of them getting safely to the coast had been minimal. Now he didn't want to think of their fate if they did.

The following days took on the familiar pattern of walking and sleeping. The children were becoming wiser and warier, and on the third day they saw their first stone circle sitting menacingly on the crown of a low hill, some distance to their right. Alfie took Anja's hand and became unusually quiet. Quicksilver hurried them on until it was a distant shadow and when they stopped for a rest, he decided that it was time to expand their knowledge.

'This far north, the circles are small and infrequent. If a storm comes, we'll have no problem getting to shelter. We're following a route that's never too far from a grove. The storms here on the North Downs are not usually as strong as the one a few days ago, so we should be free of them for a while at least.' He smiled at Anja. 'Hopefully, we won't need to go into another of the shelters, and if we do, we'll not use the vents unless we absolutely have to.'

Anja said that he and Alfie could do what they liked; she'd be staying outside in the grove, storm or no storm.

'But we must keep away from the stone rings,' he continued, ignoring her remark, 'because if we're caught near a large one in the open when a storm comes, we'll be in danger.'

'What about those big black birds I saw in my dream?' Alfie asked.

Quicksilver shuddered. 'I hope we never see any. They are ravens and don't belong in this part of the Land. They're a portent of danger. If you ever see one, no matter how far away it is, tell me.'

Anja felt that this lecture was primarily directed at her. Alfie had been furiously nodding his little head in support of Quicksilver's warning. She would talk to him later when they were on their own.

'Tonight, I'll show you the proper way to get in the shelters,' he said to Alfie, 'then you can get things from them as well.'

'Like a bath,' Anja quipped.

Later that evening, when they'd made camp, the boys went into the nearby grove whilst Anja prepared the evening meal. They found a large tree in the centre. 'There's always one in each grove,' Quicksilver said, walking Alfie around it. Alfie started running his hands over the surface. 'That's exactly how to do it,' he said, not realising that Alfie was merely copying what he had seen him do during the storm. 'Tell me when you feel a slight change in the surface.'

Alfie continued and on his second circuit, stopped. 'Here it is,' he said.

'Right,' Quicksilver congratulated his beaming friend, 'now push, not sharply but with constant pressure.'

Alfie braced his feet and, using two hands, pushed. He felt a slight give and then resistance. He kept up the pressure and a gentle cracking sound started. At first, he couldn't see where it was coming from, then he saw a faint line emerge and spread, tracing the shape of a small door. A very thin top layer of bark had grown over it that parted perfectly when pressure was applied. It swung inwards. Alfie was delighted.

'That's what should have happened to the other one,' Quicksilver said, 'but if they're not used for a long time, they grow back into the tree. Over the years, I've visited most of the groves, but there are still some I haven't, like that big one the other night.'

He didn't tell Alfie that there was no discernible difference between the surface of the door and the rest of the tree. Alfie would either intuitively know it was there or wouldn't. Quicksilver knew that his suspicions about Alfie's development were correct. They entered the shelter and searched it.

'Never take more than you need. None of the provisions will be replaced,' he warned.

When they got back, Alfie told Anja about the doors in the trees. She listened politely but seemed distracted; something was on her mind. 'Are you unwell?' Quicksilver asked. Their health had been extraordinarily good, apart from the odd headache or stomach problem during the first few weeks. Since then, they had suffered no illness at all. He had a vague idea of what sickness was but had never experienced it.

'No. I just suddenly thought about Toby, I can't explain. It upset me a bit, that's all.' She looked close to tears. 'I often think about him, but since we were told that no harm would come to him, I've been more concerned with reaching him. I know it sounds silly, but it's almost as if he called to me in my head, just now. I can't shake it off.'

Quicksilver didn't seem surprised. 'Then he did,' he said, as if she shouldn't have doubted herself. 'It proves that he's alive and needs you. You can't do more than you're doing, Anja. We can't go faster.'

'How much further left have we got to go?' Alfie asked. Questions like this only popped into his mind when prompted.

Quicksilver was not sure whether to divulge all the answers. Would it be better not to let them think that far ahead? he wondered. In the end, he decided that Anja needed to understand what they were facing. 'If you take a straight line from the Great Forest to the bay, I suppose we still have about ten times the distance we've covered so far, without detours.'

Alfie thought about it for a moment and then his face fell. 'Ten times!' he repeated. 'We've been walking for weeks and weeks. My legs will be worn away. We'll never get there.' He collapsed backwards in disappointment. Anja also looked disheartened. They had touched on it before, but it had not sunk in how far their destination was. The sound of Toby's voice haunted her, and she ached to press his little face to her cheek.

'He can't possibly survive until we get there,' she said brusquely. 'He's only a baby.' She stopped voicing her thoughts; the images were too horrible to contemplate.

'Toby will still be alive, even if we take a year to get there,' Quicksilver said emphatically. 'I've been told that the creature will keep him alive until you arrive, it's what happens then that we don't know.' They both stared at him. 'But it's not going to take us a year to get there. Remember the Great River I talked about? Soon, we'll come to it. We've been cutting across the Downs to join it below the last rapids. It's not navigable for us further upriver. Our journey will be mostly by boat.'

Alfie's tiredness left him for a moment. 'Have you got a boat? I've never been on a boat, not a real one.' Anja also felt a thrill of excitement, realising that their journey would not be so long. 'How long will it take us then?'

'I can't be exact, but we'll be on or near the river for about a month, maybe a bit longer. Then we leave it before it widens into the estuary entering the Southern Ocean.

After about four more weeks trekking across to the coast, we should reach the bay.' Anja sat trying to calculate how long it would take altogether. Quicksilver realised and forestalled her. 'Don't expect that to be precise. I simply wanted to reassure you that it wouldn't take as long as you feared.'

'So we get there, and rescue Toby, then have to come all the way back with him; just a baby. We're never going to get home, are we, not really? It's going to take years, Mummy and Daddy will think we're dead.' She stared at him; no emotion showed on her face. 'We will be older and they won't recognise us.'

'Why not?' he asked, puzzled.

'Because we will have changed, got older, especially Toby.'

'Why would you change? You will be the same.'

'Not if it's two years, we will have grown older.'

Quicksilver still looked puzzled. 'I don't know what you mean. Two years might pass until you can return to your parents, but you will still be the same. Two years is nothing, is it? Perhaps you might look a bit older in a hundred or so years, but not in just a few years.'

Anja shook her head. 'You're so weird.' Then she sighed, realising he hadn't understood her. 'Sorry, that wasn't nice, I didn't mean it. When will we reach this Great River?' she asked, trying to change the subject, and needing a goal to bolster her hope.

'Just a few more days,' he replied nonchalantly. 'Then the excitement starts.' Anja was speechless that he hadn't told them the Great River was so close. Alfie tried to press him for more, but he wouldn't be drawn. 'Getting on the river is really exciting,' was all he offered.

As promised, a few days later, they came to the end of the first phase of their journey. Quicksilver and Alfie stood on the edge of a precipice. Directly across from them, looking deceptively near, was the other side of an immense canyon. The scale of the incredible view made them feel like ants. Peering down, Alfie could barely hear the roar of the Great River far below.

'How are we going to get down?' Anja asked, staying some distance from the edge and dreading the reply.

'We could try climbing down,' Quicksilver began, but stopped as he saw the look of panic on her face. He nodded towards a belt of trees growing along the top of the cliff a few hundred yards to their left. 'Or we might find a better way down over there.' As they approached the trees, Anja could see that it was one of his groves.

Once within its lofty shade, he left Anja to make camp, ably hindered by Alfie, who was seething with excitement which had turned to frustration when Quicksilver had not reappeared for some time. When he finally returned, Alfie was napping. 'Come, walk with me,' he invited Anja. Back along the clifftop, some way from the grove, they sat on a rocky outcrop as near to the edge of the canyon as she would go.

'Watch,' Quicksilver said.

The sun setting behind them picked out every feature on the huge golden rock face opposite, the shadow of the cliff on which they were sitting slowly rising up it; a long line of darkness. It was beauty on a grand scale. Twilight crept across the vast panorama and the sky softened in hue until, first a few, then many and eventually multitudes of stars blazed down from the dark heavens.

'Is there such beauty where you come from?' Quicksilver asked.

'I didn't know everywhere,' Anja replied. 'I only know where I used to live.'

'Used to?'

'You know what I mean. It seems such a long time ago, at least to me it does.'

'What will you do if… when you rescue Toby?'

She shrugged, ignoring the "if". She'd never dared think that far ahead.

'We *will* go back home,' she replied eventually.

'What will you tell them?'

Anja shrugged again. 'I don't know. The truth.'

Quicksilver was watching her face lit by the starlight. Her sadness was profound.

'How are you going to get home?' His pressure was gentle and paced.

'I don't know, but Pan will help us.' She looked at him; a defiant edge had crept into her voice.

'Of course he will. What you said, though, will they understand what happened?'

Anja's tone relaxed, knowing that he was only asking things that she needed to consider, however difficult.

'I try not to think about it, rescuing Toby is all that matters for now. Anyway, none of us might come back. If we do, I'll worry about it then, but I must return to Pan. I promised.'

Quicksilver nodded but didn't comment.

'What about you?' Anja asked defensively. 'You're not just any ordinary boy, are you?'

She didn't get an immediate reply so continued to probe.

'How long have you lived here?'

'I don't know, not long.'

'You came with those Folk, didn't you, how long ago was that?'

'I am not sure, I can't remember being with them, only everything that happened when they were here. I've always been like this. Time doesn't mean anything here.'

A vague timescale crept into Anja's mind; longer than he'd implied. Later, she would understand how this happened.

'So, you never get any older. What are you then, some sort of Peter Pan?' A hint of vindictiveness entered her voice.

He didn't know who Peter Pan was. He didn't need to; he could feel her hostility.

'I came with the groves. I was somewhere else before, for a long time, I can't remember. I understand what you mean about getting older, but I think you're mixing different sorts of time.' The hostility changed to confusion in her eyes and he decided to leave explaining that to someone else. He hadn't meant to talk about all this.

'Nothing could have helped the Folk,' he said, almost to himself. 'The shelters didn't make any difference in the end. They couldn't stay in them forever. They should never have entered the Land.'

Anja found herself drawn into his tale. 'Why didn't you go with them? Don't they need you now, wherever they are?'

He smiled glumly. 'I am what I am, I belong with the groves. The Folk were destroyed, that's why I'm helping you rescue your brother from the creature. The Land might accept me then.'

'Did the creature kill them?'

'No, but I think it exists because they died.'

'The Land does accept you, though.'

'I'm not sure, there's something powerful that lives beneath the Downs, it controls the stone circles. It doesn't want the groves, and I belong with them. If it kills me, the groves will eventually die.'

By unspoken consent, they decided that each had revealed enough of themselves for one day. They ambled back to the camp. Anja thought about their conversation for a long time before she slept; she still didn't know what Quicksilver was but wasn't so suspicious of him. He was still annoying though, and she resented how much she relied on him.

Within a few days, that estimation had multiplied. It started the next day as he led them into the belt of grove trees.

'Where are you taking us?'

'To get a boat, but we have to get down the cliffs first. The way down is through the grove. Not like the last time, just a short walk through some tunnels and then we go down the cliffs. It won't be dark. There's no climbing and I'll have a torch.'

Anja was not convinced. They reached the largest tree where, much to Alfie's delight, Quicksilver allowed him to locate and open the door, proudly showing off his new skill. Quicksilver crouched to enter the tree, but Anja stubbornly waited outside until the torch was lit, even though there was plenty of light streaming into the entrance. The door snapped shut as soon as they started to descend steep stairs down to the shelter. With the only light coming from the crackling torch, Anja fought to keep her anxiety under control, cursing herself for believing him again. After descending for some time they came to a door and behind this a huge room-like cave. It was large, dry and had a hearth cut into one wall. More doors and curtained openings led to unknown rooms and passages. Whilst Quicksilver lit a few oil lamps, Anja looked around.

'It's this way,' Quicksilver said, walking towards one of the doors at the far end of the room. Anja ignored him and continued to wander around. The boys turned and waited. She poked behind some of the doors and hangings. Quicksilver sighed, knowing what they hid and what was coming.

'You two go and do whatever you want,' she declared. 'I'm going to light a fire, boil some water and clean up. Do you think there are any clean clothes here like these ones?' She pulled at her tunic and breeches.

Quicksilver nodded, pointed to one of the rooms and exchanged a dejected look with Alfie. She wouldn't be going anywhere for a while. He turned towards a passageway on the far side of the cave. 'Come and help me get things ready, Alfie.' Alfie scooted after him before Anja decided to include him in the "clean-up".

Anja smiled and busied herself with the fire. She realised why she wasn't bothered; these were caves and not holes in the earth, like graves. She was going to spend as long as she needed to.

Quicksilver and Alfie followed the gradual descent of the passage. A quarter of an hour later, they reached its end; a large fracture in the canyon face. Although the opening was high and at least thirty feet wide, it was only a small blemish that would be difficult to see from the other side.

Standing on the lip of the opening, they could see the river far below. They'd descended about a hundred feet from the clifftop. A vertical fissure a few yards wide bisected the floor, creating a cleft down the canyon wall almost as far as the river below. Around the fissure a huge wooden structure spanned its width. Ropes lay coiled or hanging from huge pulleys. Nets, heavy rocks and large wicker baskets were lying nearby.

'First, we need a net.' Quicksilver got straight to work. Alfie helped him drag one of the heavy nets nearer to the fissure.

'Stand on the end of that,' Quicksilver ordered, pointing to one end of a seesaw- like contraption. Alfie complied and his companion rolled a heavy lump of stone onto the other end. Then he added another lump. Alfie rose off the ground. 'That's you done,' he said, rolling the rocks into the net. 'Now help me with this big one.'

They repeated the process for Quicksilver, and more rocks joined those in the net.

'If we find some a bit heavier than yours, they will do for Anja.' He chose a couple more and added them to the pile in the net, then hauled over one of the ropes that had a huge hook attached to its end. Gathering up the edges of the net, he hooked the whole lot together. Alfie was fascinated.

'That should do it,' Quicksilver said. 'Now help me attach it.'

They grasped the rope he had attached to the net and looped it over a large pulley wheel suspended from an axle fastened to the beams across the fissure. Quicksilver wrapped a bight of the rope around a huge rotating drum anchored to the cave floor. Then he put his weight on a large lever on the side of it that clicked into place. The heavy net was attached to the rope that now went over the wheel before being secured around the ratcheted drum.

'This one,' he said, pointing to another, larger, handle on the other side of the drum, 'winds in the rope.'

Quicksilver proceeded to pull the winch lever backwards and forwards. The drum turned and slowly the hook began to pull up the edges of the net. A great deal of effort later, the net of rocks slid across the floor towards the fissure. It reached the edge and swung over the middle of the fissure beneath the pulley, restrained from plummeting down by the winch head jammed in the ratchet.

'I'm going to put my weight against the brake. When I say so, pull that lever and release the winch.'

Alfie nodded, tentatively releasing it. The drum began to spin and the dangling net disappeared down the fissure.

He ran around to add his small-but-important amount of weight to Quicksilver's on the brake that was slowing the net's descent to the bottom of the canyon. It took about five minutes for them to control its creaking descent. When it was down, most of the rope stretched down the fissure attached to the net of rocks. What was left dangled over the huge pulley wheel with another hook attached to it.

'That's the hardest part done. When Anja's ready, all we have to do is hook the basket onto this end and it's ready to go. This is going to be really exciting,' he said, grinning.

Alfie grinned back, wondering if Anja would like "really exciting". Then he made a typical Alfie remark: 'So, what's it for?' Not having a clue what they'd just done.

'What do you think?' Quicksilver said, laughing.

Alfie shrugged amiably.

Quicksilver explained. 'The rocks are a bit heavier than we are, so when we get in the basket it won't go down, but if we take a few rocks with us we will be a bit heavier. Then down we go and up come the rocks. When we get near the bottom, we throw the extra rocks out just at the right time to slow us down.'

He went through the actions as he told Alfie, who caught his excitement but still didn't really understand. It didn't matter, though; if Quicksilver told him it was safe to jump down the cliff face, he would do so.

They returned to the caves where they found Anja waiting for them, scrubbed and changed. Alfie could not resist a quick cuddle. She kissed him on the nose before theatrically pushing him away, wrinkling hers. 'There's still time to have a bath,' she said. He scuttled back to Quicksilver, laughing.

'Ready then?' Quicksilver asked.

'Yes,' she replied breezily, unaware of what was waiting for her.

11

Anja followed Quicksilver and her brother down through the passage to the face of the canyon. They watched Quicksilver drag one of the big baskets to the edge of the fissure and push the hook dangling from the pulley through loops on ropes attached to each corner. He then hung bags of small rocks from one of the sides.

Alfie whispered a confused and illogical version of how it worked. Anja went to the fissure, looked down where the rope hung, blanched, and quickly stepped back.

Quicksilver appraised his work. 'There, shall we go?'

Alfie was about to run to him, but Anja grabbed his shoulder. 'What do you mean, "shall we go"?'

'Go down the cliff. I'll raise the basket over the drop. I release the brake and join you in it. It won't start to go down until I get in and make it heavier than the net at the bottom. The net with the rocks comes up and we go down until I throw out the weights. That slows us down as we reach the bottom. I hook onto the nets slung on the walls down there and we climb down to the floor. Then we go and get a boat.'

'That,' she pointed to the basket, 'is ridiculous. There's no way me, or Alfie, are getting in that.'

Alfie was about to say that he didn't mind, but her fingers were gripping his shoulder, hard.

'Why? It's terrific!' Quicksilver declared, disappointment entering his voice. 'This is the best part of the journey, no more boring walking for a while. Anyway, there's no other way down. It's hundreds of feet and we can't jump.'

'We might as well, because this…' she spat at him '… is stupid.'

She folded her arms to emphasis her unhappiness. Alfie took the opportunity to creep treacherously over to Quicksilver, who was losing patience.

'Anja, it's as safe as anything in the Land. Folk made this and it's safe. If you think this is dangerous, wait until you reach your brother and the creature that intends to kill you.' He stopped, breathing deeply, regretting this exchange. 'Anja, please stop getting so angry, it hurts my head, and I can't talk to you or think properly. Please control your moods.' He paused again. 'There's no other way down,' he said gently.

Anja realised that she was going to lose this battle. Alfie was jumping up and down; he couldn't wait to go. She capitulated. 'Let's get it over with then, but if Alfie gets injured, I really will hurt you.'

'Anja, it's really quite safe. Come on, Alfie and I will help you in.' As a concession to her outburst, she let them help her climb into the basket. He then unceremoniously helped Alfie in.

Quicksilver winched the basket up until it creaked and slid dizzily over the fissure. Anja sat on the floor; eyes pressed into arms folded around her knees. Alfie, who could just see over the side, was holding on with white knuckles, trying not to show how nervous he was.

'Best to stand up, Anja, your knees will cushion any jolts.' Quicksilver waited until she reluctantly did, then gingerly released the brake, ready to apply it again if the basket started to descend, which meant that he had miscalculated the balance. It didn't and he quickly grasped the side and vaulted in, almost kicking Anja in the process. Immediately, his weight changed the balance. They began to descend, within seconds picking up speed. Anja shut her eyes but immediately opened them because it was worse. Alfie squealed in fear and excitement and Quicksilver whooped and started to cut away the bags of stones. Anja couldn't release the scream that was lodged in her throat as her feet almost left the floor of the basket and her stomach churned.

The hairs on the back of Alfie's neck were still tingling when the last bag dropped away and the balance equalised. The walls of the fissure that had been hurtling past became distinct again and before they had time to realise just how precarious their drop had been, it slowed and the tops of wide nets rose around them. Quicksilver hooked one with a grapple tied to the basket and they came to a bone-jarring stop. Alfie was laughing hysterically and shaking like a leaf. Anja was ashen. An uncontrollable wave of nausea welled up and, leaning over the side, she was violently sick.

'There, I told you it was exciting, didn't I?' Quicksilver shouted. The strange, mottled tinge of his skin had deepened, quickly subsiding as he regained control of his emotions. Facing the nets on the wall, he hadn't seen Anja until he turned around. She straightened up, still gagging a little and wiping her mouth. The boys watched her anxiously, but she was beyond words or embarrassment. She peered over the edge of the basket and saw that the nets hung down to a large flat ledge. Turning around and looking out into the canyon, she could see that this ledge was still thirty or so feet above the deafening roar of the mighty river. She then craned her neck to look back up and shuddered at the distance they'd dropped.

'All we do now is climb down,' Quicksilver said, nervously watching her as he began to lower their belongings down.

'Wait,' Anja said, 'let my stomach settle. My legs are still shaking.' Secretly, Alfie was glad of a few minutes to recover as well.

Quicksilver waited patiently until Anja nodded, then used another grapple to pull the basket close to the net. Alfie and Anja climbed out and started to awkwardly climb down.

Quicksilver was lowering their bags but turned to advise them. 'Use one of the vertical ropes for your hands, with your feet stepping down either side. You'll find it easier.' They followed his advice and speeded up. As they reached the bottom, he scuttled down and joined them.

'Now what? Jump down the rest of the way?' Anja asked quietly.

Quicksilver laughed sheepishly, hoping she'd perk up. 'No, the boats are this way.' He turned and lifted up the bottom of one of the heavy nets. They crawled under it to the back of the ledge where a seeping black cavity opened into the rock face at the bottom of the fissure.

Anja's face blanched, but she could only express her feelings in a long, shuddering sigh. Over the last months, she had discovered fears she never knew existed. One thing that didn't bother her was water; she and Alfie were both strong swimmers.

Quicksilver led them by the light of yet another of the conveniently stacked torches back into the bowels of the soaring cliff. These were wet, dank tunnels where water permeated to trickle, stream, gush, and after particularly huge storms, roar its way to join the Great River on its journey to the ocean.

'You seem to know all about this. How many times have you been here?' Anja asked.

'Just once. I don't usually travel this far up the Great River. The groves tell me what the Folk did. They made the way we came down before the Great River was forbidden to them. They were familiar with boats.'

Anja didn't want to know any more. She felt like reminding him that "*they*" had all died.

On Quicksilver's advice, they removed their soft footwear for fear of slipping in the cold, slimy tunnels as they squelched their way deeper and deeper, Anja ever mindful of the thousands of tons of rock and earth piled above them. The constant dripping, strange echoes and shadowy hints of alien rock formations was all that accompanied them until a faint whispering sound gradually became louder. The passage widened, entering a large tunnel, and the sound became a deafening roar.

Directly across their path, a fast-flowing underground river cut deep into the terraced sides, washing the slippery lower banks with a hammering spray that spoke of speed and power. In the dancing light, they could just see the glistening walls of the other bank. Pendulous, twisted shapes projecting from the ceiling reflected the flickering flame.

Quicksilver had to shout above the sound of the torrent: 'Here's where we start our river journey. The banks of the canyon are still too steep and the Great River too fast for us to get on it outside. This river empties into it downstream from where we came down the cliff. The boats are along here.' He picked his way down to the rock terrace just above the river where they came across small boats placed upside down. Coils of rope, oars and sails lay beneath heavy covers.

Leading them past recognisable boats, Quicksilver stopped before a slightly flattened, large domed object. Made of thick wicker covered tightly with an outer skin, bulky rolls of padding were wrapped around the rim resting on the ground. Alfie thought it looked like a huge upside-down cereal bowl.

'Help me turn it over,' Quicksilver said, wedging the torch in a crack in the tunnel wall.

To their surprise, it was deceptively light and, although awkward because of its shape and size, after a few tries they managed to heave it over, rocking madly before settling with the padded edge now on the top, level with Alfie's nose.

'Why can't we use one of the others, is this thing really a boat?' Anja sniped.

'The other ones are too difficult to navigate onto the Great River. This one's better. It's special, you'll see. There were only two of them and I've already used the other one.' He tested the strength of a long rope and fed one end of it through an iron ring hammered into the rock floor of the bank. The rest he passed through a loop sewn into the padding, coiling it in the bottom of the craft.

He secured the rope onto the loop and then manoeuvred the strange craft into the river, where it strained against the rope as the river tried to sweep it away. Throwing in their bags and equipment he gathered from the stores along the bank, Quicksilver shouted at the children to follow his instructions. The craft was constantly bumping as it struggled to escape the rope's hold. He struggled to hold it firmly against the bank.

'Quickly, it's soft inside, so just dive into the middle.'

Anja gingerly stepped over the padded edge and unceremoniously slid in. She regained her composure and sat on one of the thin planks spanning the bottom. She rummaged in her bag and crammed her hair into her soft leather cap, preparing for whatever lay ahead. Alfie tumbled in and copied her.

Quicksilver let go and jumped in as the boat bounced violently against the bank again. He began to saw the part of the rope between the loop and the ring with his knife. When it was almost cut through, he turned to the children.

'Put your arms through the straps around the edge and brace yourselves. The boat will spin and bump as we go through the caves. I'll have to leave the torch, so it will be dark for a while.' He grinned devilishly in the flickering gloom. 'This will be fun.' He gave them a second or so to get ready, then hacked away at the last few strands. Two small yelps and one loud whoop came from the craft as the river tore it from the bank.

The craft bumped and spun madly against the bank for a hundred yards or so before being thrown into the middle of the flow. Had it not been for the thick padding, it would have been matchwood. Anja's arms ached as they strained against the straps and she could hear Alfie's constant gasps mirroring her own. They swept on at breakneck speed, expecting a fatal collision at any moment. After what seemed like an eternity, blackness turned to gloom and within seconds, blinding sunshine forced their eyes tightly shut and they shot onto the Great River.

Converging currents boiled the water and tossed the craft about, throwing it up and down in all directions. Barely able to hold on, they tumbled around and were soon soaked; Anja trying desperately to protect her bag and spare clothes. Thankfully, this only lasted a few minutes, before settling into a gentle, giddying spin as the boat steadied itself in a fast undisturbed current.

Quicksilver picked up a sturdy oar-shaped piece of wood from the bottom of the craft and fed it through a gap in the hide between two willow uprights. He then swung around to sit with his back against the side, clasping the handle tight to his body. As he strained against the current, the boat gradually stopped spinning. They were all, even Anja, laughing hysterically, recovering from the shock of their brief violent launch onto the Great River.

'You're good at this considering you've only done it once before,' Anja shouted, still bracing herself. He seemed very skilled with the strange boat. 'How did you get so good at it?'

'I just know what to do,' he said matter-of-factly. 'I sense what to do. I don't think about it.' He considered this enough of an explanation. Anja held on to his gaze for a second or so before realising that was all she would get.

'You're strange,' she said in a flat non-committal way, moving closer to him.

'I know,' he replied. 'It's how I am. I've heard about your land and wonder what it would be like for me to be there.' He weighed his next words carefully. 'Everything is different here, even the simplest things. Nothing's the same as in your land, not even you. You're also strange, Anja.'

He expected her to argue, but she didn't; she just looked at him. He held her gaze, taking in her enigmatic, beautiful face, hair half tucked into the leather cap, and her eyes; hazel brown, flecked with gold. She turned away to watch the cliffs sweep past. *Perhaps your people would find me normal by comparison*, he thought.

Idle times followed as the swift waters carried them between the echoing walls of the canyon. Their stops were infrequent at first, taking advantage when the sheer walls meandered enough to allow a small sheltered rock-strewn beach to exist and, to Anja's relief, to spend the night ashore and extend her a little privacy. But mostly they slept on the boat, the canyon constricting the starry sky between its towering black walls. Often, they were hungry, especially during the first days, there being nowhere to find fuel or make a fire. The river dictated their pace. Quicksilver was often quiet, but relaxed and content. Soon the canyon widened, the cliffs diminished, and the river became less aggressive. Anja proved an able apprentice with the tiller, so Quicksilver often joined Alfie at the front of the craft, eagerly scanning ahead for somewhere they could stop that promised kindling to burn.

'What happens if a storm comes?' Anja asked one day, shuddering at the thought of being on the wide river if that happened.

'There won't be any,' Quicksilver replied. 'The storms only occur on the Downs to the west of the river and south of the Great Forest, where the stone rings are.'

'Does it rain at all here then?'

'Of course, just as it does in the forest. For a couple of days you might get a steady downpour, then the sun comes out again. When there is a storm on the Downs, the Great River is swollen and fast, and the rain is heavier, but the storm never crosses the banks.'

This description of the weather seemed illogical to Anja. 'What about winter, or spring, you know, the different seasons?'

Quicksilver looked confused.

'Is it ever cold?'

'No,' he replied, 'not here. It's always warm. Sometimes,

the nights become a little chill, or mists may form in forest hollows or here on the riverbank. As we travel further south, it will get much warmer, though. Pan has told me that high in the mountains to the far north, beyond the Great Forest, it becomes colder, but I don't travel there. I don't go far from the groves.'

'Not even if you wanted too?' Alfie's voice piped up, joining this long and interesting conversation.

'I could, but don't want to,' Quicksilver answered. 'I go into the forest, or just across the river, but not much further. So, what are "seasons"?'

'It doesn't matter,' Anja answered. Although she now felt more at ease in his company, she still found it hard to accept their dependency on him and begrudged that Alfie treated him like a big brother. She'd hoped Alfie would take up the conversation now in his usual blunt manner, but he didn't, accepting Quicksilver's explanations of this bizarre land as if it was perfectly normal.

Alfie's curiosity wasn't blunted in any other respect. Too small to help with the steering, he spent some of the time on one side or other of the craft, kneeling, dangling his hand over the side. One hot afternoon, whilst staring at the spray sparkling against his hand, he noticed something attached to the outside of the boat, snaking back in the water. He leant right over the side to watch it dance in the wake. Perplexed, he sat back, intending to ask Anja, who was steering, near to where it hung, what she thought it was, but she was concentrating on keeping the boat on course and he thought better of it. He leant further over to get a better look, only to receive a curt rebuke from

Quicksilver as he manoeuvred to take over the tiller. He tried ignoring it, but his curiosity would not allow him to. He tentatively tried to awaken the interest of his sister, but he should have known better; her face should have warned him.

'Anja?' he wheedled.

Her face flopped around towards him. 'Not now, Alfie,' she said reproachfully, too sleepy even to get annoyed.

He turned back to the water and continued to watch the annoying thing from the corner of his eye. It was still there, stretching behind the boat on the surface of the water. He had to know, so he tried Quicksilver.

Moving around carefully so as not to rock the boat, he leant over again, as near to the back of the circular craft as he could, but just as he located the thing again, Quicksilver hoisted him back, gripping his belt.

'If you fell in, your sister would probably leave you.'

'There's something dangling from the side into the water. I can't see what it is.'

Quicksilver had a good idea what Alfie had seen. 'Be careful and look all around the sides of the boat,' he said.

Alfie eased his way around. 'There's more of them, but they're tied to the boat. I didn't notice them before.'

'They've always been there, that one must have come loose.'

'What're they for, tying up the boat or something?'

Quicksilver laughed. 'They wouldn't hold the boat for long against this current, not individually. No, they're for another reason. I told you, this boat is special, it's not a Folk boat.'

'They didn't make it. Aren't you going to tell me?' Alfie asked.

'No, that would spoil the surprise.'

Anja had been listening. 'Can't we have a rest from "surprises" for a while?' she chipped in sleepily. 'I'm beginning to find "surprise", "this will be fun", or "really exciting" annoying.'

'Just wait. This is a surprise that you really will love.'

She made a face and closed her eyes.

12

Far to the south, deep beneath the Valley of Great Stone Circle, the Master of the Downs was scrying the northern reaches of his domain. He had lost the progress of the youth. Having sensed him emerge from the Great Forest and, extraordinarily, with human company, the Master was now aware of him disappearing near the Great River. He also sensed something else, a spark of intense rage at one of the northern stone circles. Another human? He knew humans, having lived many years ago in their land. But there was something wrong with this one. He was curious and gently extracted it, because that was his nature when possible, but had this failed, he would have used firmer methods...

Rob woke and scratched at his eyes; he was blind. In a frenzy of madness, he thrashed about, grasping for the comforting hardness of his spear.

A voice spoke from nearby in the blackness, chiding him softly.

'You won't be needing your little needle. I wish you no

harm, I am curious to understand why you're here in the Land, and so small. I've never seen such a tiny human. Have you always been like this?'

Rob's befuddled mind was calmed by the beguiling voice. He tried to speak rationally but was far from lucid and stumbled through the story as best he could remember, spitting out how he was lured from his cottage by the children and the horror that he woke to.

The voice was silent throughout his garbled tale of woe, but when he'd finished and began shouting and weeping, it silenced him, though not unkindly.

'Stop. Please stop this noise.'

Rob shook his head, trying to rid himself of the voice. 'Who are you and why am I blind? Where am I?'

'I sensed your rage and brought you here. You are not blind, there is no light. I can see well enough and find it more comfortable than the sunlight that illuminates the beautiful Downs above us. Who am I? I've had many names, but the one that I prefer, and you may recognise, is Hades.'

Rob stayed silent. Of course he recognised the name, but couldn't recall anything good about it. He couldn't get his thoughts together.

'Your mind is in turmoil, but I also sense strength and determination. You could be useful. Sleep will help, so rest for a while to allow it to recover. When you wake, we'll see what can be done.'

'I'll kill the children, then go home,' Rob muttered.

'Ah, you will never be the same human you were before this little adventure of yours began. You've been changed, little man. All I can do is perhaps adjust things.'

Before Rob could rage back, he was asleep.

Weeks passed before he was gently roused by the soft voice. It took him a while to come to. Anger was still there, but he felt calmer. He remembered and knew he was being watched.

'Good, do you feel better? I'd have let you sleep longer but I have news that I wanted to share with you.'

'How long have I been asleep?'

'Oh, a while; you endured a lot.'

Rob took a few seconds to think; the key memory was still missing, but he could think lucidly, coldly. 'You said that you were Hades, so are you The Hades, the Greek god? Am I imagining you, is my mind that broken, or is this all one insane dream?'

'Yes, I am that Hades, but I'm not a "god" as you call such entities. The Land gifted me and some others certain powers and attributes, to maintain the balance. We found that when we entered other lands, these powers became amplified and I am afraid we were too naïve to recognise the danger and consequences of our actions. We each have different attributes and mine left behind a certain reputation. No good came of our time in your land, so we returned and decided never to openly visit it again. I've little inclination to do that, though. And I can assure you that this isn't a dream.'

'Where are we, this Land? I don't remember coming here.'

'That is complex. Think of it as being in another land, or world, in a different universe.'

'So, how did I get here? It wasn't a mistake, I was lured here.'

'I also wonder. Perhaps you simply blundered into the Land, but I am fairly sure that indeed you were lured here. I'm not sure how, why, or by whom, although I have a suspicion.'

'Children, it was two children.'

Hades smiled inwardly. *Perfect*, he thought.

'Ah, now, the children. I must admit that I did doubt your insane ramblings when we last talked, but things have happened since then that make me more inclined to believe you. There are few sentient, intelligent beings here, and those who are here are mostly known to each other. All are usually changed in some way or another for reasons known only to the Land, which is also sentient and we live here by its grace.'

'What about me?'

'Even you. Although perhaps being so small, it didn't notice your existence.'

'I'm strong, I survived.'

'Indeed, but your luck was running out, and your sanity certainly suffered. But let's continue with what I want to tell you. There is another in the Land, who has the appearance of a youth. He doesn't belong here and is an itch I cannot scratch, but the Land seems unwilling to do anything about him. My little domain is but a small part of the Land. I cherish and sustain the Downs and the Underland. This boy came with others – the Folk, whom the Land did not want, and are now gone – but he remains, with his trees, and travels wherever he wishes. I feel it is my responsibility to cleanse him from the Land, as I helped cleanse it of the Folk. Recently, he has been travelling across the Downs again and this time I will catch him.'

Hades explained this in his soft, friendly voice, without a hint of malice or anger. He paused before giving Rob another juicy titbit.

'However, he is not alone. Can *you* guess who he is travelling with?'

Rob felt the surrounding blackness enter his head, but calmed himself.

'Two children.'

'Exactly, quite a coincidence, isn't it? It is probable that these are the ones who are of such interest to you.'

'I'll kill them.'

'Oh, I think they might just tread on you without knowing it. Also, they are here by the grace of the Land, and they travel with the youth, who I have found very difficult to catch, despite my considerable power.'

'They must pay for what they did to me.'

Rob could not see the satisfaction spreading across Hade's face. 'Perhaps, but you must help me capture the youth; he's cunning. I can help you in many ways, but you must agree to serve me. I'll give you back your size, but there will be changes.'

'I'm already changed, look at me. I'm tiny, nothing can be worse than this.'

'Possibly not, so do you agree?'

'Yes, if I can be my normal size again.'

'Good, now stand up and please remove that ridiculous

132

smelly thing you are wearing. Hopefully, change will also cleanse the rest of you. You really are an offensive little thing at the moment.'

Rob stood up and cast off the moleskin cloak.

'What's going to happen?'

'I'm not sure. I *can* gift you change, but I don't know *exactly* what will happen, and the Land must approve. Do you still want to go through with it? They are only children after all, and many small creatures live out long, happy lives in the Land.'

'They are not *only* children, and I don't want to stay like this.' Rob's voice was tight, barely controlled.

'Yes, I suppose appearance can be deceptive, especially in the Land. So, if you are sure, we can begin.'

If Rob could have seen the smile on Hade's face, he may have been a little less eager. For a long time, he stood perfectly still in anticipation and nothing happened. Gradually, he felt a slight prickling on his head, and naked shoulders, then more, slowly spreading to every part of his body. He squirmed as it reached his most tender areas. Then the pinpricks expanded in his skin, like thousands of needles being slowly pushed in. He cried out as the pain increased; his whole body on fire.

Hades watched in amusement, wincing at Rob's discomfort.

'Stay standing,' he urged, as Rob seemed ready to faint with pain. 'It won't last long.' *I hope*, he thought.

The pain didn't stop, but Rob weathered it, whimpering until at last it was over, replaced by soreness that accompanied the slightest movement.

'Is it done, am I back to my normal size?'

'Yes, well, I think so,' Hades answered pleasantly, 'perhaps a little larger if anything.'

'Why am I so sore?' Each word was agony; he could hardly move his lips.

'There's a little healing to do, but the worst seems to be over. Now, to complete the process, I need to name you formally as my servant.'

Rob brindled at the term servant but was so sore that he didn't care. 'It's Rob,' he said, just able to get the words out since the pain in the area around his lips was getting worse with each movement.

'Ah, this is a formal ceremony, my friend. I need your true name, not your given name.'

Rob groaned. 'It's Hemmer… oh,' and the soreness around his mouth prevented him from finishing.

'Yes, a good strong name.' And before Rob could say any more, Hades raised his voice a little and declared, 'From this moment, you are Hamma Half-Raven, servant of Hades.'

Rob was about to protest at the mistake regarding his name, when the full impact of the words sunk in.

'What! What was that? What's the Half-Raven thing?'

'Perhaps you should see,' the voice quietly replied, 'for yourself.'

An image appeared before Rob. Initially, he thought he was looking at a picture, then he moved his hand and gasped. Mirrored before him was the shape of a man, but it bore no similarity to anyone, or indeed anything, he recognised. He was black, not a shade of black, but a deep iridescent black. Despite the soreness, he leant closer and gasped again. It was not his skin that was black, but the thousands of tiny feathers that coated his body, even his face.

'What have you done to me?'

'You agreed to change, and the Land has permitted it. I didn't know precisely what would happen, but you're magnificent, quite stunning, and you're back to at least your normal size. You might have become Mole-Man. You were really quite attached to its skin.'

Rob mumbled a few more painful protests before he realised that he was alone, and the image was gone. He sighed and stood as still as possible for some hours as the soreness gradually wore off. He couldn't guess how long it was until Hades returned, but during that time he noticed that the darkness he'd lived in for so long was giving way to shadows and dull shapes around him. He felt Hades' presence and then saw an indistinct figure sitting nearby watching him.

'How are you now?'

'The soreness has gone. So, is this it, is this me now?'

'Not quite, but no more pain.'

'My name, it's Hemmersley, not Hamma. I couldn't talk properly.'

'No, it's Hamma. It's a formal thing. Besides, Hemmersley Half-Raven doesn't sound right. You'll get used to it. Now, there's more, an important part of your new self you need to understand. Quite exciting really. Picture a raven in your mind.'

'Why?'

'Humour me, just close your eyes and do it, the biggest and most magnificent raven you can imagine.'

'Will one appear to do my bidding?'

'Oh yes.'

As Rob closed his eyes, an image of a raven filled his mind, so real that it was a few seconds before he could draw his mind away from it and open his eyes. When he did, he was confused, since the seated figure was now huge. Then he realised that he could now see Hades clearly; a young, handsome man smiling at him.

'Excellent, and now you know why you are Hamma Half-Raven.'

A horrible realisation made his head reel and he cried out, but what he heard was a loud croak. He panicked and almost toppled over as he tried to manoeuvre his head to look down at what had been his feet, only to flap about wildly trying to control his new wings and body. Hades chuckled until Rob managed to control himself enough to stay still.

'Priceless. But I'm being unkind. Now shut your eyes and picture what you saw in the mirror.'

Rob pulled himself together and did so. There was no discernible sign of any change but when he opened his eyes, he was a similar size to Hades.

'You mustn't think too much, just do; it's instinctive. You'll be able to fly and function as normally as any raven, but try to control your thoughts. It would be a bit disconcerting if you changed back while flying. You'll get used to it.'

He nodded to his right. 'That passage will eventually

take you to the surface and you will always be able to find me, at any time, since you're now bonded to me. I gather that you can see perfectly well here now...' He paused whilst Rob nodded. 'I guessed so. Now go, and remember you are Hamma, I will not recognise any other name. Oh, and lastly, there are thousands of ravens scattered around the Land, and you are their master. They will do your bidding so use them. Locate the boy and these children and have them tracked, but don't let them know it's happening.'

'I'll kill them.'

'NO!' The command sliced into his mind.

'No, not yet, just find them.' Hades' voice returned to its normal friendly softness. 'Vengeance has to be savoured, and they may not be as easy to kill as you think. They will come to me. Have them watched, carefully, for they must not suspect anything. We will think up a special fate for them. Particularly their companion.' In his mind, he added, *The children are of little consequence to me.*

'Return soon, Hamma, my beautiful friend. I miss you already.'

With that, he abruptly disappeared, leaving Rob, now Hamma, alone to ponder his future; one more than ever focused on the children...

*

On the river, languid days became weeks and miles were eaten up. The valley through which the river carved a wide path eventually broadened to become distant, rich, verdant riverbanks, hemmed with

137

reeds where tall birds fished with sword-like bills. The task of minding the tiller became less arduous, until one morning Quicksilver tied it in place and thereafter only guided it when heading for the shore each evening. They spent long days half-asleep, caps pulled down to shade their faces from the increasingly hot sun.

Quicksilver slept most of all. Anja wondered if he was all right; it was becoming difficult to rouse him at times. Maybe it was the glare of the river or her drowsiness, but when he was sleeping, his tanned, lightly mottled face became serene and blotchy. When he eventually woke, he would stretch not only his limbs but also his face with enormous yawns and grimaces, rigorously rubbing his eyes and cheeks with his fingers, as if massaging himself back to life. If he caught her watching or she was deliberately trying to wake him, she noticed that for a while, his eyes looked back with half-recognition before intelligence deepened their gaze. She wondered how she would cope if something was wrong with him, which set her mind thinking about herself.

Ever since leaving the forest, she had felt something in her head that had not been there before. Briefly, it had driven her to distraction, but as the weeks passed it bothered her less and less, until she almost became used to it. Sometimes, she could almost control how it affected her, and welcomed its presence. At first, it had surfaced when she was angry, or excited, but now she began to feel for it at will. Alfie didn't notice, but she was sure Quicksilver did. When she sensed it, a glow filled her body and she felt euphoric; as if something beautiful was just beyond her reach. It heightened her senses, especially when Pan's music haunted her.

As each day passed, the Great River became increasingly beautiful. Small inlets began to appear where rising fish dappled the surface and huge jewelled insects hovered and droned over fields of wide water lilies that alternated with reed beds bordering its banks. Single birds became flocks feeding in the shallows as the far banks sat below wide horizons or lush thickets. Animals raised their heads from drinking to watch them glide by. Each evening brought the heady scent of fragrant blossoms drifting over the water, enticing them to land and sleep on soft beds of grass and fern, lulled by twilight songbirds.

To Anja's relief, Quicksilver gave up his day-long slumbers and peered again for long hours ahead of the boat, scanning the river, whilst Alfie took in everything, each new sight and sound. She yearned for the woods that populated the western side of the river, to inhale the soft scents of the flora and luxuriate in the cool shade of leafy glades. When they beached each evening, she would wander into them, to be alone and dance to music that no one else could hear. She longed to do so in one of her beautiful dresses but thought it would be tempting fate to change from her travel clothes.

One morning, she caught Alfie staring at her for an annoyingly long time. After trying to ignore him, she eventually told him to stop.

'It's your hair.'

'What about it?'

'It's long again.'

Quicksilver became interested. 'He's right, it's like before.'

'So, it's grown back.'

Alfie's eyes widened. 'Not that fast.'

She thought about it, and then her face expressed confusion. 'But yours hasn't grown at all, all the time we've been here, has it?'

'Not really, didn't you notice yours growing, though?'

'No, my cap has stretched. I just pull it down, I didn't notice.'

'Hair doesn't change, it's always the same,' Quicksilver commented. Neither of the children could think of anything to add after that, and since he had made the confusing remark without taking his eyes from the river in front, they didn't notice his gaze sharpen. He smiled secretly to himself, then nonchalantly turned to them.

'I think you're about to find out what the straps on the side of the boat are for, Alfie.'

13

Anja and Alfie searched the river ahead but couldn't see anything that might have prompted this announcement. They waited for a further explanation, but Quicksilver sat back, smiling. After several fruitless minutes, Anja decided that he was playing with them and went back to thinking about her hair. Alfie was about to ask him what he had meant when the water around the boat suddenly erupted.

Anja and Alfie screamed and fell into the middle of the craft, which swayed crazily, threatening to capsize and throw them into the river, whilst Quicksilver, helpless with laughter, hung on to the internal straps. Anja disentangled herself from Alfie, saw Quicksilver was laughing and tried to hit him. Realising that his laughter meant that there was no danger, she pulled herself back against the side of the boat to see what had happened, treading on Alfie as he tried to do the same.

The water was still boiling around them. Anja wiped the spray from her face, trying to see what was causing it, then screamed again and fell backwards as a brown shape launched itself out of the water in front of her. She recovered and saw a narrow head and paws hanging on to the side of the boat. With a wriggle and a squeak, the rest of the creature appeared, and it flopped over the side. It was large, wet, very smelly and immediately jumped on her, snuffling and burrowing its nose into her neck. She yelped and struck out wildly. Everything was suddenly calm.

'He only wants to be friends,' Quicksilver said in an injured voice, causing Anja to glare at him from where she was lying unceremoniously between his feet. Alfie was rubbing his bruised legs where she'd kicked him. Quicksilver had the animal in his arms, dripping on her and appraising her with quick, intelligent eyes. By this time, two more had climbed in, sprawled across the seats. Another watched her from where it was clutching the padded top of the craft.

Sheepishly, she raised herself up. A hard paw touched her lap, and its owner stretched its neck to delicately sniff her face. Its whiskers tickled and she giggled; her eyes now bright with emotion at such a beautiful moment.

'What are they?' Alfie asked.

'They're otters, aren't they?' she whispered, fearful that it would stop.

Quicksilver nodded. 'They're what the straps are for.' He leant over the side and began to undo them. As he did so, and to Anja's regret, the otters all jumped back into the water and swam in tight circles around the boat. When he'd untied all of them, he held one out. One of the otters shot towards it and pushed its head through. In rapid succession, three more slipped their heads into nooses and they began to swim downstream. They took the strain and as the craft gained momentum, their powerful bodies settled into an easy rhythm that doubled the speed of the current.

Alfie had been busy. 'There's eight of them,' he declared.

'Four to pull and four to rest,' Quicksilver explained. 'Even otters get tired.'

'Where are they taking us?' Anja had noticed that they were now angling across to the left side of the river, in a direction that meant they would reach its bank in the hazy distance. Quicksilver played his usual "wait and see" game by nodding towards that distant point.

A combination of current and otter power soon brought them to there. Anticipation built as they approached a small creek they could easily have missed. Both children craned their necks and tried to make out their destination. The air became crystal clear despite the heat, each tree and leaf vibrant with colour. The wooded banks were thick with vegetation and large exotic blossoms.

The otters swung the craft out of the Great River and pulled it against the current up the creek. Further upstream, their work became easier as it slowed. Stillness surrounded them. Huge, graceful willows formed a leafy tunnel, the strong sunlight lancing through and dappling the water. Alfie broke the silence.

'Anja, there's more otters, hundreds of them.' His eyes were wide with excitement.

She gasped. Although nowhere as many as that, there were a lot, mostly following, which was why she had missed them; dozens of little triangular heads making small wakes but hardly a sound. They filled the shady little river behind them and more loped along the bank. Then they rounded a curve, and Anja forgot the otters.

The trees thinned on the left bank where a small wooden jetty straddled the gently running creek. As they drew nearer, an assortment of craft were moored along that side, mostly small, but the last one so large that it belied the size of the creek. The grass and rich vegetation glowed, highlighted by sunbeams streaming through tall willows and birches. Constant flickers of movement as otters plopped into or shook themselves out of the water should have distracted their gaze from the jetty, but nothing could draw their eyes from it.

A beautiful young woman was waiting. Involuntarily, Quicksilver whispered her name, his eyes shining with love and awe: 'Aphrodite.'

Anja's heart quickened and her breath caught in her throat. Her eyes flashed from Quicksilver to the woman, as if she was an apparition that he was conjuring.

Alfie stood slack-jawed beside his friend.

The woman smiled widely as they approached, and waved. Quicksilver waved back and Alfie hesitantly copied him.

Anja sat in shock, unable to respond. She couldn't move, mesmerised by the sight of the incredible young woman. Quicksilver glanced momentarily at her, rewarded to see the effect he'd hoped for. Then, as the boat gently bumped the jetty, he jumped out and crushed himself into the woman's embrace, becoming the boy he was. She gently kissed his cheek. He turned and helped Alfie climb clumsily onto the jetty. Alfie reddened but did not pull back as the young woman crouched down to meet his eyes. She brushed his hair to one side and kissed his forehead.

'Do you like honey, Alfie?'

He nodded vigorously and she laughed. 'Of course you do! I've the best honey that you have ever tasted.'

He swallowed the saliva that filled his throat and licked his lips, unable to control this reaction to such an unexpected question. Quicksilver sniggered and Alfie quickly covered his mouth with his hand to catch the spray that accompanied the burst of laughter he didn't have time to control. Luckily, the woman had raised herself back up, saving him more embarrassment.

Anja stood alone in the boat, waiting. Nothing that had occurred had registered; not even Alfie's usual unforced antics. Her eyes still fixed on the young woman, she couldn't formulate her thoughts.

'Hello, Anja, I've been waiting, and so looking forward to meeting you.' This simple greeting threatened to unravel months of carefully suppressed emotion.

She couldn't reply. Having dismissed Quicksilver's talk about a slight detour and yet another surprise, this was more than she could bear. She had kept strong, enduring everything that had happened; things that shouldn't have been possible and the changes in her head that constantly bothered her. Now, these few words threatened to unpick carefully constructed barriers.

'Come, walk beside me to my home,' the woman said, puncturing this bleakness. 'The boys can bring your things. I am Aphrodite. I've had other names but it's the one I like best.'

Anja took her proffered hand and gracefully joined them. Intuition told her that the woman understood. Still holding hands, they walked away from the creek and along a narrow path through the woods. Quicksilver winked at Alfie and, gathering up their few belongings, followed a short distance behind. Anja constantly looked up at Aphrodite, who squeezed her hand and smiled back; each complemented the other's beauty and charm.

'Is she your sister?' Alfie whispered.

'Oh no, she's much more than that Alfie, and she's a Great One, like Pan.'

Alfie wondered but unusually did not ask what he meant; too surprised by what they were approaching.

Aphrodite's cottage was a bizarre mixture of familiarity and strangeness. Like a country cottage that had grown wild, it was impossible to figure out what was natural and what was not; with living trees embedded in the structure, at some corners and in its walls. Thatch entwined within branches and all alive with blossoms and leaves. It was also big; just how big a mystery: rooms branched off corridors that turned off other corridors, none of which were either straight or level. There were stairs, rising to baffling levels or leading down to cellars and caves. And many windows, but whether they were framed using live gnarled tree branches or constructed of ancient, twisted wood defied logic. Yet, inside, each room was bright with whitewashed

146

plaster on the walls and ceilings, shaped to follow natural forms and structures, few surfaces flat or angles square. Cosiness, comfort and safety cocooned those who stayed there. A pervading smell of sweet wood, herbs, spices and baking wafted through sultry breezes that still held promise of the hot sun outside.

Everywhere at Aphrodite's homestead were otters, not only along the banks beside the jetty and the woods but also in the cottage, never more than two or three and these mostly kits; they came and went as they pleased.

Quicksilver and Alfie could have had a small room each, since there were plenty, but they dumped their bags in one of the larger ones and there they stayed, content with each other's company. Along a short corridor and up a twisty staircase, Aphrodite led Anja to a room of her own. Two small windows were cut deep under the low thatch, looking out over a wild, natural garden, barely distinguishable from the surrounding open woodland.

'This is yours, and mine is just along the corridor,' said Aphrodite. 'The boys can stay below where we can't smell them. There's a tub room across the way, only for our use, and I've prepared lots of hot water. You can have a long soak and by then it will be time to eat. Come down when the sun sinks enough to show its face in your windows.'

She was about to leave. For the first time since their meeting, Anja spoke. 'We can't stay long; we're going to find my brother. He's still a long way away. I don't really know where he is. Quicksilver's taking us.' She made a small futile gesture. 'He's only a baby. We've been travelling for ages. I hope he's still all right. I don't know what I'll do if I can't find him.' She sat on the bed, her hands in her lap.

Aphrodite went over and sat beside her. She took off Anja's cap, brushed her hair away from welling eyes and put an arm around her.

'We'll talk properly tomorrow, I know what has happened. You shall stay for as long as I think is right. We've a lot to talk about. Your little brother will still be there when you reach the coast, however long it takes. It's you that concerns me, Anja. You need my help. We'll spend time together because I must explain things to you.' Anja leant against her, determined not to release the sob caught in her throat. 'You and I will become great friends.' Aphrodite kissed Anja's forehead. 'I'll knock when your bath is ready.'

It was the smell of fresh bread that prompted Anja to glance towards the windows; the afternoon sun was now framed within them and she quickly blinked away. She had soaked until the water in the tub was tepid, luxuriated afterwards with exotic oils and essences, and groomed her hair with finely worked combs and brushes.

Returning to her room, she had found her dresses hanging in a wardrobe. Even though they'd been subjected to the rigours of the journey, they looked as if they'd been newly made. The other dress was almost identical to the one she had tried on in the shelter; only the embroidery was slightly different. She chose that one and put it on. There were more cupboards built into or against the walls. It was not easy to be sure, and inside one of the wardrobe doors was a long mirror. Whether faced with glass or some other material, it was difficult to tell, but it gave a deep, clear reflection.

She gasped; it was the first time for many months that she'd gazed on her own image, and hardly recognised the girl standing there. This stranger was slimmer, with deep, dark olive skin. Glossy almost black hair fell to her shoulders and large, deep brown eyes heavily flecked with gold stared incredulously back. And she was beautiful. Even her teeth were pearly white, though they hadn't felt the abrasion of brush or toothpaste for months. But she looked no older than she remembered.

Turning away, she slid her bare feet into soft brown buskins and fastened a silver filigree chain across her hips. Then, returning to the mirror, she pinned the delicate silver and pearl filigree skullcap to her hair, adjusting it twice until it looked and felt right. The image in the mirror captivated her for a full minute or so, not with vanity but disbelief. Familiar voices floating up broke the spell. Anja firmly shut the wardrobe and left to join the others, following their voices down to the kitchen and, self-consciously realising that the clothes were influencing the way she carried herself, went in.

The conversation stopped. Three pairs of human-like and a couple of sets of otter eyes turned to her. She couldn't stifle the smile that lit her face. Quicksilver flashed a quick glance at Aphrodite, who ignored it, went over and kissed Anja's cheek.

'Oh, my little lady, we do have a lot to discuss. You've no idea what's happening, do you? This is all so exciting.' She walked Anja to a chair beside the table. 'Sit down, eat first then tell me all your adventures so far, everything that's happened, right from the beginning.'

For a while, there was no conversation. Small plates of preserved meat and rich wheat cakes preceded scones, butter and honey, followed by a large sticky dessert, which only a glare from Anja prevented Alfie from devouring like a famished wolf. It was a rich meal, the likes of which they had not eaten since their arrival in the Land. They wanted to eat and eat, but managed only a paltry amount. Alfie forced himself to eat as much as he could, and despite feeling sick and bloated afterwards, looked at the food still on the table with regret.

'I want to eat it all,' he said sadly.

'You'll soon be able to eat more,' Aphrodite commiserated. 'You're not used to rich food, or very much at all by the look of you. I expect your stomachs will complain for a day or so. It will be back to a meagre diet when you leave, so I want to treat and build you up while you're here.'

Anja was already feeling a mild cramp and was relieved to hear that there was nothing wrong. Aphrodite poured a warm herbal brew and as they sipped it, the discomfort slowly subsided.

'Now, tell me all about your journey.'

They told her everything, and it was difficult. Anja's telling was quiet and factual; in some areas, her voice grew faint and she stumbled over a memory she was not sure she wanted to share. Now and again, Alfie took over, determined to express his importance in the sequence of events, especially when they'd been in the Great Forest.

Anja was content to let Alfie cover this part, not wanting to elaborate on her own time there.

Aphrodite listened and even when certain events begged a fuller explanation, didn't probe. But her keen eyes watched their faces and noted their reactions. They would tell her everything, but now was not the time to push. It was just the beginning; they needed time to relax and recuperate.

Alfie spent the next day exploring the woods and river around the house, annoyed that Quicksilver had gone off somewhere without telling him or asking if he would like to go. Anja stayed for most of the morning in her room, before emerging to sit shyly in the kitchen. Aphrodite smiled inwardly and went about her normal routine, subtly encouraging Anja to accompany her, to become comfortable and trust her before broaching difficult subjects.

They visited small cultivated areas in the surrounding woods; gardens in which Aphrodite grew small patches of crop; here, an area of cereal for cakes and bread, there, fruit trees, both laden with produce that continuously grew. There were hives in old tree stumps, buzzing with life, where she culled the sweet honey that graced each meal, even goats that supplied her milk. They walked with the otters to the jetty, playing with them and accepting their gifts of fish. The afternoon and early evening passed in a kaleidoscope of lovely moments.

Alfie tried to be alone and depressed, but the lovely little haven forbade it. He found his way to the creek and sat on a tree root watching the water slide past. A small wet otter scampered out of the river and before long he was laughing at the antics of the smelly, playful beast. By late afternoon, he had a band of willing companions who needed no more than a stretch of river and riverbank for contentment. By the time the girls joined him, he had stopped trying to be unhappy. Evening wore on and Quicksilver missed tea. Aphrodite didn't seem in the least concerned, as if she expected it. Alfie asked her if she knew when he would return.

'He never stays anywhere for more than a few hours. I suspect he isn't far away. He looked a bit drawn yesterday. There are some trees, not far, where he finds comfort and peace. I suspect he's there.'

'We know about the groves and how he is with the trees,' Anja said. They hadn't mentioned what they had seen him do.

Aphrodite looked at her keenly. 'Yes, it is a grove he's gone to, a very special one, though.'

'I thought he would've taken me with him,' Alfie grumbled. 'I like exploring the groves.'

'I expect he's gone there to think. I talked to him last night. You're like a little brother to him, Alfie. He's been alone for a long time, except when Fox travels with him. Having a young human friend is something he needs to process, he'll be back soon.' This cheered Alfie up. 'Listen and learn from him, Alfie. Your dream in the grove chamber was not by chance. Wait here for him in the morning.'

Anja was watching and listening carefully. Aphrodite turned to her. 'Tomorrow, I'll wake you earlier, Anja. We'll go for a long walk.'

Anja nodded; there was much she wanted to discuss with Aphrodite, so much. They both gave her a kiss before they went to bed. It seemed a natural thing to do.

Aphrodite sat and watched them go. She hadn't known what to expect prior to their arrival and realised she had to rethink all she'd assumed. Maia was probably still indisposed with her daughter or the whims of the Land, so she hadn't heard more from Pan and had assumed he'd been charmed by the innocence of the girl, remembering the many times that had happened in the distant past, but now they were here, she was re-evaluating that assumption.

They shouldn't have survived. Surely, by allowing them to live, the Land was helping the creature who was waiting for them with their brother. Before their arrival, she had considered denying the entity its prey and wondered why Pan had not done the same instead of encouraging them. Now she realised that the Land was not simply letting them stay, it was intervening; changing the girl. Pan had sensed there was more than her being bonded to him. She had sensed it when she'd seen Anja, but the moment Anja had entered the kitchen that evening, she understood. They had to go on. Anja would fulfil her destiny; she would face the creature and probably not survive the encounter, but it was the will of the Land. Up to now, they had watched with distaste as his ghoulish little kingdom grew. Now the Land was reacting, and Anja was part of its plan.

What was exciting was that the girl was changing in a way that was different; unlike anything the Land had done before. All Great Ones drew adoration, but Anja generated powerful emotions that affected the mind, but had to learn to control them and how they affected others. Then there were her eyes. Suddenly, as if prompted by these thoughts, Pan filled her mind and she detected the familiar melody of his pipes faintly caressing the night. She knew that Anja was standing by an open window in her room, sensually moving to the music.

Quicksilver had still not returned when Alfie fell asleep. He'd kept awake for as long as he could, hoping, but the softness of the fragrant dried-moss-filled mattress drew him to slumber. His next awareness was of being pushed on the shoulder.

'Come on, wake up.'

His eyelids refused to stay open. 'Where've you been?' he managed to slur.

'You'll find out when you get up. Come on, breakfast's in the kitchen.'

Alfie fell out of the lovely bed and staggered over to the window. Although the sun had already banished the last tendrils of river mist and was setting the glades aglow with its golden radiance, he could only think of wheat cakes and golden honey. Pulling on his clothes, he splashed his face with some water from the large jug and bowl. Content that he'd washed, he stomped sleepily after his friend.

He was soon chewing noisily on a massive wheat cake, drenched in honey. 'When I've finished, I'm going to tip Anja out of bed,' he stated bravely, which Quicksilver heard as a barely understandable mumble coming from his full, sticky mouth.

'She's been up, breakfasted and out hours ago. They

have gone mushroom picking. They looked in on you, but all they could see was a bump under the sheet.'

This revelation had no discernible effect on Alfie except to prompt another mouthful to join the half-eaten one already there.

'Hurry up and finish,' Quicksilver laughed. 'I'm going to show you somewhere special.'

'Is it where you went yesterday?' Alfie licked his lips and swallowed the last of the food.

'Yes, it's not far, we'll be back by tomorrow afternoon.'

Alfie didn't know whether to be excited or not, thinking about the soft bed and two missed meals. Quicksilver read his mind. 'We'll take something to eat.'

'Take lots of honey. Won't Aphrodite and Anja worry about us?' he asked, prioritising his concerns.

'No, Aphrodite will know where we are.'

Alfie went off to get his bag and knife whilst Quicksilver gathered provisions together. He was waiting outside when Alfie returned. Alfie greedily eyed the table, hurriedly dousing another cake with golden nectar, before running after Quicksilver with it dripping from his hand.

The Land had never taken such close interest in his servants, its awareness necessarily spread throughout its entirety. Since detecting the threat, it had decided to become more corporeal, and with that came empathy, a feeling it struggled with. The girl was interesting; strong, captivating. It was investing in her more than it had intended.

14

Anja was having a blissful morning. Aphrodite had gently roused her just before dawn and she luxuriated in the sparse comforts of her room after the privations endured during their journeying, savouring the simple things which in her past life had been chores, like brushing her hair and washing properly. There was even a simple toothbrush. But best of all were the small toilets on each landing; simple but welcome after times she'd been thankful for a stream trickling nearby.

She slipped on the same dress she'd worn the evening before, clean clothes each day an improbable memory after sleeping and travelling in the same ones for months.

They breakfasted frugally and without much conversation. Anja knew that Aphrodite was studying her but didn't feel uncomfortable or embarrassed; content to let their conversation develop in its own time, she took the opportunity to do the same.

Aphrodite was young; probably in her early twenties, a little above average height, with a shapely, athletic body that Anja could only dream of. She was extremely beautiful, with flawless olive skin, light brown hair and ageless, impossibly bright, sapphire blue eyes. Anja could sense the dignity and power pulsing within her, even when she was engaged in the most mundane of household duties. Anja admired, but was a little embarrassed by, Aphrodite's short white tunic, plainly the only item of clothing she wore. Anja had come to terms with not wearing underwear in the Land, but at least her dresses were not *that* short, or revealing.

What small talk did take place was about Alfie. Aphrodite had looked in on him and Anja laughed at her description of her brother's deep slumber. She also learnt that Quicksilver had returned during the night. They relaid the table for the boys, took a large willow basket each and left the cottage.

'Do you like mushrooms?' Aphrodite asked.

Anja nodded, not sure that she always had, but now ate anything edible, and mushroom had been a welcome supplement to their foraging. Two of the younger otters appeared, obviously intending to join their morning walk as they set off towards the deep woodland in the angle between the creek and the Great River. These woods were magically gloomy and overgrown, with patches of mist hanging over the dankest parts. Strange, brightly plumaged birds flitted or perched just within sight, their raucous calls echoing around them. Now and again, they skirted still pools laid with large lily pads, where small amphibians croaked and splashed, each sound loud in the prevailing stillness. They began to talk.

Aphrodite peeled away levels of Anja's emotions as they searched for plump mushrooms. Firstly, about her siblings, then herself; her fears and worries, then delving deeper, into areas that Anja had suppressed: feelings of guilt and blame she harboured for the responsibility she refused to let anyone take from her, carefully touching on her parents. Gently, she asked about Pan and finally Quicksilver. She realised that both children were more aware of what they'd seen and experienced than she'd expected. She knew that Anja had only adapted to her predicament at a superficial level. What she'd not done, because of her age and the mental trauma she had barely survived, was understand or accept that she was changing. As she probed, laughter and tears followed in quick succession.

Aphrodite then began to heal; she soothed, explained, listened and listened more, as Anja poured out her heart. She also realised how deeply Pan's music had woven their patterns. Each time Anja's mind raised a fear or dark thought, the seductive music drifted in to replace it. Aphrodite knew Pan as she would a brother. His music could charm for many reasons, but in his bonding with Anja she could detect no intention but kindness. However, it hadn't been pity that had drawn Pan to her; the Land had decided to save Anja for reasons of its own.

Maia had arrived months ago, relaying Pan's concern, telling her that she was with child and wouldn't be available for a while. Pan had decided to keep the children with him until he knew more. Fox and Quicksilver had undermined that. Even when his hand had been forced, he had not just sent them on their way, but to her. She now realised how concerned he must have been. The Land was gifting the girl slowly but immeasurably. Pan had bonded her to him; now she could feel the same happening to her. Anja had an aura of vulnerability; she was so beautiful, so innocent, but underlying this was a will of steel that was denying the growing gifts the Land was burdening her with.

There was no doubt the children had to go on; their destiny was set. If the creature's barren realm expanded to the mouth of the Great River, the results would be catastrophic. Could the Land not destroy the creature itself? If that was the case, was it developing Anja as a sacrifice, a saviour, or both? Whichever, it was her role to prepare her, despite her growing affection for her.

'You shall stay for ten days, and then it will be time to go on,' she said abruptly. Realising how harsh this sounded, she gently laid a hand across Anja's shoulder and added, 'Any longer and you'll become so comfortable that you'll not want to leave.'

'Yes, it is lovely here, and you're so kind, but we must find Toby.'

'I insist, though. Ten days.'

Pouring out her heart to Aphrodite was like a warm breeze entering one ear and blowing her troubles out of the other. She felt so content and happy that she began to dance. Aphrodite sat in the shade, entranced by Anja's grace, and smiled. She could feel the nascent power radiating from the girl. *Who knows how this is going to end?* she thought. Once, she would have been jealous of such budding power and beauty, but that was before the return. She was no longer that person.

When Anja finished her impromptu little performance, they continued, meandering slowly back towards the cottage as Aphrodite taught her more wood lore, charming her with the ease of one used to gaining the devotion of others, so much so that Anja felt comfortable sharing something very private with her; something that had been bothering her.

'I've stopped.'

Aphrodite looked at her for further validation of this comment.

'You know, it wasn't much but it's stopped. It hasn't happened since I came here. Mummy said it would get heavier as I got older, but it's stopped completely.'

'Oh, oh right, now I understand, that's what you're asking. It's a very long time since I've considered it. It was something that caused a lot of discussion between us women when we went to your land. We hardly age, Anja. Everything slows. Bodily functions don't, because we still eat regularly, although we don't really need to, and we sleep each night. Again, we don't really need to. But our ability to reproduce is stopped. The Land maintains its balance. When we went to your land, it came back again, slowly. The longer we stayed, the more this happened, with predictable consequences.'

'But did you still love each other when you were here?'

'Love is complex, Anja, it's not simply about sex. I'm assuming you do know about sex, having babies?'

'Of course, I'm not that naïve. Don't, it was excruciating, so embarrassing when Mummy tried to talk about it, and I knew all about it anyway.'

'Hmm, did you? Well, we still have that desire but are not fertile.'

'So, is that what's happened to me?'

'Yes, it's a sign that you are becoming like me.' Aphrodite did not want to continue with the line of conversation; she deviated slightly. 'Anyway, love is not sex. It's deeper and more meaningful. You love your parents, don't you, and Alfie and Toby?'

Anja dutifully nodded.

'And Pan?'

Anja stared at her for a moment, and then gave a tiny nod.

'I know, Anja, I know how deep bonding goes. I'm also bonded to someone. But love isn't simply about sex, it's something much deeper.'

'I think I love you too.'

Aphrodite closed her eyes. This was now getting far too deep too quickly, but she couldn't reverse what she'd started. 'You're new here, Anja. I still exert adoration on you.' She wanted to bring this strand of the conversation to a close, because her young acolyte was already struggling enough with the mental changes she was experiencing. She'd used Anja's lovely, innocent confiding to introduce complex subjects; it was enough for now.

'So, it's quite natural that you've stopped. Let's just say that it's not necessary here, which is a blessing, because the Land prefers us to be infertile while we remain here.'

'So have you tried to have children?' There was a twinkle in Anja's eyes.

'Right, that's enough. I've shared enough for today.'

However, Anja had seen something in Aphrodite's face, a sadness; momentary, quickly covered, telling.

*

Five or so miles across the creek, Quicksilver and Alfie were following a downstream path parallel with the Great River, half a mile or so inland. Alfie badgered his friend about their intended destination. At last, Quicksilver gave in.

'We're going to the place I came from.'

'Where you were born?'

'No, it's not where I was born, there was somewhere before. I don't remember where that was. This is where I came from in the Land.'

Alfie was running backwards so that he could face Quicksilver, who always seemed to speed up his pace whenever Alfie wanted to know something.

'Why do you never tell me properly? You just say a bit and when I want to know more you don't tell me,' he whinged breathlessly, trying to talk and skip backwards. Then he almost fell and turned back around, falling in step with his tormentor.

Quicksilver mischievously changed the subject, pointing to a rabbit sitting further along the path. As they approached, it vanished into the undergrowth.

'You'd think that we'd have seen more rabbits on the Downs, wouldn't you?' he said blandly. Alfie snorted, uninterested in rabbits.

'You hardly ever see more than one or two. The

storm flooding might be why, or perhaps they just don't like it.'

For the next hour, Quicksilver kept up this diverting conversation, presumably to advance Alfie's education of the Downs. As usual, he was either unaware of or taking a silent delight in Alfie's exasperation at not finding out what he wanted to know.

Late afternoon was drawing on as they passed through dense woodland. The ground sloped steadily down towards the river and they angled towards it, walking pleasantly beneath canopies of leaves sheltering them from the sun. The soft droning of insects filled air laden with the scent of pungent herbs that grew in small sunny glades. Just ahead, a forest of larger trees loomed. As they entered it, Quicksilver stopped and stroked the familiar hued trunk.

'They're grove trees, aren't they?' Alfie exclaimed. 'Right in the middle of these woods.'

'Not right in the middle, they grow from here, down to the river and along for about half a mile. It is a very big grove.'

'But I thought that groves always grew on their own.'

'All those that grow on the other side of the river do, usually near the stone circles. But this one is special.'

'Why?'

'Because it wasn't a sanctuary, there are no storms here. I think there are small rooms and tunnels underneath, but no passages to get into them from the Great Tree. This one wasn't planted for the Folk.'

'Are you really not one of those Folk?' Alfie had wanted

to ask that question for a long time, but somehow it had never seemed right to do so. Now it came out quite naturally.

'I'm not one of them. Aphrodite found me here, just after they had gone. I'm not sure how I got here. The Folk were frightened of this side of the Great River, but some began to explore it. They were the ones who made the way down the canyon and the dock in the cave. There are more remains of their work near here, by the river. Aphrodite stopped them using the Great River.'

'Why did she do that?'

'Because they didn't belong, the Land didn't want them. They thought that they could settle here, but they were wrong. They were upsetting the balance.'

'I saw it in my dream. I saw them trying to pull down the stone in the circle, and all their boats sinking. I even saw them arriving.'

Quicksilver's eyes widened. The dream may have ended as a nightmare, but as more details came out, he realised that his little companion had learnt more about what happened to the Folk than he'd thought. He hadn't been sure whether he should bring Alfie here but was pleased he had.

Alfie sensed the drift of his thoughts. 'Do you want me to tell you everything I dreamt that night? I can remember all of it.'

'No, I know what happened. What I don't know is how they came to be in the Land, because they shouldn't have been here. I don't think that even the Great Ones know why so many arrived. It's the same for me, like a dream, but the only way I could be here is if I came with them. Aphrodite says she doesn't know either.'

'Is Aphrodite a very powerful Great One?' Alfie asked.

'Yes, she's more powerful than Pan, though they all pretend they don't care about power anymore.'

'Did she find you when you were a baby then, did they leave you behind?'

'No, Alfie, I told you, I'm not one of the Folk. I was here in this grove. I don't know what I was before Aphrodite came and found me.'

Alfie looked astonished. 'But you must've started as a baby, everyone does.'

'Well, I didn't, I was just like I am now. I came from the Great Tree. Aphrodite told me that. The Folk didn't care for the groves but were sort of protected by them. I don't know who planted them, but someone must have. When the Folk left, I appeared. That's all she told me.'

'Is that why you can put your hands into the trees?'

'Yes, I'll show you the Great Tree tomorrow. There's no door, though.'

'If there's no way in, how can there be anything underneath them?'

'I don't know. I can sense it but haven't been underneath. The Great Tree doesn't want me to.'

Then Alfie's young mind threw up a very mature question: 'Why did the Land kill the Folk when they were already going? This world is so different to ours.'

'I know a bit about your world, your land. Aphrodite and Pan have told me about it. They said humankind are smothering it, and take everything. Perhaps the Land thought that the Folk were the same. The Land is very alive and powerful, Alfie, it didn't want them. Then there's the terrible entity beneath the Downs. It's also very powerful and serves the Land. It drove the Folk from the Land and destroyed them. Afterwards, the creature appeared, and then you.'

'Why?'

'I don't know, but it's all because of that,' Quicksilver replied. 'That entity really dislikes me,' he added.

'Why?'

'Because of the groves; they're all over the Downs and it can't destroy them. I belong with the groves. I look after them.'

'Are you like a tree then?'

'I don't think so, but I can become like one.'

'Wow! Why did you come alive?'

'Aphrodite says because of the Land. If it doesn't like you, you won't live. But it can change anything to be part of the balance here. The entity doesn't like me, but the Land must, I'm still here.'

'Have me and Anja changed? I don't feel any different.'

'Haven't you noticed anything different about Anja?'

She was a bit different, definitely moodier. He didn't want to talk about her. He shrugged and the conversation ended.

Quicksilver led Alfie down through the grove until they reached the trees that loomed massively over the Great River, their sinuous roots delving thirstily towards the water. They leapt from root to root, sure-footed, follow-my-leader, and when the excitement of that game waned, moved back into the depths of the grove. The trees grew larger, much broader towards the centre, and Alfie marvelled at their height and size. Quicksilver suddenly put his hand over Alfie's eyes. 'Now you mustn't look,' he said. 'I'll lead you.'

After a few more minutes, they stopped.

'Now, open your eyes.'

If the other trees were big, the one in front of Alfie dwarfed them, standing alone in a large depression, as though its weight was pushing it into the earth. Its huge canopy darkened the whole area except for thin beams of afternoon sunlight that managed to thread though the soaring branches, speckling the ground.

They walked a little way down the slope until they reached one of the massive roots radiating from it. Alfie wandered down a narrowing gap between two until he reached the point where they emerged from the tree, the tops twice his height. Quicksilver called him back and it took them ages to walk around the circumference of the depression.

Quicksilver climbed onto a huge root at the point it burrowed, far from the trunk, deep into the soil, then helped Alfie up. They made their way up its smooth surface, so wide there was little danger of falling off. As they neared the trunk, it joined another, forming a lumpy platform. Directly before them the trunk had split beneath a large knot, making a cavity big enough to enter, its interior so dark that Alfie couldn't tell how deep it went. The tree was so massive that they hadn't noticed it from the top of the depression. Just inside, Alfie's eyes became accustomed to the gloom. Quicksilver whispered in his ear. 'This is where I came from.'

Alfie thought that it smelt and felt a bit creepy but

didn't say so. They backed out onto the bumpy root platform and sat down on its knobbly surface.

'How do you put your hands into trees?' Alfie asked, hoping that Quicksilver might now be comfortable talking about it. His friend didn't answer him. Instead, he got up, turned and faced the great wall of trunk. Alfie shuffled around to watch.

Quicksilver placed his hands flat on the smooth bark. He gently massaged his palms against the surface and slowly his hands began to sink in, then his wrists and elbows. Concentrating for a second or so, he removed his left hand. Turning towards Alfie, who thought that he had finished, he kept turning, with his right arm still in the tree. Facing Alfie, his shoulder started to sink in. He laughed at the expression on Alfie's face as his whole body followed. Before his face sank in, he quipped, 'Bye, Alfie,' and was gone.

Alfie went to where his friend had been seconds before. There was only smooth hard wood. 'Quicksilver!' he called.

He suddenly felt very alone, as if Quicksilver had never existed.

'Don't worry, I'm still here.'

Way above, Quicksilver stood on a branch, smiling broadly down at him. Then he jumped straight at the trunk, hitting it with his arms spread wide, and slowly slid down until he was standing back on the roots. He'd used his fingers to slow his descent.

'Wow, I wish I could do that,' Alfie said, serious with admiration.

'You can't, Alfie. I'm me and the only one there is. Anyway, you're human.'

Alfie's face creased with disappointment. 'But I've seen lots of the things you have, in my dream. We could be blood brothers.'

'The groves have communicated with you and the dream shows that… what's a blood brother?' Quicksilver asked, suddenly catching Alfie's last words.

'It's where you both cut your hands…' he demonstrated on his palm '…and then hold your hands together.' Again, he demonstrated. 'Your blood mixes together and you are blood brothers. Cowboys and Indians used to do it.'

Quicksilver looked at his palm. He placed both hands against the tree and closed his eyes. When he opened them again, he was smiling. 'We can do something like it, but the tree has to be part of it as well. It's happy that I'm here, it doesn't usually like me delving into it.'

Alfie nodded eagerly.

'I'll show you what to do. But first, do you really want to be my blood brother? Are you really sure?'

''Course I'm really sure,' Alfie replied.

Facing each other, Quicksilver told Alfie to put his hand on the trunk, then he reached across his chest and put his own hand on the tree.

'Now clasp my free hand, palms together as hard as you can.'

'We haven't made the cuts yet,' Alfie said.

'We don't need to.'

Alfie put his right hand against Quicksilver's, who gripped it firmly.

'Ready?'

Alfie nodded.

'Squeeze hard. NOW!'

Alfie screamed and tried to pull his hand away, but Quicksilver tightened his grip. The little boy's face was ashen, but Quicksilver held on. Eventually, after about a minute, he let go.

Alfie held his hand to his body, tears welling from his eyes. He did not want to cry, but his hand stung unbearably. Quicksilver held his right hand out, palm upwards to show Alfie. From the pad at the base of his thumb, a large thorn had grown. The thorn and most of his hand was red with Alfie's blood. The stinging subsided to a dull ache.

'Are you all right?' Quicksilver asked belatedly. He seemed to be as surprised as Alfie at what had happened.

Alfie sucked in his breath as he opened his clenched fist. There was a large puncture at the base of his thumb. His hand was also bloody, but it had stopped bleeding.

'Nothing dug into *your* hand,' he complained, sniffing.

'I didn't know that was going to happen, Alfie. I just knew what to do.'

Alfie looked unconvinced.

Quicksilver looked seriously at his friend. 'Something did happen, though. That wasn't pretend.'

Alfie looked back at his hand. The ache had gone. Instead, he felt a warm glow surrounding the wound. 'It's stopped hurting. Do you think that we're blood brothers now then?'

'I think so,' Quicksilver reassured him. He didn't know what had just happened, but it was meant to; he was sure of that.

15

Quicksilver and Alfie walked back down to the Great River and stood quietly on the bank, letting the huge expanse of flowing water calm them. In the distance on the far bank, the trees of another smaller grove stood out.

'There was a sort of crossing here,' Quicksilver explained. He pointed to nearby remains of a structure that had been built on massive legs, some straddling the water. It didn't look very safe; where there had been handrails, most were missing, broken or leaning over. A set of rickety stairs climbed the side of the structure.

'They built this out of ordinary wood. I suppose they didn't want to cut any of the grove trees.' He picked at a fallen piece which crumbled in his hand. 'See, it's nearly rotten, falling apart. Might even be something the Land did. Normally, things don't rot like this. The structure on the cliffs hasn't.'

'Did they come across in boats from the other side?'

'Sort of, but it wasn't an ordinary crossing. This grove

is different. Aphrodite said a special person used to tend it.'

'Why didn't more cross over if it was safe here?'

'It wasn't, Aphrodite never allowed it. Only that one person was allowed. The Folk who made this were too frightened to return once it was made. They shared the fate of the others.'

'What, frightened of Aphrodite? I can't imagine her scaring anyone, she's lovely.'

'She is lovely, but she's powerful. All Great Ones can be fierce. There's a cellar full of bows, spears, weapons of all sorts and armour, made especially for her and others – under her home. It's hidden away but she showed me once. I don't know why they need such things.'

He hesitated whilst Alfie goggled at this. 'She told me that even before the Land decided the Folk should go, she'd made them fearful as soon as they got near to the Great River. Pan did the same at the Great Forest. Only the special one came after that.'

Alfie considered climbing up the old stairs.

'So, how *did* they get across, before she stopped them?'

'There were two wheels like the one on top of the cliff, only laid flat, one on each bank, part of the structures, with a big rope going around them in a circle. A small boat was attached to the rope. One person could pull it across on their own. The river's too wide and strong to try to row a boat straight across. Aphrodite can do it, but she has the otters to help and, anyway, she can control the Great River.

Alfie was only half listening and wandered over to

the rotten structure. He absently tried to pull off a bit but only a few paltry rotten strands came away, so he swung his leg lazily back and tentatively kicked the stair support where it looked crumbliest. The result was spectacular; wood and dust exploded everywhere. Encouraged by this success, he swung his leg back and forth, systematically destroying more and more.

Alfie lost interest in the history of the structure; it was much more fun wrecking it. He decided to try a little harder. He stepped back and, with a little hop and a skip, put his full weight behind a mighty kick. A whole area disintegrated, collapsing in a cloud of dust. The stair emitted a sickly creak and sagged a little. Quicksilver stood back out of the way, watching with amusement.

Alfie lost himself in the enjoyable destruction and with one wild kick after another, destroyed the steps. One large post remained of the area the steps had been built against and once this was gone, he reckoned that it would all tumble down. He turned, laughing, to make sure that Quicksilver was watching, and launched himself at it.

His foot hit the post and stopped abruptly. Its core was solid. Soft buskins proved scant protection and he hopped away, screaming, holding his foot in a haze of excruciating pain. Quicksilver, convulsed with laughter, launched himself after Alfie to see if he had done any real damage. He caught him and, still laughing, managed to grapple him to the ground. Ignoring the little boy's tearful protests, he pulled off the buskin and surveyed the damage. A couple of toes were already turning black and beginning to swell.

'Good game?' he grinned, dodging Alfie's other foot as it lashed at him.

'Stop laughing. I've really hurt it, I can't walk.'

Quicksilver caught hold of Alfie's good foot and dragged his protesting friend over to the nearest grove tree. He helped him hop up onto a root and sit down. Then, propping him up from behind, he told Alfie to put his injured foot against the trunk.

'I can't put it on anything, it hurts too much,' Alfie sobbed.

'Of course you can, rest it against the bark.'

With much sucking between his teeth and other pitiful sounds, all of which Quicksilver ignored, Alfie did as he was told. The bark was cold and soothing on the sole of his foot as he eased his toes against the tree.

'Now press your heel.'

Alfie pressed gently, bracing himself against the older boy. His heel flattened against the surface as the pressure increased.

'Harder.'

Alfie closed his eyes as pain lanced through his injured toes.

'Keep pushing.' Excitement had entered Quicksilver's voice.

'I *am* and it really hurts,' Alfie remonstrated.

'Why don't you have a look?'

Alfie did so and gasped. His heel and most of his foot had almost disappeared into the surface of the tree. He could only see the tips of his damaged toes.

'Try to relax and keep pushing.'

Alfie watched his injured big toe sink into the wood. He didn't feel any restriction. If he could explain what he felt at all, it would be that it was as if he had placed his foot in a lukewarm bowl of water. The pain ebbed away.

'Better?'

Alfie nodded.

'Try to pull your foot out quickly.'

Alfie braced himself. He pulled, nothing happened; his foot was locked tightly into the tree.

'It won't come out.'

'First lesson: when it went in, it was still your foot. When any part of you is inside the tree, you move it with your mind. Now think about your foot coming out and gently withdraw it.'

Alfie thought about his foot coming out and instantly understood. Gently, he withdrew it. He gingerly stretched his toes and let out a groan of pleasure. No pain, just a nice, muscular sort of soreness. He was healed.

'When your foot was part of the tree, it was made better because it wasn't flesh and bone anymore, it was tree. If you went completely into the tree, you could flow through it and come out anywhere. You just think yourself coming out, and as you do, your essence becomes you again. It's your mind that's important.'

Alfie was examining his foot. 'I can still sort of feel it hurting, although it doesn't really.'

Quicksilver gave Alfie his buskin. 'That's because it gets better so quickly that your mind thinks it can still feel the pain. I suspected what had happened when we did the "blood brother" thing, but I was going to wait before

175

trying. Don't tell Aphrodite or your sister yet, I'm not sure what they'll think.'

'I don't care what Anja thinks. Am I the same as you now?'

'You're not the same, Alfie. You've been changed by the trees so that they can help protect you. I wouldn't want you to be like me, but we are "blood" – or "sap" – brothers now.' He laughed at his own little joke. Alfie looked at him blankly and Quicksilver playfully ruffled his hair.

'Come on, we'll sleep here tonight and travel back in the morning. It's getting dark.'

The boys returned to the magnificent Great Tree and nestled down within the comfort of its massive roots.

*

Earlier, seated in the kitchen, Anja and Aphrodite had just finished a meal of fish and fresh wild mushrooms. Aphrodite poured herself and Anja a sparkling drink in crystal tumblers. The strange, lightly scented drink cleaned Anja's mouth and effervesced all the way down her throat and into her stomach. It also bubbled into her head. Her eyes opened wide as she experienced the strange sensations. Aphrodite laughed and took a sip of hers. 'For special occasions; it's a sort of wine. It isn't strong but has some unusual properties.'

Anja took another tentative sip.

'Now, I'll tell you more about the Land, and myself.'

The drink and her hostess's relaxed manner prompted

Anja to be unusually forward. 'Are you and Pan the same, I mean, are you magical or something?'

Aphrodite smiled. 'I know what you mean by magical, and in your land, it might have seemed that we were, but we're not. Here, the Land decides how to maintain its balance. We so-called "Great Ones" have been given gifts and attributes by the Land to help it do so.' She sighed. 'When humans first walked your land, they understood the balance; the ways of animals, weather, plants, of everything. They listened to your land and understood what they heard. Humankind call it the "balance of nature". We just call it the "balance". Your ancestors understood their land was alive and aware. Everything that lived on it understood.'

'How did it change then? We spoilt it, didn't we?'

Aphrodite nodded her head sadly.

'Yes, but we didn't help, although we could have.'

'What do you mean, you could have?'

'Well, Anja, we went there, but we didn't help.'

Anja frowned. 'I don't understand.'

'There were more of us then, not a great many more; there can never be very many *Great Ones*.' She put a contemptible emphasis on these words.

'We found the portals, gateways to your world. As you're now aware, it's like the Land, yet so different. Here, each of us uses our gifts to maintain the balance. Pan, the Great Forest: me, the Great River and woods. Others have or had different responsibilities. We were gifted attributes and some power, but we were naïve and selfish.' Aphrodite sipped her wine and gave her young guest a haunting look, a look so sad that Anja wanted to look away.

'Your land was alive and aware, but not the way the Land is. When we crossed into your world, not only did we still have our attributes and powers; they were greatly magnified, and we had no responsibilities or restraints.' She paused again, wanting Anja to digest each word.

'Initially, we acted responsibly. Humanity was in its earliest stage of development and we made small interventions that we considered harmless. However, even the smallest intervention is never insignificant and can alter everything. Your ancestors were grateful, naïve, worshipped us and we bathed in their adoration. We did whatever we desired.'

'Do you still go there?' Anja asked, but Aphrodite was not ready to answer questions.

'Each of us did as was our nature. Pan roamed the great forests that covered your land. Humanity held him in awe, but also feared him, although he never mixed openly because he's so different. We all drank deeply of that adoration. The more we received, the more we wanted. Our powers flourished with such veneration. You named us gods and we liked it.'

Anja rephrased her question slightly. 'Do you still go there?'

'When we returned to the Land, many never came back. But I have, only very rarely, not to be noticed and not to interfere.'

'Are any still there?'

'No.' She held Anja's hands in hers. 'Some were so corrupted by human behaviour and adoration that they cared less for your land's... your world's... balance, because it spoilt their enjoyment. It was not the Land and could not control them. We told them it was wrong, that we should all return. They refused. Argument turned to anger, hatred, and we fought. After a terrible conflict, we overcame them; their gifts, attributes, had been corrupted. With great sadness, those few of us who survived returned to the Land.'

She squeezed Anja's hands. 'We can do so much, Anja, but we couldn't change human behaviour; its urge to compete, and uncontrollable fertility. Your species reproduce faster than any other. Such huge populations inevitably destroy the balance. Humanity has so many attractive traits, but they have used up your land. The Land understands humans, Anja. It knows its traits.'

'So, what about me?' Anja had become confused at the sudden, intense change that had come over Aphrodite.

'The Land has sensed something about you. It is changing you, gifting you power that will enhance you.'

Aphrodite saw that Anja was becoming wary. Nonetheless, it was time and she decided to push on.

'Everything, Anja – your age, gender, personality, the circumstances coming here – all convince me that you must understand what is happening and accept it. It's developing quickly and you must learn to control it.' She leant forward. 'Do you understand what I'm saying, Anja?'

'Mummy says that I'm strong-willed.'

'I am not asking what your mummy says. Do *you* understand what *I* said?'

'I've always been like that.' Anja was closing down.

Aphrodite took her hands in hers. 'Have your friends always flinched when you are angry and told you that you are hurting them?'

'No.'

'But they do now, don't they, and how often do you hear Pan's pipes?'

A stronger flash of wariness entered Anja's eyes, but it was too late to stop. 'When you first arrived, Pan was there for you. I know the power of his pipes, what they are capable of doing, Anja. I know why he plays for you. You are bonded to him, Anja. Only the Land could allow that, and I am drawn to you too. I genuinely care for you, and so does Pan.'

Anja shrugged and looked down at their entwined hands. 'I don't know what you're talking about.' Aphrodite waited. After a second or so, Anja looked back at her.

'So, I do a bit, but I don't know why *you're* so bothered. We'll leave soon, find Toby and go back to the Great Forest. Pan will show us how to get home. I don't need all this rubbish about powers and change.' Her eyes softened. 'Oh, that was really rude and I didn't mean it, Aphrodite. You have been so kind, and so has Pan and Quicksilver, but no one said you had to help us. All this about changing and the Land... If I had any powers, I would put all of this right. And what do you mean by "powers" anyway? All this is my fault and I have to put it right, and now you're making me think about things; things that are not important and I don't want to talk about.'

'It's hard, Anja, but it's not your fault, and we do have to help you. The creature is a great danger to all of us and we still don't know if helping you is right. The Land hasn't asked *us* to destroy it, not yet. Therefore, the Land has something planned that you're part of. Pan *had* to help you, and so do I.'

Anja tried to pull her thoughts together. 'So, what have I got to do when we get there, when we get to the coast?'

The first thought that came to Aphrodite's mind was *nothing*. Anja was being used and the children's fate rested with her. The Land would watch, learning. 'You'll do whatever you can, Anja. Use your instinct. Don't think about it now…' *Because I can't bear to discuss what will probably happen.*

Another vague answer. Anja pursed her lips. 'Were you human once?' Surely, Aphrodite couldn't dodge that one.

'It doesn't matter what I was originally, I can't remember my beginning.'

'You look human.'

'The Land changes us as it pleases.'

'I'm human, and only a child. Why does the Land want me if it doesn't like us?'

'The Land doesn't like or dislike anything, Anja. It's an entity and only considers itself, its balance, and we are all part of that. You were drawn here and it senses something within you. Pan and I do as well, but maybe not what the Land does.'

'There are billions of us in our world. What's so special about me? Is it because I don't like what's happening in our world?'

'It might be. In your land, the balance has already

been destroyed. Vulnerable species capable of correcting the balance have been driven away or are hiding. Your land is unable to stop the dominance of humanity.'

'What does that mean?'

'It means that only humanity can control itself. The urge to reproduce and the ability to do so quickly and in large numbers has led to complex behaviour; sometimes abhorrent but often compelling, exciting, attractive. When we found your land, it was still early in both human and our development. We were naïve when exposed to humanity. They were exciting and we corrupted the power gifted us by the Land. We took on human traits.'

'And the Land let you return?'

'Not only let us, welcomed us; those who survived. The human traits we acquired – skill and willingness to go to war, experience, caution, remorse – made us better guardians.'

'And me?'

'You possess raw, uncontaminated human traits. Enormous potential that hasn't been corrupted by age, knowledge or experience.' She did not elaborate on the significance of this. 'That's enough for now. Your confusion is understandable, Anja, and to be honest, I'm a bit confused myself. Let's sleep on it. Those two rascals will be back in the morning, so I'd better be up early to bake some fresh cakes. I'm sure that your brother eats his own weight in scones and honey every day.'

Anja retired to her room, thinking about the conversation. There was no doubt now that Aphrodite and Pan were similar, even if they looked different. They spoke in riddles and used words and expressions she couldn't make sense of. Aphrodite was beautiful and wise, but Anja wanted reassurance and wasn't getting it, just talk about changing and powers. She wondered what it would be like to have real power. Of course, she didn't have any. If she had, she would know, wouldn't she?

Falling into a deep sleep, she was back in the Great Forest with Pan, dancing through the woods, trying to find Alfie, who kept appearing, before melting away from her into the trees. It was the chorus of birdsong calling to her through the open windows that gently roused her, and she lay comfortably between sleep and waking for a long time as another day slowly opened, until in the distance she heard her brother's voice drifting through the woods.

They were back.

16

'There is no sign of them, Master.'

'They have left the Downs, my dark friend.'

'We will search along the river, and the other side.'

'NO, you will not. They will return to the Downs; have patience.'

'Why wait? If we look beyond the Downs, we can track them.'

'Have a care, Hamma, there is much you don't understand. Do not leave the Downs. Have some of your minions spread out and watch carefully near the river, but do not expose yourselves. I want to know when they cross back. The youth will be visiting someone dear to me. He will feel safer when he crosses back, will take less care.'

'But the children…'

'Have patience.'

'Can you not just grab them, as you did me?'

'No. They will avoid my stone circles. Heed my instructions, Hamma, do not disobey me. Gather all your minions. Keep all but your scouts away from the coast and the river side of my great circle.'

'Of course, Master. You have a plan?'

'They will come to me.'

*

Breakfast was a lazy conversation dwelling on what the boys had done, although much was left out, prompted by mutual looks that were not missed by Aphrodite's intuitive eyes. Her own day with Anja was briefly glossed over, and although she and Anja both intended to dip into subjects already broached as soon as they were alone again, neither was in a hurry. Talk moved to the journey ahead.

'Take great care when you are crossing the southern Downs,' Aphrodite cautioned Quicksilver. 'It's been unusually quiet nearer the coast, with few storms, and even those not severe, which is not normal.'

Quicksilver shrugged. 'I'm always careful. As soon as we've finished on the Great River, we'll cut directly across to the coast. Fox should have arrived there weeks ago and will meet us, then we'll make a plan.'

'I'm not talking about when you reach the coast. First, you must pass near the Great Circle. It's dangerous for you, Quicksilver. Give that area a wide berth, even if it adds a few days to your journey.'

Quicksilver lightly agreed, as if it was of no consequence, but Aphrodite held him in her troubled gaze.

'Really, I'll take care,' he reassured her.

They discussed matters concerning the journey until Alfie started to become bored and began playing with one of the otter cubs. Their antics distracted everyone, and serious subjects were gratefully dropped. Anja caught Aphrodite's eye and her wish to talk required no prompting, the boys pretending not to notice or care when they rose and walked outside, hand in hand.

As they passed out of earshot, Anja's eyes narrowed. She turned to Aphrodite. 'They're keeping secrets from us.'

Aphrodite smiled. 'You noticed as well. I wonder what really happened at the grove.'

Anja giggled. 'It was so obvious. If I get Alfie on his own for a couple of minutes, I'll soon find out.'

'No, leave him. I'm sure you'll find out soon enough. There are not many secrets that can be hidden when you're travelling together. It's better to wait. Now where shall we start?'

'All this about powers. I can't really have any powers, can I?'

'It's not easy to explain. It depends on what you understand by "powers". As yet, your natural traits are amplifying, and that affects other people's feelings and thoughts. You almost shouted in my mind that you wanted to talk a little while ago in the house.'

'I didn't know I was doing that.'

'Because you can't control your mind yet. I'm very receptive, so I would recognise it happening. Others wouldn't realise, they would simply feel the need to talk to you. Do you understand?'

'I suppose so. Then it's not really a power, is it?'

'Oh yes, it's a strong sign that it's growing, Anja. The ability to influence other minds is an unusual power and I don't know how strong it will become. If it can affect me, here in my own domain, in the Land, imagine what it will do in your own land. Remember what I said yesterday; abilities, or, in your case, powers, are gifted by the Land. If, rather when, you return to your own land, I'm not sure what effect it will have. That will depend on you controlling your mind and, particularly, your emotions.' She lifted Anja's chin with her finger and knelt in front of her. 'Was that plain enough? I've been wondering all night how I could convince you. Do you understand better now?'

Anja sighed. 'I understand, but what's the point if I don't even know that I'm doing it?'

'As I said, it's only beginning. That's not all, Anja. There is something else, something that I recognise. You are beautiful, Anja. When you came into the room wearing the clothes that Quicksilver gave you, you were so beautiful that my heart ached for you. Even in your travelling clothes, you are beautiful, even when you're tired.'

'You are as well, that's how I felt when I saw you on the jetty. I almost fainted. I could never be as beautiful as you, Aphrodite.'

'Anja, you *are* becoming like me. What do you see when you look at me, exactly?'

'A beautiful woman.'

'No, *exactly*: age, type, shape?'

'Oh right; a woman about twenty-something, dark hair, very fit but curvy as well, really beautiful.'

'And what do you see in the mirror in your room?'

'A girl, I suppose, sort of teenish, dark hair, not very curvy.'

'Beautiful?'

'I'm not sure.'

'If anyone else was asked that question, I tell you what they would say, exactly and without hesitation. They would say "beautiful", "adorable". Not pretty, or nice, or anything else. There will come a time, as with me, when your beauty will be so overpowering that someone from your own land will not be able to look at you unless you protect their mind. You may have to cover your face, particularly your eyes.'

Anja looked dubiously at Aphrodite. 'What makes you think that?'

'What colour are your eyes?'

'Brown.'

'I'll ask you again. You've used the mirror in your room, I know you have. What colour are they?'

'Brown,' but Anja knew what she was asking. 'You mean those flecks?'

'They are not any old flecks, Anja, they are golden, and more are appearing each day.'

Anja nodded.

'What colour are my eyes?'

'Bright, bright blue, incredibly blue.'

'Originally, my eyes were grey. One of my first memories was when they gradually became flecked with this blue, then they turned completely. Your eyes will be golden, Anja, purely golden.'

Anja didn't say anything again for a while, then she stood up and faced Aphrodite. 'If, and only if, all this is true, will it help me get Toby back? And I just want to take him home.'

'I don't know, I don't think it's happening fast enough for you to control and use. If the creature was human, from your land, maybe, but I don't know if this creature can be influenced by anything. He's an entity; you will have to act intuitively if you confront it. I think that's what the Land has in mind.'

Anja did not want to contemplate facing the creature. 'What about this Fox friend of Quicksilver and Alfie's? They talk about him making a plan. Will he help? He's just a fox.'

Aphrodite smiled widely.

'Fox is a good friend to have. I asked him to take a message to Pan when Maia had to leave, and it *was* him who thought that you needed to start your journey.'

'Yes, but how can he talk, is he a Great One as well?'

'No, I don't really know what he is, apart from a talking fox. He doesn't speak about himself, but the Land must have made him what he is. He is kind and clever.'

'Can he change back, be an ordinary fox or whatever he was before?'

'I don't think so. Who knows what he was before, perhaps not even a fox? But I've only seen him in fox form. He appeared just before Quicksilver did. So many things happened then. Some changes are permanent, but others are the ability to become something else when you wish to. I have changes I can make when I want to.'

Anja perked up. 'You can change, into what?'

'Oh, a few different things, some that Land gifted me, and some another powerful Great One gifted me with the Land's approval.'

'What, change into an animal?'

'Yes, other creatures, or a different female form,' she replied, laughing. 'Some of the other female "gods" of your land were me, but in slightly different forms. It was stupid and selfish, as if having one group of people worshipping you wasn't stupid enough.'

'Does it hurt, changing?'

'The first time can if the other body is very different. Your essence is manipulated to accept the changes needed; it can be painful. After that, it is instinctive. Most living things are made up of the same components, just in different ways. Billions of little parts, all attached to one another. If you're gifted the ability, those parts are trained to reconfigure, sometimes a little, sometimes a lot. It happens so quickly that you have to be ready for your new body. It can be quite disconcerting going from two legs to four, or none.'

'I didn't want to be gifted at all. Doesn't the Land ask you?'

'No, it doesn't. Pan was one of the first and hasn't any change attributes, but I'm sure he was permanently changed to what he is now. I can't imagine that he was born like that, can you?'

They were sitting against a low bank of grass. Aphrodite put her arm around her young laughing companion. She realised how lonely she had been all the long years since the return. Her mind turned back to those stupid, wondrous days when they'd found another land, before it had all fallen apart…

The huge river to her left glowed red, partially from the reflected sun that was rising over the flat horizon and partially due to the red soil it deposited on the wide flood plain holding back the desert. From her high vantage point, everything was covered by a thin, even mist, but even now, before the rising sun had time to slowly burn it away, she could hear thousands of voices rising to the great ziggurat upon which her golden throne was placed. Thousands of her devotees, spreading far into the distance, their low hypnotic chants answering the clear, sweet call of the priests. She lowered the barrier she had raised around her mind and her presence spread over the kneeling masses, their foreheads pressed tightly to the ground. A gentle groan broke from the multitude, washing backwards until it rumbled like distant thunder.

She stood and opened her arms, translucent robes framing her beautiful form like dazzling wings as she whispered, 'I am come.' As one, the people raised their heads, and sighs of devotion and joy faded to silent anticipation. She knew that even the most distant, aged eyes could see her with the same clarity as those who knelt like ants over two hundred cubits below. She savoured the adoration that poured into her mind, filling an unquenchable need until its sweet pain became an agony of pleasure. She then sent it back in a wave that surged through her subjects, their heads snapping back in the ecstasy of that perfect moment. The priests cried out her names and titles and the ecstatic people wildly chanted their love in fervent harmony, voices delirious with supplication. She watched with sated benevolence until they were exhausted, then whispered again, 'Silence.' And her sweet voice, like ice, caressed their spines and they sobbed with humility. Shrouding her mind, she sat back on her throne. The sun blazed, the river flowed, and all was well…

'What are you thinking?' Anja's voice snapped her back and she laughed.

'Oh, Anja, we were so stupid and arrogant. Never be naïve enough to think that wisdom comes with power, because it doesn't.'

Anja smiled sweetly, snuggling Aphrodite tightly, and closed her eyes. A time would come when both would realise such advice is easier to give than take.

The days passed blissfully in the backwaters of the Great River. Alfie and Quicksilver exploring the woods and creeks. Anja with Aphrodite. She began to copy her ways, particularly how she spoke, much to the amusement of Alfie, despite him doing the same with Quicksilver. She shared her deepest worries, and Aphrodite coaxed her to talk about her parents, but the pain of their memory and her betrayal of their trust were so traumatic that Aphrodite calmed her, letting the forest music weave its healing charm. As Anja danced dreamily before her, she understood more than ever that what had happened in the Great Forest couldn't have been avoided.

Aphrodite left Anja alone for the last few days to relax and enjoy the serenity of her homestead. She went early to bed, sleeping deeply until late in the mornings, the music running though her body and often staying with her long after. Alfie saw the return of the secret, faraway smile when he caught her unawares. Eventually, the tenth day loomed. It was time to leave.

With heavy hearts, they sat down to their last evening meal with Aphrodite. When the plates were finally cleared, they stayed at the table to discuss the resumption of their journey. Aphrodite led the conversation.

'Only travel down the Great River for about half of the remaining distance to the coast. Then land and cut across the Downs.'

'Why can't we go all the way?' Anja asked. 'It goes all the way to the coast, doesn't it?'

Quicksilver answered her question: 'The river changes as it approaches the sea. Miles inland, it becomes a vast estuary. There are many islands, currents and tides. I haven't the skill to navigate; we'd be taken out to sea.'

Aphrodite nodded: 'Back on the Downs you must be vigilant. Don't push your luck, Quicksilver.' She waited for an assent before continuing. 'Keep well clear of stone rings and always watch for the signs of danger. Do you understand the signs, children?'

'I've told them, but I know you will go through them again.'

Aphrodite's look cautioned him for his carefree attitude. 'Quicksilver carries danger with him there. The entity beneath the Downs is often dormant but should never be underestimated. The groves are a constant reminder that its power was challenged. Quicksilver has become an unbearable irritation.' Quicksilver pulled a face, but Aphrodite was unmoved, as anxious for him as she was for the children. 'The dangers are the same. On the Northern Downs they are slow to develop, on the Southern Downs, and in particular the area you must cross, the speed and ferocity of the storms make escape, if you are caught in the open, almost impossible. Watch carefully for the signs: small dark clouds; close, cloying air; yellowing of the sky. At the very hint of any of these, find safety, quickly. Its wrath will come down on you with unimaginable speed.'

She paused to emphasis the next sign. 'One sign you must never miss: a distant speck wheeling high on the thermals, a croak carried from afar on the breeze. If you hear or see a raven, then flee as fast as you can to the safety of the nearest grove. From sunrise to sunset, from the moment that you leave the river, constantly watch for ravens. There is rumour that a Great Raven has appeared, one that speaks and all creatures dread.'

If her point had been to frighten the children, it worked. The memory of the storm they had already encountered was still fresh. *How much worse can a storm get?* Anja wondered. She was not sure what a raven was, something like a big crow, but she knew she would recognise one if she saw it. Alfie's little face looked more troubled. Aphrodite was satisfied that her warning had made its mark. She moved on to their eventual arrival.

'When you get to the coast, don't go near the cliffs until you've met Fox. Hopefully, he will have gathered information by the time you arrive. I think that you should wait for him at the last grove. Did you make any arrangements before he left?' She looked expectantly at Quicksilver.

'Sort of, he finds me wherever I am when he wants to.'

'Then wait there and make your plans as best you can.

194

I have been asked not to journey with you, as was Pan. We have free will, but are servants of the Land and must trust it. Anja, when the time comes, use your intuition and act quickly. The longer you hesitate, the more chance there is you will be discovered, and the chance of a stealthy rescue lost. It's waiting for you, don't signal your arrival.'

'Please could you come with us?' Anja asked in a small voice, knowing that she shouldn't have. She'd asked Pan the same and knew the answer.

'No, my love. You don't know how hard this is for me, but I will sense your progress.'

'That's what Pan said.'

Having not really contemplated reaching the coast and finding Toby, there was now grim resolve in Anja that gave Aphrodite some satisfaction that their stay had not been wasted, though her heart bled for the innocent eyes looking at her; eyes that begged her to change her mind.

Anja looked away, realising that the Land intended her – and her alone – to either rescue Toby or share his fate. There was no other future, because she couldn't go back without him. But she could keep Alfie safe. She'd considered asking Aphrodite but knew she would have offered if it had been possible, so was determined to leave him with Fox and Quicksilver when they reached the coast and go alone.

As they left the kitchen, she took Alfie's hand and led him with her. They cuddled to sleep on her bed; she needed him close.

17

*T*he child was weak. It had never kept a child alive before, but it only had to survive until they arrived. It could slaughter it now and the others later, but its meagre blood was not enough on its own.

The creature shifted its grainy gaze away from the distant cliffs to look painlessly into the burning sun, basking in its searing rays. The infant would survive. Along the base of the cliffs some hapless creature would stray into its clutches, like the small brown animal he had so nearly caught. If not, he would raid the nests of the gulls. The child needed sustenance; a regular supply of eggs would suffice, but the mashed carcass of an animal would supply enough until they arrived.

The gulls feared and hated and mobbed it whenever it took form in the open. It neither cared about nor felt their pain, as it hadn't those children whose pitiful, desiccated corpses and skeletons now decorated the bleached bones of the ships that had carried it to the seabed. It had gorged on the blood of those who had sunk with the ships when its miniscule body had escaped from the smashed phial that had been so carefully hidden. With each drop of blood, each iota of essence

196

that drained into the dry seabed, its awareness grew, its control over the sand increased.

The cruel parody of those whose terrible death had brought about its existence flowed back into and through the huge edifice it had copied from the image that had briefly flowered in the innocent mind of one of its first victims, seconds before her consciousness was torn from her on the hot sand. On the parched seabed, it spread its myriad grains beneath the burning orb shimmering above…

*

When she was sure her guests were asleep, Aphrodite slipped out of the cottage. A low whistle, and four sleek shapes glided to her side, escorting her to the creek. Five otters silently entered the water, and the vee of their wake was the only sign betraying their swift progress through the moon's reflection on the Great River.

Dawn had barely broken when the children and Quicksilver gathered in the kitchen.

'Where's Aphrodite?' Anja asked. Reluctantly, she had decided to leave her dresses behind and was dressed to travel. Only the bare minimum, the very least, was packed. They were ready, physically and mentally, for the final part of their journey.

'She's on the Great River,' Quicksilver answered. 'Don't worry. We'll see her before we start walking.'

Anja sighed. After becoming so close to Aphrodite, she knew that her bond was not the same as Quicksilver's.

At the jetty, Quicksilver fetched the craft he'd chosen

to carry them on the final stage of their river journey: a heavy, wide canoe. When their bags were carefully stowed, they took their places; Anja in the prow, Alfie in the middle and Quicksilver in the stern. Anja picked up the paddle that lay beneath her feet; it seemed the right thing to do.

'You won't need it, Anja,' Quicksilver said.

She felt a slight flush of embarrassment, then held on to the sides as he pushed off and with a couple of deft strokes, turned them downstream towards the river.

'Keep your feet and knees apart, it helps balance the boat.'

A hundred or so yards downstream, the banks suddenly seethed with life, and practically all the otters from the small settlement slid into the creek with them.

Anja now knew what to do and felt for the straps she guessed were tied to the prow, quickly releasing all the nooses. There was a small commotion as the otters took their places, vying with each other to be first to pull. With a gentle jerk, they were off.

All the way down the creek, the otters jostled and squabbled with each other to take their turn to pull the craft, the rest swimming before, beside and after it. When the waterway became too congested, some jumped out and ran along the bank. This strange arrangement continued until the whole company spilled out into the Great River. After negotiating their entry, the otters had little to do as the fast current drew them downstream.

Soon they reached the place, on their left, where the grove trees lined the bank. 'Look at that,' Anja shouted as they passed the ruined jetty, and the boys grinned, sharing their secret.

Although their task was largely redundant, a large group of otters continued with the travellers. On either side of the craft, two lines formed. As the sun began to burn off sporadic riverside mists, they settled into the beautiful monotony of river travel.

Many miles later, they sadly watched as the beautiful woods on their left thinned out and the scenery returned to the pretty but unchanging meadowlands. To their right, along the western banks, the Downs undulated against the long skyline. Occasionally, on the crown of a distant low hill, raggedness would betray a brooding stone ring. No one mentioned or pointed them out, but they all glanced at these reminders of the dark dangers ahead.

At night, they slept within a smelly nest of bodies that constantly snored and squeaked; a wonderful lullaby, even if Anja sometimes woke to giggle and push away a cold fishy snout that had invaded her slumber. With each day growing even hotter, Quicksilver rigged up a makeshift sunshade to shelter them from the searing midday rays.

A few more days of this uneventful cruising and they came to the end of their Great River journey, heralded by a flurry of action from the large leading otters. Without any obvious prompt, they nudged the canoe until Anja realised what they wanted and held out the harnesses. They began a slow pull to the west bank. Throughout that morning, they powerfully kept this course until they had crossed the mile-or-so width of the Great River and entered the mouth of a tributary; one of many that clustered the upper neck of the estuary, swelling its waters as it widened, many miles across, signalling its unity with the ocean ahead.

Quicksilver recognised the lead otters as those that usually attended Aphrodite and realised they had rejoined the pack the previous night. The rest of the company fanned out ahead in a great vee to combat the powerful current they now fought as they made headway up the tributary.

Quicksilver didn't stop Anja this time as she clumsily plied her paddle to help. Her arms were beginning to ache, and she was about to give up when she spied Aphrodite ahead, waving to them from a shingle bank. With a final bump, and an awkward disembarkation, they were on the Downs again.

Leaving the canoe, they walked onto grassy tussocks beyond the shingle. The usual snuffled wet greetings were exchanged between Aphrodite and her sleek friends and they settled down to a frugal lunch; the last of the honey cakes they'd brought had gone days before.

Anja looked for Aphrodite's boat, still mystified as to why she hadn't travelled with them, but there was no sign of one. A big hug from her soon banished the thought from her mind.

'Keep the line of the sun to your left in the morning and over your right shoulder in the afternoon and you should reach the coast, near the bay, in a few weeks.' Aphrodite was discussing the journey later with Quicksilver.

'I know the way,' he replied confidently. 'There's a more direct route, we'll get there quicker than that.'

'No,' she said adamantly. 'After a week, you must make a wide detour eastward. This will ensure that you don't go near the Great Stone Circle. The others you can skirt, but you must keep well away from the big one. Promise me, Quicksilver.'

Anja couldn't understand why Aphrodite kept on about this. They all knew how dangerous the circles were, no one more than Quicksilver. He'd been their only guide and mentor up until they met Aphrodite. She was just about to say something when Aphrodite turned to her, as if she knew what Anja was thinking.

'I am more worried than I thought I'd be. I want to come with you, but I'm not meant to. There are signs; the weather is too hot. It's always very hot on the South Downs, but not as constantly as this. I've sent a messenger to find Fox and tell him of your approach and where to meet you. Quicksilver *is* acting responsibly,' she gave him a look that melted his heart, 'but my concern is as much for him on this part of the journey as it is for you. This advice is not given lightly.'

'I won't take any chances,' he said seriously, then stood up. 'We should make a start.'

Anja was surprised; she'd thought that they would camp there and leave the following morning. Aphrodite saw her disappointment.

'Quicksilver's right, I must not stay here much longer. My presence will be felt and will compromise your journey. You must start today, but before you go, Anja, come and walk with me by the river.'

Anja jumped up, her face glowing. They wandered

out of earshot, leaving the boys to prepare for the long walk ahead. When they returned ten minutes later, Anja's eyes were damp and red, but she was smiling. Alfie hid a look of boyish contempt behind her back, which was gone when she looked at him. 'Thank Aphrodite for her kindness,' she said. 'Remember all the scones and honey that you've gobbled up.'

His face lit up with the many lovely memories of their stay with her. Bashfully, he ran over to her. 'Can we come back afterwards and stay with you for a while?'

Aphrodite almost crushed him with her embrace. 'Oh, that's all I can wish for, Alfie.' She took his cap from his bag and pulled it down over his head. 'Not much protection from the sun, but better than nothing. Your body will soon adapt.'

Quicksilver received her parting kiss with an adoration he could never hide, not even when she was chiding him. Then he turned and, motioning the others to follow, walked away. A few of the younger otters scampered beside them for a while, reluctantly turning back when they realised their elders hadn't.

As the three small figures grew smaller in the distance, Aphrodite threw her head back in frustration. She didn't want to stay out of this, yet she was hampered by old decisions, and recent direction. Now those seemed hollow. She pushed the canoe onto the water, harnessed otters to it and instructed them to take it home. Then she walked into the river with the elder ones. Within minutes, the area was deserted.

Any softness in Anja's and Alfie's muscles gained

during the time they had spent on the river and at Aphrodite's homestead soon toughened during the long slogs up and down low hills in the relentless heat, and knowing they had embarked on the last stage of their long journey spurred them on. What would happen on their arrival at the coast they pushed to one side; meeting Fox was their next goal. Only once did Anja imagine a time where she was hugging Toby, his little face beaming at her, but she quickly buried the image and scolded herself. She dare not allow herself such a tantalising fantasy; there was too much scope for failure, which she ardently refused to contemplate.

As their meagre supply of fresh food ran out, they resorted once more to foraging and the bounty of the groves. There were many more of these and seldom a time when one wasn't within sight; a haven of shade and respite from the burning heat. Stone circles too, but always at a healthy distance, and they watched constantly for signs of trouble.

One afternoon after a long ankle-stiffening climb, Quicksilver stopped to scan the horizon. Anja watched him carefully whilst trying to adjust the piece of cloth she'd tucked under her cap to gain some protection for her neck, her hair unable to block the strong rays. It fell on the grass and she cursed in frustration and discomfort.

Both boys exchanged looks of mock surprise at this uncharacteristic slip.

'How did the Folk put up with this heat?' she asked Quicksilver.

'It's always hot this far south,' he answered distractedly,

still scanning with his hand shading his eyes, 'perhaps not always as hot as this. The Folk were used to such heat; they often wore big round hats for protection.' He stopped, realising that Anja was staring at him in a way that made him feel uncomfortable. He smiled weakly, realising why. 'What, do you want me to get you one? There's usually some in these southern shelters. I don't like them myself. The sun doesn't bother me, I'm used to it.'

'I don't care how stupid they look. Why didn't you say? Please get one for me and one for Alfie.'

'I'm not sure I want one, Anja...' Alfie began to say, but her murderous glance silenced him. It wasn't a choice.

'All right, I didn't realise.' Quicksilver sighed. 'I should've thought.'

'I know. I'm sorry I went off again, I just want some shade.'

Quicksilver looked around; he pointed to a grove in the hazy distance to the left of the crown of the hill that they were climbing. 'We'll make that one in an hour or two.'

On reaching it, Anja stayed in the welcome shade of the towering trees whilst the boys trooped off to find the central tree, returning later with extra provisions and hats like big flat mushrooms. Alfie's was far too big and when she fastened it under his chin with the cord provided, his head almost disappeared. Hers was also very wide; made of thin, strong parchment stretched over a light wicker frame with a soft pad to rest on the crown of the head. She played around with the adjustable pad until it seemed comfortable, then tied it on. Alfie, tipping his head back to see, went into a fit of giggles. She tipped hers back a little and turned to Quicksilver, who'd been watching, waiting for a comment.

'Perfect,' certain that they'd chosen the widest they could find for her, and she meant it: a big sunshade. Who cared what it looked like?

'Are we still on course to avoid that big stone circle?' she asked.

Quicksilver peered out of the grove, towards the south. 'Yes, I don't travel this far south often, but I can read the groves and reckon if we turn slightly south tomorrow, or early the next day, we'll skirt a large grove. Then I can estimate where we are in relation to the great circle. We'll pass well around it.'

Anja wondered. He sounded confident but their stop earlier had been the third in an hour, as if he'd been getting his bearings.

'We should try to make a bit more progress today,' Quicksilver said. 'There's still plenty of daylight left.' He wanted to caress the familiar coolness of the last tree as they left the grove but denied himself, determined to maintain his confidence.

*

Hades hushed the hot, waiting Downs.

The boy was back, delving beneath the groves; a constant reminder of their presence. The Land had allowed him to stay but he suspected Aphrodite was involved. Beautiful Aphrodite; the groves hadn't infested her woods as much as they had the Downs, their great roots challenging him. He had taken no pleasure in scourging the Folk. The Land had requested it and he had complied. The unforeseen rise of the creature was an irritation, like the youth.

In self-inflicted isolation, Hades was unaware of what was unfolding. Obsessed with the boy, he reasoned that the groves would wither if his essence was drawn and confined. The children were of little interest; Hamma wanted them, and although he didn't condone needless cruelty, he would let his servant have them. So, for now, the stone circles could hold their menace, ignoring the travellers. The storms stayed tethered and the Downs remained parched. Hamma hid his minions. He'd followed the children from a distance; their hated high-pitched voices hurting his keen ears as he fought the overwhelming desire to tear them limb from limb. Hades' coercion was too strong. He seethed with anticipation; the trap was primed.

*

The largest otter suddenly broke away from the head of the pack travelling upstream and sliced through the water towards the downland bank. She bounded out and stood on her hind legs in the lush grass, sniffing the air. Her pack, most of whom had gone with the canoe, settled around her, silent and still. Suddenly her anxiety blossomed to a terrible fear and she squealed an ear-splitting warning that she feared would not penetrate the minds of those she desperately wanted to warn.

Had Quicksilver heeded the urge to place his palm on the grey trunk in the grove, the warning would have laced through him. Hades felt it, shook his head and smiled. He missed the intrigue, the games. He would take the boy's essence and dear Aphrodite would just have to accept it. In the bay, the creature mindlessly felt its echo, and nearby, slinking down the cliffs, a long whiskered snout felt it burn like a tiny ember. Its owner leapt in a frenzy of worry and after a moment of hesitation, decided to abandon his plans. He raced back towards the top of the great white cliffs. Far away in the depths of the Great Forest, Pan heard it clearly and strode towards the border with the Downs.

Meanwhile, the three friends, having missed the warning, continued to the next grove. They settled down for the night. Quicksilver didn't need to find the chamber, having successfully foraged earlier. Gnawing anxiety became a restless night, and still he misunderstood the cause. Alfie slept fitfully amid fearful images, and Anja, constantly worried, relied on Quicksilver to filter her fear.

The following morning, Quicksilver's urgency was uncharacteristic; he seemed distracted. Anja sensed his disquiet.

'Is everything all right?'

He nodded but didn't look at her as she stretched her pace to keep up. Alfie was almost trotting.

'What's wrong?' She stopped him with her hand.

'I don't know, I'm not sure we're going in the right direction.' He looked at her at last, as if he'd made up his mind to admit he was concerned. 'Usually a few miles here and there make no difference, but here it could be crucial. I felt something in the grove last night. Something's niggling me.'

'Alfie was very restless, weren't you, Alfie?'

Alfie scampered in between them, holding his huge hat on with his hands. 'I had a weird dream, sort of like the other one, only I can't remember what it was about.'

'It must be the effect the Great Stone Circle has on everything in this area,' Quicksilver said. 'That's what it is; it casts its shadow over everything, but we must be more careful than ever.'

'Why don't we go back until you get your bearings again? Or better still, take an even wider loop to our left, just to make sure?' Anja urged.

'No, I feel all right now. We'll stay to the left of the bigger hills for the next few days, just to make sure.' His confidence grew as he spoke and didn't waver. Nor did the heat.

During the rest of the day, they changed course three times to avoid small stone rings rearing up on the landscape, following a carefully placed ribbon of groves that had obviously been planted in the valleys to counter them, but why so many? Anja worried.

18

After another early start the following morning, they passed a massive grove a quarter of a mile or so away to their right. Quicksilver ignored the welcoming shade of the trees and a few minutes' relief from the sun, wanting to push on. Anja adjusted her hat, looking back longingly as they climbed away from it.

'I don't think that I could do without this,' she said fervently. 'I'm not really affected by the heat or sun so much now, but this is really hot. Doesn't it bother you?'

'No, I get hot, but that's all.' He was scanning the surrounding hills. 'I'm not absolutely sure, but I think that we must have skirted far enough eastwards. It's well over a week since we left the river. If we keep going directly south-east, we'll be past any danger and, in another week or so, be approaching the coast. Then we'll find the last grove.' He pointed ahead. 'Come on, there's nothing on that big hill. We'll get to the top by early afternoon and see where we are.'

It took longer than expected and their walking had

slowed to a trudge. An hour later, they still hadn't reached the deceptive crown. Quicksilver stopped and peered ahead, reassuring himself that he could see the summit. 'We're almost there. From the top, we'll be able to see for miles.'

Neither of his companions answered, their tough legs now feeling the pace, ankles and thighs aching. The sun felt as if it was beating through the wide shade of their hats. As the hill began to level out, it took effort to put one leg in front of the other. They were breathing hard, even Quicksilver. Alfie pulled at the neck of his tunic and took off his hat, wiping his face with his sleeve.

'I'm really tired and sweaty, Anja.'

Anja nodded, feeling trickles of sweat down her back. Quicksilver turned, horrified. The sky was not as blue as it should have been. 'Oh Aphrodite, no! Stay there, don't move.' He sprinted up the last few hundred yards to the crown. Slumping to his knees, he held his head in his hands.

Spread below him was a great bowl-like depression. Within this squatted the Great Stone Circle. Movement on one of the huge stones, great black wings flapping, spurred him into action. He leapt up, running helter-skelter back down to the waiting children. Panic preceded him, and they turned, racing down the slope. Alfie tripped and blundered into Anja, who fell heavily, leapt back up and dragged him to his feet.

'Quickly, the grove,' Quicksilver gasped. 'We—' His voice cut short as a heavy drop of rain hit his face. Another, and then many, many more. His pallor reflected the changing colour of the sky. Fighting the urge to race away to the security of the grove and leave his slower companions, he calmed himself. He had to get them to safety. 'Run. Keep together, it's starting.' He swallowed, grabbing their hands.

Below, in the distance, they could just see the salvation of the grove. As they sprinted down, fierce gusts began driving rain into their faces; they could scarcely see or keep to their feet on the steep slippery grass.

Latent energy, confined and nurtured for weeks, exploded. Lightning crackled continuously, accompanied by heart-stopping peals of deafening thunder. The coiled tempest engulfed them with howling ferocity.

Alfie was blown over. Quicksilver caught him and together they were whipped into the maelstrom. Anja grabbed his foot and hung on for her life. Buffeted, tumbling and gasping for breath, they clung together in a scrum of bodies and limbs. Agony erupted in Anja's head as her eardrums ruptured, her screams lost in the pandemonium. The pain became unbearable and she let go to cover her ears. As the wind increased to greater and even more destructive intensity, she had a fleeting glimpse of Alfie's flailing body spinning downwards before the world spun and the ground came violently back to meet her head with a crunching collision that knocked her senseless, sprawled across Alfie, who had met the same fate.

Neither Anja nor Alfie saw Quicksilver being sucked into the black tornado, nor its departure and the numb silence it left behind. Gurgling runnels of water cascaded down the hill and around the two inert bundles of human flotsam splattered with mud and blood. Since Quicksilver's cry of horror, just ten terrible minutes had passed.

*

*A*nja, I gave you strict instructions that Toby was to be in bed by eight. Now Aphrodite tells me that he's missing. I can't trust you with the simplest task.'

Anja couldn't bear to look at her father. He was livid. She loved him so much and now she'd let him down again.

A stabbing pain in her back.

'I thought that you were old enough to take responsibility. I trusted you, and this is how you reward me.'

The stabbing pain was getting worse.

'And where's Alfie?'

She looked around but couldn't see him. He must be hiding behind one of the chairs. His voice was coming from somewhere.

The pain was becoming unbearable. She tried to tell her father about it, but no sound came out of her mouth. He was talking to Pan. Couldn't he see that she was trying to tell him something?

'Anja! Anja, get off.'

She couldn't stand much more of this pain…

*

*A*nja, get off me, I can't breathe properly.' Alfie's voice sliced through her nightmare, bringing her to consciousness. The pain in her back was still there. She tried to open the one eye that was responding to her dazed mind. A flood of light blinded her, and she shut it again. The pain came again sharply, and her ears hurt.

'Anja, wake up and get off, you're crushing me.'

It dawned on her that the pain was coming from Alfie's elbow, grinding into her kidney.

Groaning with effort, she slowly rolled off her brother. Now fully conscious, her dream nightmare replaced by a real one. Try as she could, only the one eye wanted to open; her head was throbbing, ears hurt and she felt sick. She pulled herself up onto her hands and knees.

'You look terrible,' Alfie said, sitting up near her. 'Your eye's really swollen, and you've got big cuts all over your face.' The pain in her ears was dulling.

She rolled over, lay back on the grass and closed her one good eye again. Slowly, her head stopped spinning but still thumped like a drum. She remained still and quiet for a few minutes more to let the nausea pass and try to piece together the jumbled memories of what had happened, wincing as they reformed.

'Quicksilver's gone. We've got to find him.' Alfie's voice drew her back to the present. She moaned and sat up, although all she wanted to do was sleep. Alfie was standing over her. He had her hat. She took it and sighed with relief as it shaded her injured eye from the glaring afternoon sun.

'I don't know, I think he got pulled away by the wind. He could be anywhere,' she mumbled. Her mouth was swollen.

He knelt to peer at her under the ridiculously wide

brim. 'He's over the top of the hill. It's the place in my dream. It's the Great Stone Circle, Anja. He's lying right in the middle, on a big stone.' He pointed towards the top of the hill. 'Over that way.'

'How do you know?'

'We're blood brothers. I know that he's there. Something horrible is happening to him. We have to go and help him. Now, Anja.'

Intuitively, she knew he was telling the truth. She held her hand out and he gallantly helped her up. Briefly, her head spun again and then settled. She was thirsty and looked for her flask. If ever there was an emergency, this was it. It was not there. She cast around but couldn't see it nearby. Instead, she found a small deep puddle of rainwater in a small hollow. She drank and tenderly dabbed water on her face and head.

'Are you feeling a bit better now?' Alfie pleaded. 'We've got to help Quicksilver.'

'Wash your face,' she told him. 'You're covered in blood and mud as well. I want to see where you're hurt.'

With a sigh of frustration, he did as he was told. He didn't have a mark on him. Anja frowned, but didn't ponder for long. All the pain she was experiencing was easing and her head was rapidly clearing. She was beginning to grasp their predicament.

'Okay. Let's find our stuff and then we'll see what we can do.'

They did not have to look far. Their frugal possessions – bags, flasks and, important to them at that moment, their knives – were scattered along the route they'd tumbled down. The climb up was slippery, but the sun was rapidly drying everything, including their clothes.

Alfie, fretting wildly for his friend, beat Anja to the top, where he urged her to hurry as he pointed down the other side. Breathing heavily, she reached him and shuddered at what was revealed. In the middle of the strange bowl-shaped valley stood two enormous circles of stone-capped pillars, one within the other. On a huge flat stone, in the centre of this great monolith, lay Quicksilver; small, still and vulnerable. Around him, on every lintel balanced across the upright stones, were crowds of large black ravens; thousands, silently watching his inert body.

Anja was now looking down upon this ghastly scene with both eyes, and her other injuries were also rapidly healing. Clear-headed and becoming as resolved as her brother, she took his hand and began to stumble down the slope. The massive lintels across the two tallest pillars formed a gateway through the first circle, and this was repeated on the inner one, forming a corridor to the centre. The children walked obliquely down the hill towards them. It seemed the correct thing to do, although they could have walked between any of the other great standing stones. As the slope flattened, they stopped, Alfie's fingers digging into Anja's hand, but she didn't notice.

A few yards away, the first gateway rose; incredibly tall, its lintel yards wide. They couldn't see all the ravens roosting on it, just the backs of those on the edge. They were ignoring the children, facing inwards, watching the body on the slab. Anja took a deep breath and they walked on. Alfie's determined little face matched his sister's, yet neither could help nervously glancing up as they passed under the first gateway and approached the second. The ravens still ignored them as they passed through it. The flat stone lay about fifteen yards ahead. Just within this inner circle, they stopped, a sudden dread gripping them. Anja turned and glanced up. In the centre of the first row of birds on the inner gateway, gripping the edge with huge talons and dwarfing all the others, perched Hamma Half-Raven. He moved his head slowly and transfixed her with a stare from a strangely human eye. As Anja held his gaze, Alfie tugged her hand and hissed, 'Hurry, Anja, the circle's really hurting him, I can feel it.'

Rage and contempt filled Anja's mind and Hamma recoiled, flicking his stare away from her. The feeling of dread increased and, as if bolstered by some invisible help, the huge raven's beak opened and to Anja's horror, it spoke, its rasping voice clear and loud, echoing across the valley.

'His essence is gone, body ready for my comrades to feed. They will tear it apart, gorge on his entrails, pluck out his eyes while you watch. Then, your turn. First, your brother. Finally, when your mind is as destroyed as mine, I will tear *you* to pieces. This is my revenge.'

Alfie frantically tugged Anja's hand, turning her away from the vile bird. She saw what concerned him; Quicksilver's face was turned towards them, his eyes open. They raced over as he tried to raise his head.

With the roar of air being beaten, the ravens rose in a huge black cloud that blotted out the sun. Hamma marshalled his forces. Rising high, the dark cloud circled ominously. Then dozens of his largest minions hurtled down towards them. The rest gathered in a shrieking host, ready to follow.

Anja and Alfie had just enough time to clamber onto the slab and drag Quicksilver off, resting him limply against it. They drew their knives and waved them above their heads in an attempt to discourage the beaks and talons descending on them. Anja raised her flimsy hat in her other hand like a shield. It was torn from her grasp.

Beyond the host of black ravens, they failed to see the sky darken again. An ominous crackle of lightning laced across the hills. The only sounds they were aware of were their own screams and the coarse cries and flapping wings of the attacking birds. They dared not raise their heads for fear of heavy beaks. All they could do was slice the air above their heads, hoping to damage or keep at bay some of the heaving mass of pecking black rags.

Alfie, his arms numb and scarlet with puncture wounds, dropped his knife, tripped, and fell on Quicksilver. Anja, fired with rage, was beyond pain and fear. One hand shielded her face and the other flailed her knife wildly. Injured ravens began to tumble and hop away from the battle. Others recoiled from her blazing eyes. Yet hundreds massed above to take their place.

Another battle was taking place over the hills. From the far north and the south-east, strong winds began to blow, one laden with the dark fragrance of the forest, the other the tang of the river and sea. The threatening storm fought to unfold but was unable to combat the concentrated power assailing it from the Great Forest and river and it faded.

Anja sensed the help, and her mind responded, a screaming banshee of blood and feathers that made Aphrodite, frantically sensing the young girl so far away and beyond her help, gasp with pride as battle madness seized Anja. Suddenly the birds broke away and Anja seized the opportunity to take in a great gulp of air, but what she saw as they moved aside chilled her heart. The huge raven was diving, talons first, through its flock towards her. Barely having time to defend herself, she covered her face with her free arm and swung up her knife.

19

Hamma let out a screech of triumph. Beating his wings, he spread his talons to rake her face. His mighty beak hammered down and Anja shrieked in pain as it punctured her left eye. It lifted again to deliver another blow when a scream of rage preceded a russet blur that streaked through the circle and launched into the air, clamping the neck of the great raven between rows of needle-sharp teeth. With a violent shake, it tossed Hamma's broken body aside, landing, still snapping with fury, beside Anja.

'Fight, Anja!' Fox snarled, sneezing feathers from his nose. 'Fight, help is coming.'

The couple of seconds' respite and disarray caused by Hamma's fall passed and the ravens fell upon them again with redoubled rage. Fox fought like a demon. Anja, sobbing and screaming with shock and pain, was surrounded by ravens recoiling from her fury. Even Alfie, who had found his knife in the brief lull, took heart from Fox's arrival, adding his small effort to the fray.

Across the river, Aphrodite, tear-stained and furious with herself, felt the Land's presence and redoubled her effort to bolster Anja's mind, as did Pan from the Great Forest. The skies cleared above the battle and a strong breeze from the south swept in from the sea.

Through the seething masses, a broken black bundle of feathers and blood came plummeting down, then another and another. Hundreds of ravens rose to meet a new unseen foe. As the mass directly above them thinned, Anja could see through them again with her undamaged eye.

High above, arriving from the south, a river of white seabirds, hundreds upon hundreds, great ribbons and squadrons riding the high thermals, streamed towards them. Gulls with huge hooked beaks threw themselves screeching into the fray. The desperate ravens fought as only the possessed can but were vastly outnumbered. Black carcasses rained down.

Soon, gangs of grey-white gulls chased and mercilessly slaughtered the last few injured ravens as they tried to flee amongst the impotent stones they had so imperiously perched upon not long before. Then it was over, the twilight sky filled with the gulls' tumultuous victory cries. Below, the valley was an amphitheatre of death, carpeted with black corpses interspersed now and again with the stark whiteness of gulls, witness to the ferocity of the battle.

Alfie was slumped beside Quicksilver. Anja's undamaged eye had lost the shine of battle and was now dull and unfocused with shock, her hair a torn, tangled mess. They were both slick with blood, whether it was their own they couldn't tell, but they could feel the many punctures and deep wounds that had been inflicted on them.

'I think my eye's gone, Alfie.'

'Fucking hell, Anja,' Alfie whispered, seeing her damaged face and unable to control his emotions.

Fox stood over Quicksilver, eyes and heavy panting betraying his worry. He'd not escaped lightly and his pelt glistened darkly in many places, but he gently licked Quicksilver's few wounds. The children had sheltered him from the worst of the onslaught, but the harm had already happened on the slab.

'Forget your injuries, children. Quicksilver needs you.'

*

Below, Hades was mystified. It had been going so well; all Hamma had to do was take his reward. He'd expected a little interference from his peers but was confused by such a level of intervention. The battle was lost but he wasn't greatly concerned; he'd taken most of the boy's essence before the children had arrived. A pang of concern had disturbed him when Hamma fell. He would see to him later. No, something else was at play; he had missed something, and that wouldn't do, not at all. Perhaps it was time to reconsider his self-imposed isolation. No, he wouldn't do that lightly, not until he had to. But he had misjudged the situation; there was something important about these children.

*

Quicksilver's essence had been almost completely drained from his body. Had his young companions not arrived, by dusk he would have been a juicy husk for the ravens to tear apart. He lay unmoving, his skin grey and glistening, breathing weakly, his eyes flickering, barely open. Alfie knelt beside him. He knew Quicksilver was trying to communicate something. He put his ear to his lips.

'Take me to the grove just beyond the gap between the hills to the south. You'll know what to do. Hurry or it will be too late, Alfie.'

His loyal little friend nodded furiously.

'What did he say?' Anja asked. Alfie winced at the mangled mess in her eye socket.

'We've got to take him to a grove over that way. I don't think it's far. If we don't, then he'll be gone forever. Your eye, Anja?'

Anja groaned but pulled herself up from the ground that she had thankfully collapsed on minutes before. She knew it wouldn't happen without her. 'Come on then.'

'Your eye, Anja?'

'It isn't hurting so much now. I can't do anything about it. We have to help Quicksilver.'

Fox watched this exchange quietly, focused on Anja, his expression serious and unreadable.

It wasn't easy for them to lift Quicksilver up. He was heavier than them and fading fast could do little to help himself. They began to half help, half drag him through the circle. Painfully slowly, the little group, including Fox, who fussed and encouraged them because he couldn't help, staggered out of the valley tainted with so much death and suffering.

*

Hades sensed what was happening. Fingers pressed to his eyes, thinking, he drew them down each side of his nose and laughed. He had fixated on the boy. Arrogant and stupid, he should have listened instead of dismissing the ramblings of poor Hamma, who had been right all along. What had occurred had not been about the boy; it had been about the children. No, not both, the girl; it had all been about the girl. Aphrodite and Pan had intervened because of her and the Land had supported them.

He had felt the blossoming power erupt from her when she'd been in mortal danger, protecting the boy and her brother. Today had been his doing, but the Land had used it, testing her, directing his peers to support her and she had responded magnificently. His frustration melted away, replaced by curiosity and excitement. Who was she and what was she becoming? He must meet this girl. But first he should see to poor Hamma; he had let him down, ignored his ramblings.

*

The sad little party reached a gap between the low hills on the southern side of the valley. Because he had left the great circle, or was approaching the

223

grove, Quicksilver gathered his last strength and their progress speeded up.

A quarter of an hour later, as stars began to pepper the skies above them, they thankfully collapsed in a heap under the eaves of the welcoming grove.

'Sorry, Anja, we can't stop yet. We have to take him to the middle.'

Alfie tugged at Quicksilver's arm and he staggered up, his eyes rolling, skin almost transparent. Reluctantly, but knowing that Quicksilver would not survive another move, Anja supported their friend deeper into the grove. Reaching the tree at the centre, Alfie urged Anja to make one final effort to hold Quicksilver upright. Alfie stood with his back pressed against the expanse of the trunk. Anxiously, Fox watched on.

'Lean him against me, with his back to me so that I can put my arms around his waist.'

Anja struggled. Alfie was so much smaller than Quicksilver that his face was pressed against his friend's shoulder blades, his arms wrapped tightly as far around his waist as they would go.

'What are you doing?' she asked weakly, leaning against the trunk to support her aching body. He ignored her.

At first, she didn't notice what was happening. Then she realised that her brother was sinking backwards into the tree. She gasped and turned to Fox to make sure he was seeing this. Alfie turned to her and his face displayed no emotion as it gently disappeared. Soon he had gone, except for his arms around Quicksilver. Then Quicksilver began to go, entering the tree rapidly, as if it was sucking him in.

She and Fox were alone. He seemed as stunned as her. 'Well, things have changed,' he muttered.

Anja looked down and remembered how she had reacted when Alfie had first told her about him. 'Things certainly have,' she agreed, and they both waited patiently, glad the other was there and because there was little else they could do. She had to adjust her face to see anything on her left side.

Eventually, a small bulge appeared in the trunk and then another. The bulges became lumpy parts which in turn developed into limbs, and then Alfie's body and face followed. As his bottom finally detached from the tree, he smiled sadly. 'He's gone, with the groves again, but he's not dead.'

'Will he come back?' Anja asked.

Alfie shook his head. 'I don't know. I could just about feel him in the tree. I don't know.'

'I didn't know you could do that,' Anja said, a hint of accusation entering her voice.

'It's not important. Your eye, Anja, it's terrible. Fox?'

Fox didn't get up; it was as if he wasn't concerned. 'Does it hurt?'

'No, it's sort of warm.'

'There's a stream just over there. It runs through the grove. It's gushing with water now. Go over and wash all the mess out of the socket. In a few days, we will see how it is.'

She shuddered. It was the last thing she wanted to do.

Waving Alfie away, she found the stream. Kneeling over a still area, she saw her reflection and was violently sick. She finished retching and moved to a faster-flowing place. Gingerly, she felt where her eye should have been and wept as her fingers found little except a slimy mess. She tried to wash it, but realising the futility of using her cupped hands, swore and immersed her face in the stream. The cold running water was a shock at first, then felt so nice that she only lifted her face out when she had to breathe. Gently fingering the socket, it felt cleaner; everything had washed away. It wasn't even bleeding.

Snuggling down at the base of the tree with Alfie and Fox, her last thought was that all animals were smelly, but foxes didn't smell as much as otters, and this fox had saved them. Alfie, although exhausted, was last to sleep. He relived what he'd just done, the memory so fresh in his mind of how he had felt the brief fluttering of Quicksilver's fading consciousness urging him on; the weight of his friend squeezing him against the trunk, and then the realisation as he'd looked at Anja that he was entering the tree; blackness and a moment of panic.

Then a voice entered his mind, like Quicksilver's but somehow different, sweeping through him like a calm wave: *Don't fight or try to move, close your eyes and relax.* He had, and the panic subsided. *Now stretch your arms and legs in your mind, stretch them until they reach high into the sky and deep into the ground.*

Again, he had found it easy to follow the instructions and stretched and stretched, sensing the evening breezes playing in the topmost twigs, and the earthworms tickling the deepest roots. He heard the grove sighing as it recovered Quicksilver to itself and all the groves in the Land. The experience did not reflect the gloom of the night but the beauty of the great grey trees in the moonlight. Feeling the tree sap coursing through his essence, Alfie felt the weariness of the terrible day lift, then his mind was gently touched.

'Is that you, Quicksilver?'

'Fox will guide you. Say goodbye to Anja for me. It has my essence, Alfie, find it for me. Go to the Great Tree.' The faint voice faded away and he knew that Quicksilver had gone. Alfie wondered how to get out of the tree again, but even as he remembered his body flowing out, Alfie was asleep, memory drifting into dream.

In the morning, they woke to find Fox gone. They moved to the edge of the grove. Anja's smaller injuries had faded but the deeper ones were still red and swollen. Her tunic and breeches were torn and dirty and her hair slick and matted. Alfie kept his gaze on her mouth, to avoid looking at the place where her eye had been. Apart from his torn clothing, he didn't appear to have a scratch on him. She felt resentful.

'So, you're a tree boy now?' she muttered.

The sarcasm bounced off him and he simply nodded in agreement.

'And the trees heal you as well?'

He nodded again.

'I'm sore, and my eye is gone, and I'm upset that Quicksilver is as well. He did so much for us.' Her voice was trembling.

'He hasn't really gone, not forever. Not like he's dead.'

'Do you think we'll see him again, I mean, if we get through all this?'

Alfie shrugged. 'I don't know. He's with the trees now, but I don't know if he'll ever be Quicksilver again. That horrible stone circle took the part of his essence that made him Quicksilver.'

For the first time, Alfie looked at her properly and, with the first hint of normality, said, 'He asked me to say goodbye to you.'

Her one eye countered, *Be very careful, little brother*, then she smiled. 'Did he really?'

Alfie nodded, no hint of mischief.

'I wasn't always nice to him.'

'He didn't mind, Anja. He just liked you.'

Anja felt herself welling up and changed the subject before Alfie noticed.

'Does that big tree have a proper chamber under it?'

Alfie nodded again.

'And is there a doorway?'

He nodded again.

'And is Quicksilver still in that tree in any way?'

Alfie's brow furrowed. 'No, he isn't even a boy anymore. I think whatever's left has gone to the grove by the Great River, by Aphrodite's home. He isn't anything now, there's just the tree bit left.'

'And has this chamber got a washroom and a tub?'

Alfie suddenly caught on. He snorted. 'Oh. Well, it's a big grove, but I'm not sure. Shall we have a look?'

Anja nodded. 'We need new clothes and stuff and some food.'

Fox trotted up, and two gulls swooped down and landed nearby.

'Ready to leave?' he asked.

'No,' Anja said firmly. 'I can't start out again like this. We're safe here in the grove, so I'm going to clean up and find some new clothes, even if it does mean going underground and losing half a day.'

Fox lay down, panting, with a look that said that he had no intention of arguing, whilst Alfie shut up, in case he said something wrong. Anja yanked him off towards the big tree.

Fox waited patiently, moving with the shade to avoid the heat of the sun throughout the morning. The gulls stayed nearby some of the time and at others scavenged locally. At last, Anja and Alfie came back.

Alfie had found a new tunic and breeches, and another big hat. Anja had bathed and pampered herself. She had found a dress; not as nice as the ones she had left at the cottage, but she decided to wear it for the time being, although she'd also found a new set of boys' clothing that fitted her. New buskins and a large wide hat completed her outfit. The bath and oils had soaked most of her injuries away, except one.

'Ready?'

'What are we going to do now, Anja, without Quicksilver, and your eye?'

'We are going to finish what we came for. Otherwise, Quicksilver will have helped us for nothing. He got us this far. We are going to get Toby. That's what we are going to do. My eye doesn't matter; it doesn't even hurt. Aphrodite told me I would become so beautiful that everyone would adore me. So much for that.' She cut a strip of cloth from the hem of her dress and tied it around her head, covering her eye.

'I'll guide you and do all I can to help,' Fox said. 'The gulls will, too.'

*

Under the eaves of the Great Forest, Pan stared across the Northern Downs, his face etched with anger and worry. A small voice interrupted his dark contemplation.

'Aphrodite sends news. She will not leave Anja to her fate and is heading to the estuary. Quicksilver is lost, Fox and the two children survive, but the girl is injured. They are carrying on to the coast.'

'I sensed most of this. Maia, how bad are Anja's injuries, and what of the Land?' His voice was controlled, despite his inner turmoil.

'Most will heal quickly, but she lost an eye. The Land will let her fate play out.'

Pan swore an ancient curse. 'It should have asked us to help her.'

'You know it has reasons for what it does. Do you have a reply for Aphrodite?'

'No, will you take a message to Anja?'

'Go back to the camp. She will sense you better there, she feels your support.'

Pan growled, but Maia was gone.

20

With no warning, Anja turned on Fox. 'What's happening, Fox? There's hardly anything intelligent in the Land and yet anything that can talk or think is either helping or trying to kill us.'

Fox was panting. He thought that over the days she had recovered from the trauma of losing an eye and even more the loss of someone she had refused to acknowledge had done so much for her. He snorted and replied in kind. 'What if it's not about you, Anja? Could it be that you arrived in the middle of something, something bigger than you, something more important? And just because creatures don't talk doesn't mean they're not intelligent or can't think.'

This was not the answer she wanted; her mood deepened.

'We didn't just arrive, this creature stole Toby and brought him here and I couldn't just leave him. We didn't *just arrive*.' Her last words were sharp, and Fox recoiled.

Anja felt his discomfort and she bent down to him

in alarm. 'Oh, Fox, I'm sorry. You've just saved us, and I'm being so ungrateful. I'm so confused, and with what happened to Quicksilver and everything…' She sucked her lip and stroked his nose.

He licked her hand and shook himself. 'You really do have to be careful when you get angry,' he muttered. 'All I was trying to say is that you're part of this, but so is everyone else. It really is not just about you and Alfie. Something's been wrong for some time, but with your arrival things *are* changing. The Land only understands what it has experienced or learnt. Nothing like this has happened before.'

Anja shook her head at this explanation. It would be hard to convey the snuffling and sneezing that had accompanied it. She felt a bit better after her little spat. 'Whatever,' she said. 'I still have to get Toby.'

Fox gave his version of a shrug. *Such a strong little human*, he thought, pondering her growing power. *Will it be enough?*

The Downs changed over the following days. Rolling hills evened out and slowly descended to their left.

'Ahead is where the western coast of the estuary climbs towards the cliffs above the Great Bay. The bay has been corrupted by the creature. It's where your brother is.'

Anja nodded. She could almost smell the sea, and the constant mewing of gulls flying above told her their destination, and their fate, was close.

Over the next days, the grass grew patchier and coarser; sand began to soften their walking and before long they were wending their way through tussocks and small scrub- covered dunes.

'When do we see the sea?' Alfie asked the next roasting afternoon, his tired voice coming from beneath the brim of his outlandish hat.

'We've been looking at it all day,' Fox replied.

Alfie and Anja both stopped and peered ahead. Through the haze they could just make out a line towards the limit of the horizon that was a slightly different shade of blue to the sky.

'Are you sure? I can't tell.'

'That's because of the haze. Tomorrow morning, you'll see it better before the sun fully rises. We're almost there.'

As they sat quietly around their small fire that evening, Fox decided to tell them about a discovery he'd made. 'I was exploring the bottom of the cliffs not long after I arrived when I found a small cave entrance. Normally, it would have been covered by the tides and filled with water, deep behind sharp rocks. It's dangerous to find or enter. I almost missed it.'

Anja and Alfie were listening, half-asleep.

'When I went in, it became quite big and deep. I could see quite well but was baffled by two strongly lit areas on the far walls. When I went close to the brightest, it was daylight, shining through the forest.'

They were both now wide awake, sitting up attentively.

'There are two portals, sealed by a thin veil. I poked my head into the first one. It smelt familiar: the Great Forest. I am not sure about the other one. I went back outside, so distracted that I wasn't as careful as I should have been. The creature almost caught me.'

The children listened to him.

'I think it's how he reached your land. I believe that portal opens near to the one you came through. I wonder where the other one goes.'

'Could we go home that way?'

Fox made a shrugging motion. 'I don't know, Anja, perhaps. But remember this for the future.'

Anja thought about it. Whilst it was interesting, more immediate concerns troubled her until she drifted to sleep.

The next morning, they broke camp, the first for a long time not near a grove but in the lea of a high grassy dune. From this vantage point, they could see far into the distance. Before them stretched a half-mile or so of the sandy tussocks. To their left, they saw the western edge of the estuary mouth twinkling in the low morning sun. Ahead, the foreshore masked the true distance to the sea proper, but the horizon line now sparkled as the sun glistened on the white-topped waves stretching to it. Hosts of gulls soared and hovered above, on the quickly heating breezes.

'Are we going to the sea today?' Alfie asked.

'No,' Fox replied, 'we have to make our way to the right. We are going to the eastern point of the bay. There we will see the building. Cutting across from here will save about a day.'

'A building?' Anja said. 'What, a real castle, how did it make it?'

'Another mystery, no one knows what the creature is. Except that it has a body made of sand, as are the building and a great wall that is holding and pushing back the ocean.'

'It's a sandcastle.' Alfie blew out his lips. 'Perhaps we can kick it down.'

'Your brother is being kept at the top of its highest tower, Alfie. See it before mocking it.'

'Right,' said Anja quietly, 'let's go then.'

'We shouldn't leave yet. I've arranged to meet the gulls. They've been keeping an eye on the castle. We should hear what they have to say before starting.'

Anja almost argued, but his eyes warned her not to.

The gulls turned out to be the same ones that had stayed with them during the first few days walking from the stone circle. They landed and waddled awkwardly to where the little group sat waiting. Anja shouldn't have been surprised, but still was, when one of them threw his great beak back and began the undulating cry of the seagull nation, which trailed off and dwindled into barely recognisable speech.

'The fish are rising, Fox.'

'It is a good morning to catch the wind, Gull. How is the little one?'

The gull danced around and threw his head up and down. 'He does not fare well, not well. You must hurry.'

After a few seconds making sense of the exchange, Anja recognised who they were talking about. 'What's the matter with him?' she blurted. They were talking about her brother; she couldn't believe that after all this time, here was someone, even a gull, who had seen him recently. Since that midsummer night, his existence had been her aspiration, her purpose.

'He suffers from the sun, and it doesn't feed him well

or give him good water. We have not seen him walking on the high tower for weeks. He sleeps or lays in the little shade he has. I fear for him.' He fixed her with his yellow eye.

'Right, we're going,' Anja said abruptly, her voice tight with emotion.

'What are you going to do?' Fox said quietly.

'It doesn't matter, does it? We have come all this way without a plan. We knew that when we arrived, this "thing" would be waiting for us. We've never had a plan and we are just us. We'll go and get Toby and see what happens, I don't care anymore. At least no one can say that I left him and didn't try. Whatever happens, I'm going to cuddle him, and he will know that I love him and came for him.'

'What about you, Alfie?' Fox asked.

Alfie was fired by his sister's emotional words, still ringing in his head. 'What do you mean? I'm going with Anja, of course.'

The gull chattered its beak together and stretched towards Anja's face.

'Did gulls fight and die for you to come and give yourselves to it?'

'I don't know *what* you helped us for,' she replied hotly. 'You did save us, but I still don't understand why anyone is helping us.' She remembered the many bloody white bodies back at the circle. 'Of course I'm grateful, but why did you fight for us?'

The gull settled down on a patch of grass.

'Many generations ago, we watched the Folk arriving

in their boats. They had weathered a fierce storm. Just us two are left who saw this. They were peaceful but did not listen to those who were wise. It was of no concern to us. The seasons passed, our lives went on, chicks hatched, and the fish were plentiful. Due to their folly, they woke the Land and were driven back to the sea. We said farewell, for they had done us no harm. They did not listen to the one who tended the groves, then she disappeared.' The gull took a break to preen an unruly feather.

'The Folk who survived were sailing away, across the bay, when a great storm destroyed them. We were fearful, for it was unnatural and gulls perished. But life returned to normal until sand rose above the waves where the boats had sunk. It began to push the sea back from the bay, until a wall of sand stretched from the eastern headland to the western point and the sand baked hard in the bay. The heat rising up the cliffs is unbearable, the fish are far away, and now we suffer.'

The gull paused and both birds bobbed their heads and touched beaks in a display of sorrow. 'The great building rose from the middle of the dry seabed, massive, its topmost towers as high as the cliffs. Then the creature appeared. We were curious, but if any flew near, it would crush them in its dry hands and their blood would stain it. It looks like a two-leg, but it is not, it is a monster. Now we keep our distance. Nothing dares venture onto the bay.'

Anja and Alfie sat mesmerised by the gull's strange voice and the chilling story.

'We do not see where the children come from, but watch from high above as they are dragged past the castle to the wrecks of the ships jutting out of the hard-baked sand: spars, rotten ropes, hanging shreds of canvas bleached by the sun. There, it casts the children onto sharp pieces of timber. As their blood pours down the wood and spreads over the sand, great shifting shakes the bay, the sand ripples and the wall pushes the sea back along its length. Regularly, small children meet that fate and the ocean is driven back, each time a little less. We have tried to stop this horror, but the creature brushes us aside like flies. The bay is our place; the cliffs are ours but we cannot survive without the ocean. The last time, we heard it speak for the first time. "Not enough," the creature roared. Then another child appeared on the highest tower, and there he stays: your brother. Now the creature waits for you, to spill all your blood together. The ground will heave, and the sea will be pushed far from sight. The estuary will be changed. His kingdom will grow beyond the bay and our nest sites will perish.'

'So why help us? It would have been better if we'd died at the stone circle, then he couldn't have us,' Anja asked.

'And so I told Fox. What care is it for us, the death of two more humans? If they die at the old stone circle and not on the ribs of the ships, less harm is done.

'"These are not any humans," our friend Fox replied. "They are in the care of the Land. They do not come to die but to take back their brother. Mentored by the Great Ones, they travel with the spirit of the groves, and you must help them." I asked if the Great Ones come with them, and Fox said the children travel alone but must be helped. So, we came, and many died for you to live. Even the spirit of the groves is gone. Now, after all the help you have been given, you do not care?'

Anja leant towards him. 'That's not what I meant. I don't *want* us to die. There's only me and Alfie and we came to find our brother. Toby's up in that tower. Now we're here, we'll go and get him, and that's all our plan ever was. We should go tonight before it realises that we're here. It's all we can do. We can't wait, because Toby is dying, you said so. We've got this far, haven't we?'

Fox's voice cut in sharply. 'You've been prepared, Anja, you are *not* what you were when you came through the portal. You are changed, and wiser.'

'Wiser!' Anja shook her head in disbelief. 'I am... what... twelve? – I don't know, maybe thirteen – and Alfie is eight or nine. I don't even know how old we are now. Wiser! No! Irresponsible, stupid more like, that's what Daddy will say if I go home without Toby. At least if I try, it was for something. I've never thought past getting here, and now that I have, I'm going to get him, and what happens, happens. I'm going to get Toby, creature or whatever.'

Alfie loved her when she was like this, so long as her anger was not coming his way. Her eye was so big and beautiful, hazel glistening with gold, glaring out from under the wide brim of her hat. He shuffled closer, giving her his silent support.

Fox slowly stood up and stretched out his long body. She was as ready as she could be. 'So,' he said, 'I think we should get to the east point of the bay and camp by the wall. We can then scout around for a day and make a plan.'

'No!' countered Anja, quieter this time, brooking no dissent. 'We go to the nearest part of the wall and start out as soon as dusk falls. How far is the wall from here, and the castle from the wall?'

'If we start, then we can reach it by mid-afternoon, but—'

Anja did not let him finish. 'We go tonight. If it doesn't know that we're here, we get Toby before it does, and if it does, then it doesn't matter anyway.'

Fox procrastinated. 'We need supplies, and what if you can't find a way in?'

'There are ways in,' the gull said. 'There are entrances in the corners of the walls and other places. It is not built to keep anything out. Who would choose to go there?'

'So, why a building with towers?' Alfie mused aloud. 'How does it know about castles?'

Fox turned to him. 'I don't know, perhaps it came from the mind of one of the children he slaughtered.'

Anja shuddered. 'Thanks, that's made me feel much better. It's time to go, show us the way.' She had meant to tell Alfie she was going on alone. But suddenly she didn't want to and knew he wouldn't agree anyway. She needed him; he had strengths she didn't. She couldn't go alone.

'Take that off your eye.'

Fox's unexpected remark took Anja by surprise. 'No, it looks terrible. It's not gone, it's just a mangled mess. It looks disgusting.'

'When did you last take it off?'

'I haven't, I don't want anyone to see it.'

'Take it off, Anja. I want to see it.'

She gave an enormous sigh and jerked it off. 'Oh!'

'What?' Alfie said. 'Oh.'

She had hesitantly lifted her eyelid. Sucked in sharply and closed it.

'Leave the cloth off. Let it get used to light.'

'It's grown back, that's impossible?'

'You tell me, Anja. It's your eye.'

After a couple of hours wiping away tears and constantly blinking, she could see perfectly again with both, beautiful, eyes.

'So what's the best way to get to this sandcastle?' They had been using Alfie's descriptive name since he'd coined it.

'Follow the curve of the wall where it butts against the headland, then at its nearest point to the castle, cross the seabed.'

Anja nodded. *Not much planning needed for that*, she thought.

They walked up the final slopes of the estuary valley. Dunes changed again to luxurious grass and as they approached the headland, outcrops of chalky rock appeared. Well into the afternoon, they climbed a steep path up to the spit. To their right and beyond, grassy tops of huge cliffs circled the bay.

Their seagull companion flapped down. 'Take off those hats. The sun reflects from them.'

Alfie took his off. He went to discard it where he stood, then grinned and turned back towards the steep path they had been climbing. He laughed and threw it like a skimming stone; it sailed away back down. Anja could not resist copying and hers sailed even further. She clapped her hands with delight. She'd changed back into her tunic and breeches before dawn and they both pulled on their small caps and made sure that their flasks and knives were securely strapped; they wanted to be ready for whatever they faced. Everything else had been left at the last camp.

The climb evened out. To their left, long, eroded gullies sank down to the estuary shores. To their right, the grassy top of the cliffs climbed to even greater heights, but in front of them a wide spit of rock jutted out, narrowing over many hundreds of yards. The ocean washed against the estuary side, but on the right, a high wall of sand buttressed against its far end and curved way out across the bay, holding back the ocean and bonding to a similar promontory on the western side.

The children barely noticed the wall. They were captivated by the huge bay it enclosed, spread before them as they stood high above its corner. Had it been as it should, filled with sparkling ocean, it would have been magnificent and beautiful, but without the sea, it was empty and silent, except for the haunting cries of the gulls circling them. The eeriness was magnified by the monolith squatting within it. Alfie could not have realised how apt his joke had been. It really was a massive, beautiful sandcastle.

Anja shaded her eyes from the glare of the sun on the baked floor of the bay; even at this height and with evening approaching, feeling the rising heat. The castle, as white as the bay, stood a couple of miles away, breathtaking in size yet still dwarfed by the scale of its surroundings. Towers soared impossibly above its walls, linked and supported by narrow buttresses. Anja's eyes screwed up to see these distant towers. On one, her baby brother was suffering. How he'd survived this heat for so long she couldn't imagine. His little face loomed large in her mind. She sensed Alfie looking up at her and turned to him. Had he guessed what she was thinking? She quickly rejected the image and turned away again.

'How do we get down to the seabed?' she asked, feeling Fox's presence close to her.

'There's a sort of path leading down, about halfway along the promontory ahead. It cuts back towards the shore as it descends. It's a bit steep in places but will get us down quickly. We should wait until dusk. Too early and we'll stand out against the rock face, too late, there's a danger of falling.'

They sat on a patch of grass to wait. As the sun began to sink over the other side of the bay, the small band walked out along the grassy promontory. Towards the end, Fox turned them towards the edge on the bay side. A hundred or so feet below was where they needed to get down to on the parched seabed, near to where the wall of sand butted against it fifty or so feet below, holding back the ocean. The giddying height and exposure hit both children. Alfie quickly recovered and bent forward to look down. Anja tried to copy him but couldn't control her shaking legs.

'I know that it looks like there isn't a way down, but you *must* trust me. You must lower yourselves over the edge and let go,' said Fox. 'It's only a short drop onto a narrow ledge. Then keep facing the cliff and shuffle to your left. After a minute or so, the descent gets steeper, but after a while the ledge broadens and you can turn and walk properly. The only problem with two legs is that they're not very stable. Are you ready?'

21

Nausea cramped Anja's stomach. Although the sun was sinking rapidly, she wished it was already dark and didn't have to see how high she was from the bay spread out before her. Fox crept up to the edge and, with a flurry of motion, slunk over. In her mind, she saw his small body plummeting and bouncing down to the bottom, but instead his sharp bark rose to them, confirming he was on the ledge. Alfie looked at her apprehensively, then crawled up to the edge and looked over.

'He's not far down,' he gulped, 'but the bottom is.'

Nervously, Alfie turned onto his stomach then lowered his legs over the edge. His chin scraped the grass as he gradually wriggled back until his hips and legs tipped over and he was hanging on his elbows. He gave her one last frightened look and slid over until only his hands could be seen grasping the edge. Fox yelped encouragement and then his hands were gone.

Anja almost fainted when he let go.

'Woah, that was scary.' His little voice seemed to come from a long way down.

Trembling uncontrollably, Anja crawled until she was a few feet from the edge, then turned around and backed tentatively towards it until she gave a squeak of terror when her toes in the soft buskins felt in vain for hard rock beneath them. She closed her eyes and stretched flat. After taking a second to dig deep for her last dregs of courage, she wriggled backwards; a little whimper escaped her gritted teeth as her knees lost the support of the edge and became louder as she wriggled further and felt the weight of her legs dragging her bottom over. Had she been able, she would have scrambled back up, but gravity took charge and she slid down until only her elbows and chin were supporting the rest of her body hanging over the drop. Rigid with terror, she knew she couldn't let go. Alfie grabbed hold of her foot and she screamed as she felt herself slip down.

'Stop making so much noise, and be careful,' he warned unnecessarily as she landed heavily on her feet and staggered slightly. 'It's really narrow.'

Flattened against the rock face, eyes tightly shut, her legs still threatened to collapse under her. She'd been right; she definitely couldn't do this without Alfie.

'Open your eyes, Anja. It's hard enough with them. We have to be down before it gets too dark. Now *open them*.' Fox's stern words got through. She stared first at the rock face a quarter of an inch away, then slowly down to her feet, forcing them to shuffle along, following the others. A quick glance to her left reassured her that Alfie was moving in a similar fashion, for all his bravado, a yard or so in front.

After ten minutes or so of this, she felt the ledge sloping steeply away. 'Turn around and walk properly. The ledge is steeper but wider, you need to see where you're going,' Fox warned.

She turned, still focusing on Alfie, and was able to keep her eyes forward for the first time. The exposure was not overwhelming because of the deepening gloom. Gingerly, leaning into the rock face, she forced herself to walk. The ledge was wider but so steep that soon, with her left hand behind her, she was almost sliding on her bottom.

Fox turned and smiled as only he could. 'Only about a hundred feet if you fall now,' he quipped, but night was approaching rapidly, and the climb became more bearable. By the time they felt soft sand beneath their buskins, it was dark. Although only a crescent moon hung in the night sky, countless stars illuminated the limitless cosmos of this universe, almost identical to their own.

'From here, you go on alone,' Fox said.

Alfie was taken aback. 'Aren't you coming?'

'No, I will stay with the gulls, Alfie. It almost caught me once and can sense me. I'll be more danger than help. We will be watching for you.'

Anja accepted his decision. They didn't need a guide anymore. The castle was a forbidding black silhouette, and Fox knew as little as they did about what awaited them inside.

He gave them his final advice. 'Keep to the wall until it curves closer to the castle and then cross to it. It will still be a long way across the seabed so pace yourselves, but at least at night it's cooler. When you reach it, go right. There's a small doorway in the angle of the nearest tower flanking the corner of the walls. The tower that holds Toby is the next one along the wall facing the cliffs. It climbs from the battlements, not the seabed. To reach it, climb the first tower to the top of the wall, then along to the next tower. Your brother is at the top of that one. Good luck.'

Alfie gave him a hug and Fox licked both of their hands. He was panting deeply, his tongue hanging out, eyes clouded and sad.

'Thank you, Fox. Watch for us, won't you?' Anja said. 'Well, Alfie, this is it.' Then she quickly turned away and set off along the shadowy base of the mighty wall. Alfie followed; he looked back a couple of times, but the face of the headland was so mottled with rocky shadows that he could see no sign of Fox.

They hurried to where the headland met the base of the wall, then slowed after a few hundred yards, feeling the effort of walking on the soft sand banked against it. As desperate as Anja was to get to her brother, she remembered Fox's advice to pace themselves. She still felt that finding Toby was a dream-fuelled hope.

*

Far away, Aphrodite paced outside her cottage. She had sensed the Land supporting the little travellers during their battle at the Great Stone Circle and had summoned power to weaken the storm, sensing Pan doing the same. After realising that Quicksilver was lost, she'd rushed to the grove but hadn't felt his presence there and returned distraught. The children had survived, at least Anja had, but she knew she'd been badly injured. Hopefully, Fox had found her. She made a decision; she could not leave Anja to do this alone. Great Ones were bonded to the Land, but not its slaves. She was near enough and decided that, despite any plans the Land had, she would help Anja. Whilst they were on the Downs, she couldn't directly oppose the entity beneath; it was there with the blessing of the Land. However, the bay was part of the ocean, and there she had a powerful ally who would not refuse her call for help. Her mind made up, she left the cottage and headed for the jetty. Her otters sensed that something was happening and congregated around her.

'No,' she told them sternly, 'you cannot help.' In a blur, she dived, a sleek brown shape arrowing downstream towards the Great River. There, she swam into the strongest current, heading downriver.

A few days later, after passing the point where she had left the children, the water turned brackish. Basking in the hot sun on a broad sandbank, she considered her next move. Distant hazy lines on each side marked the edges of the estuary, and ahead, larger sandbanks and small islands broke the monotony of water that was neither river nor sea.

She sat on her haunches for a minute or so, gathering the old patterns that she needed in her mind and then padded back into the water. Increasing her pace, holding her short arms close beside her body, her back legs and tail rhythmically forced her faster and faster along one of the deeper channels. Fish and lesser sea life began to flash past as she skimmed near to the surface. Then she kicked deeper for a moment and with a mighty effort lanced upwards and broke the surface. As she did so, her body instantaneously transformed; her whiskered brown snout elongating as power crackled through her. Her body grew, turned silver blue and grey and arched in a spray of water. With hardly a splash, she cut back into the channel in porpoise form.

Aphrodite exhilarated in this expression of power and tuned her mind to the ocean. *Mighty Poseidon, my love, send me help.* Her plea pulsed out as she headed towards the open sea.

*

Almost an hour passed. They had followed the curve of the wall, but the distance to the castle's silhouette didn't seem any closer. So Anja decided to head out across the bay towards it. Their pace quickened as the sand became firmer, and a couple of hours later the castle's dark walls reared up before them, blackening the night sky. They felt tiny before its monstrous size. Alfie slipped his hand into Anja's. 'Do you think it sleeps?' he whispered.

'I don't know, we don't know anything about it. Anyway, I don't care. All I care about is you and Toby, just us three. Nothing matters except finding him.'

Alfie should probably have been a bit disillusioned by this, but there was something about the way she said it, about being together again and nothing else mattering, which encouraged him.

They adjusted their approach, aiming to reach the corner tower. As they got closer, in the dark angle where it met the wall was an even darker doorway. Tiny compared with the rest of the castle, to them it was huge, and they hesitated for a moment before passing beneath its smooth, curved arch. Before they'd gone more than a few yards, they met their first setback: total blackness. They grasped each other's hand tight.

'I can't see a thing, Anja.'

'Neither can I, and just when my eye's grown back! I'm going to feel for the wall,' she responded and, remembering advice long ago from Quicksilver, added, 'Close your eyes and try not to strain them. It will help, just open them every so often.' Tentatively leading her brother, she felt to the right until her hand brushed against the gritty surface. 'I'm going to follow the wall until we find something. It's a tower; there must be stairs.'

Seconds later, she stubbed her toe and, muffling a mild curse, bent down to feel what she'd walked into. As she'd hoped, it was the bottom of a flight of stairs. Peering up, a dim light relieved the blackness high above.

'It's a stair, look, there's a little bit of light up there. Hold on to my belt and step up after me.' The steps were high, and Alfie found it difficult to reach up and hold on.

'All right, hold my hand and walk up next to me.'

The steps curved against the wall. A little while later, he let out a small cry and grasped at her.

'Alfie, don't. I still can't see anything; we'll fall back down. I keep thinking I'm going to topple backwards as it is. I don't like the dark.'

'But, Anja,' Alfie still grasped her, 'the step finishes on the other side of me and there's nothing there. I nearly fell.'

Going down onto her hands and knees, she felt past him along the step. Suddenly it finished and her hand felt space. She crawled back and stood up, leaning against the wall. 'All right, keep closer.'

They ascended slowly and carefully. The steps wound round and around, up and up. The higher they went, the more they thought about what would happen if they missed their footing. Gradually, the ray of dim light became more perceptible and they realised it was starlight shining through a narrow window. They reached it and could just make out each other's ghostly face.

'Boo,' said Alfie idiotically, breaking the tension and starting a fit of the giggles they had difficulty suppressing for the next few minutes.

After that, whenever they looked up, more dim shafts could be seen entering from two of the sides which they realised were the outer corners of the tower. They climbed slowly and steadily. Eventually, a dim light above became a larger area of gloom, and when they reached it, an open doorway led out of the tower, onto a walkway around the wall.

'So far, so good,' Anja sighed. Working their way

through the castle was taking their minds off the monster that lived in it; somewhere near. Nights were short in the Land, and each step took its toll. It was past midnight.

They crept through the doorway onto the walkway. The tower they had just left rose still higher behind them, its crenulated top looming over the corner of the wall. Alfie snuck over to the embrasures edging the wall and tried to climb up onto one. Anja grabbed him angrily.

'Stop it,' she whispered. 'You'll fall. We don't have time to play about. Come on, that's it over there.' She pointed at another tower that ascended from the battlements ahead of them.

'Are you sure, Anja? It didn't look as easy as this from the cliffs. Toby's tower is really high up, and that one doesn't look that tall.'

Anja looked at the tower. It was some way off, and they could see it all, black and menacing, throwing a slight shadow under the weak moonlight. It was the same height as the one they had just left.

'It must be it.'

She took stock again of where they were. The walkway wound around an inner wall rising to their left that the new tower butted against. She realised her mistake.

'We aren't at the top of the walls; this one climbs up like a step. We have to go up that tower to the top of *that* wall. Toby's tower must be up there.'

They hurried along the wide walkway and as they approached the next tower, could already make out the opening. The castle didn't seem to have doors, just doorways; black holes drawing them ever in, ever up.

Remembering their entry into the first tower, Anja felt her way in, brushing the walls with her right hand and feeling with her foot before placing it down. Alfie held on to her belt. A few yards in, her foot made contact with the first step. She looked up and was rewarded with the welcome sight of the pale strands of light barely piercing the darkness above, all in a vertical line, this tower not at the corner of the wall but along its length. They began climbing again.

'We'll do it the same as last time. Hold my hand and keep close,' she said.

Nearly half an hour later, they reached the top of the second tower, emerging onto a flat roof, edged with low battlements.

At first, they were too busy recovering and massaging their aching thighs and ankles to make out where they were. Then they began to look around.

'I think that it's getting light over there,' Anja said, looking towards the east, where she thought it didn't look so dark. Alfie didn't answer. He was looking the other way.

'Wow. Look, Anja.'

He'd worked out where they were. The roof of this tower stood way above the top of the second wall. On the west side of it, a narrow flying buttress arched across to a small doorway a third of the way up another tower fifty or so feet away.

Anja stared at it for some time; sure that this one was Toby's tower, and that the only way to get there was by climbing across. The eastern sky was definitely lightening, and the dizzying height they had reached was already affecting her. Alfie had come to the same conclusion and was considering the best way to get across. 'All we have to do is climb over that bridge thing to the doorway,' he said, putting the thoughts of both of them into words. 'It isn't really steep, just the first bit, then we can almost walk up. It's just wide enough.'

Anja sighed deeply, then she looked back to the east. 'Come on then, before the sun rises any more. I'll never be able to do it in the light.'

'Do you want me to go first?' Alfie offered, giving her a long, curious look.

Anja ignored it. 'Quickly then,' she said. 'Let's get it over with.'

Alfie clambered onto the base of the flying buttress, which was a few feet wide and rose at a steep angle for the first five or six yards then became gentler for the rest of the way. The sandy surface was not even, but modulated, like small waves running along its length, and, like every part of the castle, was as hard as rock. This made climbing easier, although Anja didn't appreciate it. Alfie climbed onto the buttress and began moving up. The undulations gave him enough purchase through his thin buskins to negotiate the steeper section.

Anja followed. It was even harder on their thigh muscles than the stairs had been. Every yard or so, they brought their feet together, sank to their knees and rested, then got back up like a couple of monkeys. It seemed to take forever just to finish the steep part. As the sun began to break over the horizon, the angle eased, but the light brought terror to Anja.

The castle began to feel the touch of the early-morning sun and slowly took on its customary golden white hue, highlighted by stark shadows. A fresh azure morning overwhelmed the retreating blackness of night; a spectrum of blue hues that sparkled with a few glimmering stars and the thin crescent moon that would be seen for many hours. For Anja, this spreading dawn brought clarity. The castle walls, distant cliffs and towers sharpened. Her legs trembled, the buttress suddenly ridiculously thin and fragile, ready to crumble and send her plummeting and bouncing down to the walkway or the arid seabed hundreds of feet below. Even the vastness of the castle seemed diminished from such height against the expanse of the bay clearly spread beneath her.

She closed her eyes and concentrated. This was only the most recent terror and she'd survived the others. She felt strength well up within her and knew she could do it. Keeping her eyes on the gritty white surface beneath her hands and knees, she pushed on. At least she could crawl properly now, only a gentle slope to contend with. When she next looked up, she was rewarded with not only the strangely comforting sight of Alfie's bottom a few yards ahead but the doorway and the bulk of the tower looming close. Her heart leapt into her mouth as Alfie raised himself up, leant forward and powered across the last ten feet. He reached the doorway, turned and grinned. Anja closed her eyes and swallowed the bile that had risen in her throat.

To her disgust, she found herself crawling past him

into the doorway before rising to her feet. 'This had better be the right one,' was all she could say. Alfie laughed; he was still looking at her strangely.

Within the tower, in the strengthening light, they could see stairs circling endlessly down, disappearing into the gloom. They also rose a short distance up, coming to an end in darkness pierced by one bright square opening of light. They began what they hoped would be their last climb. As they neared the top, the children stopped and listened. There was no sound.

'Toby?' Anja called softly, her eyes glistening. She couldn't bear the thought that he wasn't there; she did not know what she would do. 'Toby?' This time, she said it louder. Nothing disturbed the silence. They exchanged worried glances and Anja ran up the last of the steps. She found that the doorway had been half-blocked by a wall a few feet higher than the top of her head.

'He must be here. Why else would the doorway be blocked?' Anja said.

Alfie shrugged. 'Lift me up and I'll have a look over the top,' again, looking at her for a second longer than he should have.

'Wait a minute, Alfie, what's the matter, why do you keep looking at me like that?'

'Your eyes have gone all funny.'

'What do you mean "funny"? My eye's better.'

'They're glowing.'

'Golden?'

'Not just golden, they've been getting like that for ages. They're really bright, glowing.'

'It's probably the light, forget about it. Only Toby matters now. I'll kneel down. Climb on my back.'

Once she was on her hands and knees, Alfie planted one foot at a time on her back. He seemed as light as a feather as he steadied himself.

'Can you see him?'

'Lift me up a bit higher.'

She scrabbled about until she faced the barrier. Alfie shuffled with her.

'Put your feet on my shoulders and I'll stand up.'

Clumsily, they manoeuvred until, using the wall, she had levered herself up higher. Alfie hooked his fingers over the wall and lessened his weight on her. His chest was now level with the top.

'I can see over, but I still can't see him.'

'He must be there, Alfie,' she said, tears beginning to well up. 'Are you sure?'

She stood up straight to raise him higher.

'I'll climb over, help you up and drop down. I can't see all of the outside, only some of it through the door.' Anja heard him grunt and his feet lifted from her shoulders.

'I'm sitting on top of the wall now,' he said pointlessly, looking back down to see her staring up at him. He was about to reach down to help her clamber up when he glanced down the other side of the wall. He looked back at her, his eyes bursting with excitement, and horror.

22

'Oh fuck, Anja!'

'Alfie?' Anja gasped; at his exclamation, and what it might mean.

'He's right behind the bottom of the wall. Anja, I think he's—'

Anja cried out in anguish. He was only inches away and she couldn't see or touch him. 'Help me up,' she shouted, and with all her strength jumped. She grasped the top, kicking and struggling, and with Alfie pulling at her armpit and a heroic strength of will, she got her elbows over and slung her leg across. Straddling the wall, she looked over and saw Toby; naked, a curled-up pathetic figure, unmoving despite the noise they had been making.

Almost kicking her brother in the confined space on the wall, she threw her other leg over and half climbed, half fell onto the floor on the other side, sobbing. She lifted Toby's tiny, emaciated body; large areas scabbed with big broken blisters. Beneath him, she found the remnants of his pyjamas.

She held his limp body tight against her and kissed him, calming herself to control her breathing.

'Please be all right, Toby, please be all right. It's Anja and Alfie, we've come for you.'

His eyes opened glassily. He tried to focus and raise his head to see her. His face fell against hers. She was sure he kissed her.

'Oh, Alfie, he's so ill, he won't last long in the sun. We should have brought something to cover him.'

'Let's get him over the wall and out of here. He can have my top, the sun doesn't bother me.'

Anja nodded through her tears. 'Stay there and I'll pass him up. He doesn't weigh anything.'

She passed Toby up as gently as she could and, energised with desperation, jumped, kicked and scrambled her way up and over it again, half falling down the other side. Alfie lowered Toby down to her; he was half-conscious now and trying to talk, but his throat was so parched that just a squeak came out.

'Shush!' she said gently and unstopped the water flask that she had carried unused since the very start of their journey. A couple of drops wet his lips. He licked them eagerly. She poured a couple more. She would have loved to empty some into her own mouth but decided to keep it all for him; it was still almost full.

'Is your bottle full, Alfie?'

'Yes, I haven't touched it; forgot it was there.'

'Well, don't touch any of it. Pan must have known. Keep it for Toby.'

Alfie nodded; but now that he'd been reminded, he felt thirsty.

Pan's water had done Toby some good; his eyes were a little clearer. Alfie piggy-backed him onto Anja, half tying him on with his tunic.

'Right, let's get out of here,' she said.

They began to descend the tower, the interior now lit with gloomy light. They could see the stairs winding in a dizzying spiral, going on forever, with a fearsome drop in the hollow centre.

'Shall we go all the way down?' Alfie asked.

'No, the way we came. We don't know where this one goes.'

They didn't rush. The consequences of falling were unimaginable, and when they reached the door through which they'd entered, Anja went out into the bright morning light and stepped as quickly back into the security of the doorway.

'Go on, Anja.' Alfie's voice came sternly from behind.

She mastered her panic; something had changed within her and again she knew she would do it. She concentrated on where the flying buttress ended, on the roof of the other tower, and didn't look anywhere else. No tingling threatened to weaken her legs.

'Hang on tight, Toby,' she said softly, feeling his face nestling into the back of her neck. She didn't know whether he heard or understood, but his arms were clasped tightly around her neck, and hers were linked under his bottom. She still hardly felt his weight. 'Right, I've got him, I'm ready.'

'Let me go first.'

'Yes, just don't go too fast.'

Alfie eased past her. 'Come on, Anja, it's easy.'

Anja did not miss that he looked resolutely ahead, towards the other tower, and that his arms were slightly away from his body; something she couldn't do. She took the first step out of the doorway and then another and another. The gradual arch put all her weight on her toes. She sucked the morning air in between her clenched teeth when she eventually reached the short, steep section. The morning heat was rising and there was a steady threatening cross breeze.

Alfie ran down and waited. She hesitated, then slid her leg forward. She tried to slide the other down to it, but the slope was too steep. Almost losing her footing, she pitched forward and with a stifled scream ran down and onto the roof of the tower where Alfie steadied her. She'd kept her hands firmly under Toby the whole of the time. Stopping to adjust him, they hurried into the tower and began to descend.

*

*I*n a hall in the centre of the castle, lit by sunlight streaming through huge empty windows set high in the walls, a simple seat stood on a stark dais. The creature, aware of each grain of sand in the castle and the bay, sat motionless. It felt every breeze that caressed the bay, every insect that moved over it. Its attention was focused on two pairs of lightly stepping feet. It had followed their progress from the moment they had stepped onto the sand during the night but hadn't moved. Now, grain by grain, its body flowed into and through the throne until it was empty, as if it had never been there...

Aphrodite was far out in the ocean realm of Poseidon. He had been her mentor and much, much more, but they'd kept to the pact: to look to their own responsibilities and keep the balance for the Land each in their own way. Revelling in the ocean's power and beauty, she knew that his huge guardians were coming, the sea reverberating with their deep voices as they gathered. He had heeded her call, as he always did.

Beating towards the surface, she leapt high out of the water, somersaulting back to lance towards the bay. Poseidon's power surged within her and she whipped the sea to a fury. The top of the wall loomed massively above the rolling waves as she released the power of the ocean against it. A huge wave struck the wall and spumed high into the air along its length. Another followed and another as her wrath built and the cohort of guardians surged nearer. *You shall not have them,* her mind screamed repeatedly.

*

Anja was unaware of anything other than the endless stairs they were descending. Reaching the bottom, they hurried along the walkway towards the tower at the corner of the castle. At last, they entered it and descended the long final flight. Even Toby's tiny frame was now telling on Anja. She gasped for air, her throat constricted by his little arms, but fear urged her on. Finally, they were out.

'Which way?' Alfie shouted, all pretence of hiding now gone.

'I'm going to try to make a sort of sling for Toby and sit him on my hip. Then we'll go straight to where we climbed down. Fox will see us and be there. Don't run, Alfie. I can't keep up with you and it's going to take us ages anyway, so just walk. We just have to hope.' She looked to the distant headland, not realising how doomed that hope was.

*

It watched dispassionately as they walked away, beginning their hopeless trek to the safety they would never reach. They couldn't see it, nothing could, because there was nothing to distinguish it from the castle; it was the castle, and the bay. They were its. Since the last child, there had been a change; its voice was developing, and emotion was appearing. It craved their suffering. They were moving away from the place he had to take them. It was time.

*

The parched seabed was heating rapidly. Anja knew they had to reach safety before mid-morning. Although the sun would not damage him, it would be unbearably hot for Alfie without his tunic. She didn't want to think what further damage it would do to Toby. When they neared the headland, Fox would be there; she refused to contemplate he wouldn't. The gulls soaring high above had seen them, one already winging its way back to the cliffs. No cries would herald their return; no seabirds would stream out to greet them. Nothing to compromise their safety and alert the creature. Not long after, Fox was loping up the path to the headland, keeping hidden for as long as possible, before descending to dash across and lead them to the safety that was assured once they were out of the bay. But he knew it was all far too easy. Where was the creature?

As the tiny figures moved with aching slowness away from the castle, a barely perceptible ripple in the hard sand followed them.

'Can I have a drink now, Anja?' Alfie asked.

'No, keep it for Toby. He's so ill and can't heal like we can. I'm so frightened for him.'

Alfie reluctantly accepted her decision, trying to ignore the painful dryness in his throat.

Anja stopped. 'NO, NO, *Not now, please!*' she sobbed, turning her head from side to side, looking for somewhere to hide. Alfie's stomach told him what she'd seen.

Directly ahead, a mound of sand was growing, forming a human-like shape. It had no gender, a parody of humanity lacking any substance but sand. Ten feet in height, it stood motionless before them.

Anja bit her bottom lip and stepped back in disbelief. She had always known it wouldn't just let them go, but seeing it for the first time, blocking their escape, momentarily unravelled her ability to function. Alfie moved as he always did to her side, tugging her mind back, forcing her to take responsibility she felt so unworthy of. Then her fear drained away, replaced by loathing and anger. She felt the same strange, distracting sensation in her mind that had been there in the Great Stone Circle.

'Leave us alone,' she said, with a resignation that could almost be mistaken for pleading. Her face was wet with tears.

The creature switched its eyeless stare from her to Alfie and, with a speed that drew a scream from both, covered the distance between them and took the boy's arm in a vice-like grip.

'Anja!' Alfie cried.

The creature started dragging Alfie across the face of the castle. Barely able to stay on his feet, speechless with shock, he kept his eyes locked on hers. Sobbing again, she could do nothing but follow, struggling to keep up without dropping her baby brother.

High above, a single cry echoed across the bay and a huge white cloud rose along the length of the cliffs.

Fox heard rather than saw the seagulls take off and, realising the portent, yelped, frantic with worry. Knowing that the time for hiding was over, he turned away from the wall and headed directly across the sand. His lope became an easy run. He had far to go, and the heat was rising.

The pitiful little party reached the other side of the castle. Anja swung Toby in front of her to try to shield him from the heat she could feel on her neck. Her arms ached terribly...

*

Beyond the bay, the ocean was rising with Aphrodite's cold fury. Despite the waves crashing with unimaginable power against the wall, it held firm. She sensed the arrival of Poseidon's guardians and they slowly ranged each side of her beneath the waves, huge tentacles hundreds of feet long probing its strength. A hush fell on the ocean, a deep silence that signalled something terrible was imminent. Poseidon, sitting attentively in his halls at the heart of his realm far away, lifted his trident high and hammered it down, releasing a huge pulse of power. On the surface, a ripple formed and began to journey north, growing larger and larger, huge waves surging across the ocean towards the coast; towards Aphrodite and the bay.

*

Anja tripped. Alfie desperately cried out. The creature stopped and turned. It looked up to assure itself of the position of the sun; almost at its zenith. Then it pounced again, this time seizing Anja's arm before resuming its steady, purposeful striding. Anja felt Toby slipping. Dragged along, she tried to keep him in the tunic with her free hand. Her arm grew numb and eventually, with a cry of hopelessness, he slipped from her and fell. She threw herself back, reaching for him. Dragged to a halt by Anja's actions, the creature stopped. It released them both, and before Anja could reach Toby, it snatched him up and set off again, knowing that they would follow, as they had since it had taken their brother, then travelled so far, so long, to meet their fate together.

Through the haze, shapes appeared; silent skeletal memories of the small armada. Each pace took them closer, and eventually, Anja recognised the scene from the gull's tale and her heart sank with the awful realisation that it had been inevitable, always destined to end like this.

*

Aphrodite gave the signal. The huge, long tentacles drew slowly back and, with all the power the great guardians could unleash, crashed simultaneously against the wall. At the same time, she released a surge of power against the part of the wall directly ahead of her. For the first time, the wall shook.

*

The ground shuddered beneath Anja. Not a large shudder, but enough to break through her desperation. The creature felt it as well. It stood quite still and let its attention travel across the bay to seek the cause of the disturbance. Locating its source, it sprang at Anja. Something was happening and their tormentor was concerned. She leapt out of its reach. Striking like a snake, it twisted and, still holding Toby tightly in one arm, made a grab for Alfie instead. He barely avoided the hard fingers.

Another shudder momentarily stopped the terrible game. Anja sensed Aphrodite.

Toby opened his eyes and his little voice cried out weakly, 'Anja.'

His voice released the teasing sensation that she had been feeling. She winced as something snapped in her head, unleashing emotions unlike any that she'd ever experienced. Pan's music filled her mind and her golden eyes burned with power. The childhood conditioning that had been blocking and suppressing her disintegrated.

'*Let him go,*' she snarled.

High above them, host after host of gulls were gathering, their white wings darkening the sky. They wheeled in flashing patterns, waiting for the right moment, knowing from experience that the creature could ignore even their most concerted attack.

Still a mile or so away, Fox felt powerful forces growing. Anja needed him; she was the hope of the Land. He threw back his head and barked, redoubling his speed.

The creature turned to her. They were almost amongst the bleached remains of the sunken fleet. Just ahead, a line of horror jutted out of the hard sand. The nearest one blackened; tattered remnants of a nightdress flapping gently around the desiccated skin and skeletal remains of the small child skewered on it. Many more bones were scattered around its stained base. Other spars held similar grisly displays.

Anja's eyes blazed. 'I said *fucking let him go!*'

It recoiled from the vehemence emanating from her, then, dropping Toby, with lightning speed tried to grab her. Barely avoiding it, its hand brushed her shoulder, knocking the strap from the flask down her arm.

Far away, the Great Forest was hushed. Pan had been standing silently, without moving for hours, beside the pool. He was like stone, unblinking, his whole attention far away. He sensed the tragedy unfolding. His eyes blazed when Anja's did, and throwing his head back, he roared, louder and louder. The sound grew, the waters of the pool whipped to a frenzy. Great oaks thrashed as his roar crashed through the Great Forest and his power streamed southwards across the Downs. Hades felt it coming and added his own, answering the Land's call to aid the girl.

23

The strap caught on Anja's wrist and she took it in her hand and swung the heavy flask up and over her head. As the creature spun to reach for her again, it arced perfectly towards its face. The collision was too much for the leather flask and it ruptured.

In the forest, Pan's roar reached a crescendo. Out beyond the walls of the bay, Aphrodite, feeling the enormous power concentrated around Anja, redoubled her efforts.

Time stopped.

Anja readied herself for the response she dreaded from the creature. But it didn't move. It had felt the blow of the bottle, and the splash of Pan's Great Forest water had stung; the first sensation it had ever experienced. A dark stain spread across its face. It looked down at the small, dark splashes on its arms and hands. Hairline cracks appeared within them. Then a lump of sand fell from its face. In the Great Forest, Pan roared again.

Anja saw what had happened. Screaming abuse at the

monster, her head reeling with the power and energy that was flowing into it, she lashed the creature with her hate. Alfie was transfixed by the scene. She turned to him. He flinched but could not evade her eyes compelling him into action. 'The flask!' she screamed. 'Quick, Pan's water!' Alfie raced to her, fumbling to take it off.

The creature felt its lower face crumble and, finally realising the danger, leapt to intercept Alfie and grabbed him, loosening more lumps of sodden sand. Lifting him high in both hands, it lurched towards an empty beckoning spar. Anja sprang after them. Alfie threw the flask towards her, the movement distracting the monster for a few seconds as it tumbled through the air. Anja jumped, caught its flailing strap and, with a cry of triumph, dodged past the creature to place herself between it and the spar. With tears coursing down her cheeks, she taunted it with her rage.

'*I fucking hate you!*' she screamed. '*I'll sodding kill you.*' The creature's ruined face snapped back. Alfie twisted and thrashed, and as Anja's voice punched repeatedly into its mind, it dropped him. Alfie fell with a thump, winded on the sand. The creature turned towards its tormentor, snarling, determined that blood would pour from her squirming, impaled body into the sand and rejuvenate it, then it would inflict the same fate on her brothers.

Anja ceased her mental assault to step back and unstop Alfie's flask. Pan, knowing that Anja's first attack had barely crippled the creature, exulted as he sensed what she was about to do. The moment had arrived. Spreading his arms wide, he bellowed his support, and every creature in the Great Forest took up his cry.

Transfixing the monster with her golden eyes, Anja lifted the flask and emptied all the cold, sweet water into her mouth and down her throat until it was empty. She ran straight into its grasping hands. As it lifted her up, she gagged violently, throwing open her mouth, and vomited the water over the creature's face and body. It threw its ruined face back in a helpless plea to the sun and dropped her.

The moment had arrived. Multitudes of gulls descended. Anja got to her feet and ran to Toby, lifting him up from the sand. Then she grabbed Alfie's hand and pulled him to a safe distance. The gulls closed in on their enemy, who weakly tried to brush them off. Sand flew in the maelstrom of shrieking birds and then the sky exploded with the roar of beating wings as they ascended in a cacophony of triumph.

It was gone, just a patch of damp sand on the dry seabed. Anja and Alfie stared at the spot, hardly daring to believe, half dreading it would rise again. Anja felt that the very last ounce of energy had been sapped from her and was too exhausted even to cry. She hugged her baby brother. 'Look,' Alfie said quietly, pointing towards the castle. Fox was streaking towards them.

*

A couple of miles away, behind the wall and only aware that something terrible was happening, Aphrodite, in a frenzy of worry, signalled her great helpers to launch one last attack on the walls. She would not give up. Her power was waning, but she resolved that whilst she had an ounce left, she would go on.

The great wave was reaching its destination…

*

Fox pounded up, exhausted. He tried to catch his breath, about to say something, when a thunderous rumble preceded a shudder that shook the whole bay. When it had passed, Alfie threw himself on Fox.

'It's gone, Fox. Anja killed it. We saved Toby.'

Uncharacteristically ignoring Alfie, Fox was still panting, frantically trying to speak.

'It really has gone,' Anja said. 'I know it has.'

'Anja, you don't understand,' Fox finally gasped. 'Look, the castle.'

Slowly, the topmost towers, including the ones they had so recently climbed, were falling. Huge sections thundered down; again and again, the ground trembled and a massive cloud of sand rose slowly to a great height and mushroomed out. They watched, spellbound by the destruction.

'It's falling!'

'No, Anja, that's not it.' Fox jumped around her frantically. 'It's all falling. The sea wall's falling!'

Their eyes met and suddenly Anja understood. She spun around towards the wall around the bay and shut her eyes in disbelief.

'What's the matter, Anja?' Alfie asked. 'What's up now?'

She couldn't tell him. 'We won't have time, will we?' she whispered.

Fox shook his head.

She sat down in the sand and cradled Toby. All her fear drained away; they were all together at last. They would be together forever.

'What's the matter, Anja?'

'Nothing, Alfie. Come and sit down with me, we can all have a cuddle. You'd better go, Fox.'

Fox slumped down across their feet. 'No, it's taken me too long to get here. I'm exhausted. Anyway, I think that I'd rather stay.'

She scratched his snout.

'You will never, ever know just how nice that is,' he said, and they both laughed. Behind them, just beyond the failing wall, a white line stretching across the horizon was approaching.

'Sit around a bit and face the cliffs,' Anja said.

Alfie looked up. 'The gulls are flying back there,' he said.

One flew down and landed nearby; it was one they'd met. It strutted closer.

'There's nothing we can do,' it said sadly.

Anja put her finger to her lips and glanced towards Alfie. The gull flapped about, agitated, then rose and flew away. She didn't see it heading towards the falling sand wall.

'I think that Toby's too ill anyway,' Anja whispered to Fox, and then kissed her limp little brother's mouth.

*

Aphrodite swivelled her grey body, just in time to see the great tsunami roar towards her, driving her and the guardians over the crumbling wall. Riding it, she pierced the surface, somersaulting high and slowly in the air. She wondered how the wall had suddenly weakened but supposed that against the power of Poseidon and his great creatures, it had finally failed. She rode the crest of the mountain of water as it headed for the remains of the castle, its final obstacle before crashing against the cliffs. Suddenly she sensed sadness. As she stared at the approaching castle, the last tower crumbled. Her unease deepened, and then she saw a lone gull skimming across the waves. As she cried out a welcome, it turned and hovered above her.

'The girl destroyed the creature, They are by the wrecks, waiting for the ocean to take them.'

Aphrodite screamed in anguish, realising her error. Lancing back beneath the wave, she called the great creatures. They forced their way forward through the advancing waves until they were ranged beside her, inside the head of the tsunami as it roared across the bay. She sensed Anja, calming a tiny group huddled at the edge of the wrecked ships.

'There!' she commanded.

*

'Don't look,' Anja shouted into Alfie's ear, feeling his body stiffen as the roaring grew and the air battered their backs. To Alfie, this was as good as an order to do so. He tried to turn, but she forced his head down into her lap. She bent over him and Toby, clasping them as tightly as she could, and squeezed her eyes shut. Fox pressed his nose between their bodies.

'Anja,' she thought she heard Toby gasp.

'Love you,' she whispered, and tensed her mind and body.

Seconds ticked by like hours. The roaring was so loud, and the howling wind tore across their bent bodies. Then spray lashed her neck and the breath was driven from her body as a massive impact hit her and she lost consciousness. Alfie experienced a single terrifying second as his dream came to life, a scream driven from his lungs as the water engulfed him. The last thing he remembered was the seething saltiness as it filled his mouth.

24

On the threshold of the portal, Anja and Alfie held hands, looking out over the frosty field near the churchyard. Clear and pure, the clock struck the eleventh hour of the evening, ringing out through the freezing air. The trees that sheltered them were full-leaved and the air about them warm. Anja's mind travelled back to what had happened since she'd destroyed the creature months before.

She'd woken on the clifftop with Alfie beside her, and Aphrodite cradling Toby's body. Her head was throbbing, her back and sides battered and bruised. As consciousness grew, the headache diminished and the pain in her back began to ease. Alfie was motionless, asleep. She crawled over to Aphrodite and stroked Toby's drawn, pale face. 'Is he…?' His eyes were half-open; glazed, unresponsive.

'No, he is very ill. He will recover, I promise.'

'What happened? I don't remember anything except that the ocean was coming back. I thought we were finished.'

'I didn't realise that you had done so much, Anja. I thought I could destroy the wall and rescue Toby before you reached the bay. I was too late but luckily wasn't able to destroy the wall. Finally, I thought that I had, but it was you, Anja, you destroyed the creature and everything it had built, and all that I did was deny you time to escape. I almost destroyed you all.'

'Aphrodite, Pan was with me when I destroyed it. I felt him, and someone else. I didn't have time to think. I felt it, Aphrodite. I felt the power and I knew I could destroy it. But why didn't we drown?'

'The gull warned me just in time. Powerful servants of Poseidon were with me. They plucked you from the path of the sea and held you above the water. Seconds later, and it would have been too late.'

Anja touched her baby brother's face again. 'Are you sure he'll be all right? He doesn't look good, does he?'

'I can't lie, Anja. He is near death. The final trauma almost finished him. I've put him into a deep sleep and asked the Land for help. He is too young to endure such treatment. I will have to gift his essence.'

Anja nodded, not sure what she meant, but anything to save him. 'Alfie seems all right,' she said.

'You have both, in separate ways, gained the ability to heal and even regenerate quickly. Not enough to have survived the ocean, though. Once Alfie reaches a grove, he becomes as strong as ever.'

'What about Fox? He was there, I remember. He wouldn't leave. Where is he? He isn't…?'

'No, Fox was sorely hurt, but he is also hard to destroy.

He has done what all animals do when they are hurt. He has gone somewhere warm and safe to recover.'

'What will we do now?'

'Come home with me. The otters are arriving soon with a boat. You will stay with me until Toby has recovered, then consider your future.'

*

They stayed with Aphrodite. Anja wouldn't leave Toby's side. Just after they arrived, Alfie went on a trip with Aphrodite and returned carrying new clothes and other things from a grove on the other side of the river. Within a week or so of arriving, Toby began to recover. After a few more, he was a happy, fit little boy and spent most of his time happily tumbling and playing with the otter kits without a stitch of clothing on him. Anja was anxious when he played near the jetty and river, but Aphrodite dismissed her cares.

'Leave him to play with his new brothers and sisters, no harm can come to him now,' she reassured Anja. His face was often sticky with honey, and each evening he came tumbling in with his furry companions, kissing her with fishy breath. 'It was the only way to save him,' Aphrodite responded to Anja's shocked look the first time she realised how the miraculous "recovery" had been achieved.

Finally accepting her own change as well, she wore the green dresses, gold and silver jewels and accessories as naturally as Aphrodite wore only her skimpy tunic. Each evening, she danced. Her friend watched and smiled. One day, she took Anja's hand.

'Happy?' asked, looking into her sparkling golden eyes.

'We're all recovered, aren't we?'

Aphrodite studied her. No human would be able to look upon such beauty, into those eyes, and still command their thoughts: her embroidered dress, the fine silver chain of leaves around her narrow hips and dark, silky hair framing her face under the netted cap of small gold flowers; she was incredibly beautiful, adorable.

She forestalled Anja's next words. 'You want to go to the Great Forest.'

'I must.'

'Of course, it was only a matter of time. What will you do, go home?'

Anja shrugged, then nodded.

'You don't seem sure?'

'Do you think that I should?'

Aphrodite took her hand. 'You didn't say we, Anja, you said I, and the question is "Do you think I can?"'

'Alfie and Toby should go, they have to. But you don't think I should, do you?'

'No,' Aphrodite replied, 'not yet. Not because you shouldn't, because you can't, not yet. You're not ready.'

'But I must return to Pan, I promised.'

'Yes, you must, Anja.'

Within a few days, everyone had prepared for the return to the Great Forest. Alfie accepted the news because he'd been waiting for it.

A few mornings later, Anja and Alfie carried their bags down to the jetty. Out of the mist, the large beautiful boat drifted upstream to them. Intricate carvings laced its wooden beams. Aphrodite was standing beside a long tiller fitted on one side of the stern.

'Come on, climb in.' She laughed at their astonishment as she attached a short plank to the pier. 'Do you think that I will visit that old rogue in any old lump of wood?' Toby appeared, naked and dripping wet, with his gang of kits and scooted across to her.

Their journey back upriver to the Great Forest was quicker than the adventure that had brought them to Aphrodite's home. She hardly touched the tiller or sail as the boat powered its way upriver, and the few otters that were with them often swam in the Great River but played no part in their progress. Eventually, they passed between the high cliffs, briefly glimpsing where they had so perilously joined the river so long ago, and Anja thought of Quicksilver, how she had often been cold and unkind to him.

'Do you miss him, Alfie?' she asked, seeing him looking up at the cliffs.

He turned and looked at her. 'Of course, but he's not gone, not really.'

'Why, do you think he will ever come back?'

'Yes, I'll find him.'

'When you're in a grove, in a tree, do you feel him?'

'No, but I know he's there.'

Her face clouded. 'But what about you? You're just like him now. You can go into the trees, you even smell like him.'

'I'm a bit like him now, but I'm not him. There's only one of him. I'm still me. Anyway, I'm not as different as you are now, Anja. You're really different,' he said, deliberately avoiding a conversation he didn't want to have.

'I don't feel different, Alfie, not really.'

'It's everything, Anja, all of you. I can't even think sometimes, especially when you cuddle me. And your eyes, Anja. See, you're doing it now. All I can think of is that I love you so much.'

'Do you think about going home?'

'Yes, I want to see Mummy and Daddy.'

'To stay forever?'

'No, I will come back and find Quicksilver. It's a difficult thing to think about, I'll just see what happens. What about you, Anja? I can pretend to be normal, you can't.'

'I don't know. It is difficult.' She leant forward and kissed him gently on the lips, followed by a hard shove that sent him tumbling amongst the bags stowed under the seats. Toby and a couple of young otters scrambled over the seats to join in the fun.

The boat cut through the crashing rapids as easily as it had navigated any other part of the journey. The spray wet them, but it steadily forced its way through, sliding past huge rocks and gurgling whirlpools, sometimes tipping at impossible angles, ignoring the chaos around it. The cliffs became rocky outcrops, then the river stopped descending steeply and became deep and narrow, fringed with dark woodland until they eventually entered a wide valley bordering the northern reaches of the Great Forest. A few miles further, they branched off into a large tributary, finally entering a great lake.

The lake was as silent and still as the Great Forest surrounding it. Occasionally, the haunting cry of a bird echoed in the warm, dank air. They glided towards a sun-dappled area of lush grass that relieved the many trees leaning over their dark reflections. The boat softly slid to a halt in deep water, side-on to a long, narrow jetty. Aphrodite gracefully leapt over the gunwale and tied the craft to a sturdy post. Anja lifted Toby to her and then helped Alfie jump out, before allowing Aphrodite to help her.

She faced the forest, scanning the darkness between the trunks of the nearest trees, then bent down and pressed her fingers through the grass deep into the rich loam, bringing a handful of the black soil up to her nose, and she breathed deeply. With a little shiver, she stood up and began to walk towards the trees. Glancing back at Aphrodite, she laughed, her face bright with happiness. She began to run and as she reached the first tree, Pan stepped out to meet her.

She jumped, wrapping herself tightly around him, her face buried in his neck. He peeled her away, swinging her around before gently placing her back on the ground. Lowering himself on his strange legs, he kissed her gently on both cheeks. Holding hands, they both walked back to the rest of the travellers.

'Aphrodite,' he greeted with the same kisses. 'It's been too long.'

'Yes, it has, you old goat.'

He threw back his head and roared with laughter. 'Wonderful, as youthful and beautiful as ever.'

'We meet again, Alfie.'

He held out his hand. Alfie placed his own small hand in that of the Forest Lord and shook it once, as firmly as he could. It was his only reply.

Pan turned to Toby, who had found the security of Aphrodite's safe arms.

'And this must be Toby.' He went to lift the toddler out of Aphrodite's arms, but Toby wriggled deeper. As he did, a momentary ripple ran through his body, happening so fast that no sooner had it started than it was gone. Toby's eyes flashed apologetically at Aphrodite and she returned a disapproving look.

'You frightened him. Remember what he's been through.'

Pan smiled. 'Of course, I see there's a lot to catch up on. I have a camp not far from here. All the comforts my simple realm can provide. Walk with me.'

Pan walked ahead with Aphrodite, the pair talking quietly together. The two elder siblings followed, swinging their brother between them, his giggles spilling into the trees. He flashed a quick, regretful glance at the otters; they were staying with the boat, small splashes betraying their eagerness to explore the lake.

The next morning, Alfie woke before dawn found its way through the thick layers of foliage that covered the bower in which they had spent the night. He'd slept alone; Anja had her bed nearby, close to Toby and Aphrodite.

He didn't want to go to sleep again, just doze for a few minutes more and let the gloom of morning creep in. He listened intently for a minute or so before the warmth of his little nest gently closed his eyes; they opened again, and it was lighter. He didn't strain to listen this time; the sound that he was expecting drifted to him.

Slipping out of his comfortable bed, he walked to the edge of the bower and beneath its leafy eaves watched Anja dance. Her bare feet hardly touched the grass as she slowly weaved and spun to the music of the pipes. Her dress floated around her, her hair billowed gently beneath the silver cap, covering and then revealing her unfocused golden eyes. He felt hands grasp his waist and draw him back. Aphrodite had risen and now sat behind him on a low log bench. She clasped her fingers together across his lap and he sat back against her as they both watched. That was the moment Alfie decided to go home.

*

Anja squeezed Alfie's hand. There had been no disagreement, no heart-searching. She understood that they should go, and that she couldn't go with them. Not yet. It had been her responsibility. Neither of her brothers would be held to account; they would be welcomed back unconditionally, with tears of joy. She knew that she would also be welcomed with equal love. But she wasn't ready, and even if she was, questions would start, questions she couldn't answer. Despite everything, she desperately wanted to but couldn't face her father.

She ached for his forgiveness and to be squeezed in his strong arms, but still she couldn't go. Aphrodite had taken her aside and gently spelt out the reasons. She'd agreed; a decision shared.

So, here they were on the edge of two lands, waiting for the last seconds to tick by. On the other side, the last few minutes of the shortest day of the year ticked away. It was almost Christmas. Her mind searched for memories of freezing days, of what she was looking at, but she could only feel the gentle warmth of the night.

As the first midnight chime rang out, Alfie walked onto the field, blowing to see his breath in the chill air, his buskins abruptly crunching on the frosty grass. He turned and came back.

'I can't feel the cold, not at all.'

'Pan said that you mightn't. I don't think Toby will either. The portal will open for you if you want to come back. I'll know and come to meet you if you do, and I'll also know if anything's wrong. Don't worry if you can't sense me, I will come.'

'Aren't you going to see them at all?'

'I don't know. Let's just see how it turns out. I'll never be far away.'

With a last wistful look, Alfie took Toby's hand. 'Shall we go and see Mummy and Daddy?'

Toby nodded and Anja kissed him. They had spent a long time explaining in as simple terms as possible why neither she nor Aphrodite could go with them. They weren't sure whether he thought he was going home or just going back for a visit, so no one made a fuss about him leaving. But Aphrodite had spent a long time with him on her lap, talking softly. He'd nodded repeatedly. Then she'd turned to his brother.

'Alfie, you can't expect him not to say what happened if asked, but I don't think that either of you will be believed, even if the proof is clear. Whatever happens, you mustn't do anything that makes them suspect that you're not only different, but changed. That *will* cause problems. Do you understand, Alfie? Whatever else, remember, they will *not* understand. I don't suppose your parents will care, but others will. And simply tell them that Anja is all right, because they *will* ask.'

Her brothers, dressed identically in the only clothes they possessed, walked along the edge of the fallow field and entered the little path through the wood as the last midnight chime faded away. Toby had been persuaded during the journey up the Great River to keep his clothes on and Anja wondered what her parents would make of them. She stood there long after they were out of sight, then briefly stepped into the field, breathed the air deeply and touched the boys' minds. They both responded, and she withdrew into her beloved woods, happier now she was sure she could find them quickly.

The boys retraced the familiar route back through the little wood and down past the churchyard into the lane. Toby's feet hardly marked the path and his keen eyes began exploring. Alfie shushed him when he laughed happily, remembering the gate and stile. He could tell Toby didn't feel the freezing cold either.

They walked up the lane, along the hedge bordering

the vicarage garden, stopping beside the wide rustic arch over the path leading to the door. There was a light on in the study window and it winked out just as they reached it. As they watched, a hand wiped the condensation away and the familiar face of the vicar peered through. Alfie instinctively gave him a smile and a wave before walking on. The face disappeared. Moments later, the door opened, and the vicar carefully hurried up the slippery path. He stood out in the lane, staring after the two figures, convincing himself his imagination had not deceived him. It was definitely them; the boys, their faces as etched in his memory as they were everyone's in the village, still staring out from faded posters on every shop window and noticeboard. His heart pounded as he ran unsteadily back to the house and picked up the phone.

The brothers approached the first of a small row of cottages on their left just as the phone was being answered in the last one. The man who answered it listened intently and then quickly dressed. He'd only lived in the village for eighteen months, arriving to replace the young bobby who had disappeared at the same time as the Lovett children. None had been seen since, despite searches and an investigation still supposedly open. Now the two boys, one just a toddler, were, according to the vicar, walking hand in hand up the lane towards him. He pulled on his heavy uniform overcoat, decided against wearing his helmet and stepped out into the bitter cold. As he closed the gate behind him, he stopped, breathing heavily; great billows of hot breath clouding in front of him, but not just with haste. Two small figures were approaching on the other side of the road, their little voices clear in the frosty air. They hadn't noticed him yet.

'They won't tell us off, they'll be too happy to see us. Do you really remember what they looked like, Toby?'

The little one replied loudly, ''Course I do. You don't!'

The vicar came panting up behind them, still wrapping a long scarf around his neck. The boys turned around.

'Hello, Vicar, I thought that I saw you,' Alfie said warily, his eyes flicking to the big man with the heavy coat who had now joined them. 'We were just going home.'

Toby was tugging at Alfie's hand, trying to hide behind him.

'It's all right, it's only the vicar and…' His voice trailed off.

'I'm the new constable. Alfie, isn't it?' He offered his gloved hand to the small boy. 'Aren't you cold, the pair of you?'

Alfie shook his head. 'We're all right.'

'Going home?'

Alfie nodded.

'Don't you think that it's going to be a bit of a shock for your parents after all this time?' Constable Rose was thinking as fast as he could. 'Perhaps it'd be better if we went with you.'

Alfie shrugged. He'd pictured him and Toby knocking on the door and his mother and father laughing with delight. Now that image had been shattered and he was worried again; it *had* been such a long time. Their first question would be the most obvious, and the one he feared: *Where's Anja?* He could see it now in the vicar's eyes.

'I'll tell you what,' the constable said gently, his concern for their health in the freezing cold overriding all other considerations, 'come into my cottage and warm up and I'll let your parents know.'

Without giving them the chance to do anything else, the vicar took Alfie's hand. He had expected it to be cold, dreading that it would be icy cold, although considering their attire and the biting night air, even that would have been normal. But the boy's hand was warm; the warmth transferring to his own fingers. Once inside, the two men threw off their overcoats and the constable relit the gas fire.

'There, be like toast in a jiffy.'

Meanwhile, the vicar was taking stock of the boys. He felt his stomach tighten. They were both dressed in identical, peculiar clothing. They looked strange too; both, particularly the toddler, were very brown, as if they had been in a hot climate. But it was more than that. He glanced at Constable Rose, who was also studying them. The vicar always trusted his instinct, and he sensed unnerving strangeness.

Whilst the constable sidled quietly out of the room to make the phone call, the vicar sat in a large chair facing the boys, who sat together awkwardly on a settee.

'So, you decided to come back then?' he asked, with strained joviality.

The boys nodded in unison.

'You've been gone for such a long time. Everyone's been worried about you, and your sister. Anja, isn't it?'

Again, they both nodded. He watched them carefully

when he mentioned their sister's name. The eldest boy's shoulders sank a fraction.

'Hasn't she come back with you?' he asked lightly.

'No.' Alfie shook his head. 'She's all right, though.'

'When did you last see her, Alfie?'

'Not long ago.'

'What, days ago?'

'No, just earlier.'

The vicar could hardly conceal his frustration. The girl was nearby.

'Is she hiding? You know she won't get into trouble, none of you will. We're just so glad to see you.'

'She's not hiding. She isn't ready to come back. She will when she's ready.'

The constable had returned and sat on the arm of a chair; he'd heard most of the conversation. He told them his news.

'Well, I've just spoken to your father. He's very shocked, of course, and I told him that you seem to be okay. He's excited and a bit emotional, but he's a sensible fellow. He's going to wake your mother and break the news to her gently. I said I'd bring you both along in about half an hour, but I've no doubt they'll be here before then.'

The children looked at each other and Toby squeezed his whole body together in happy anticipation. Alfie had more of an o*h well, this is it* look on his face.

'They'll be very emotional, Alfie,' the vicar said. 'Give them time to get over the shock.' He wondered why he had said it, as if he was more bothered about the parents than the children.

There was an awkward silence and then Constable Rose leaned forward. 'How did you come back, y'know, from where you've been?'

Alfie looked at him but didn't answer.

The vicar felt the boy's discomfort.

'You don't have to tell us everything yet. It's just that we're very worried about your sister, on her own in the middle of winter.'

Alfie gave a big sigh. 'I told you, she's all right, she'll come back when she's ready. She won't if you're going to ask lots of questions.'

'I appreciate that, Alfie, but you two just turning up again like this, well, it's rather strange.'

Alfie shrugged. Toby had almost fallen asleep in the comfort of the ample cushions on the settee.

An uncomfortable silence developed and the vicar and constable withdrew from the room. There was a loud tapping on the door.

Alfie shook Toby. 'They're here.'

Toby crawled onto Alfie's lap and stuck his thumb into his mouth, something he hadn't done for a very long time.

25

Alfie's throat was suddenly very dry, and he swallowed repeatedly. He could hear his father's muffled voice. Until that moment, his homecoming had been unemotional. Apprehension and excitement had been there in varying amounts, but the instant he heard his father's voice, all the times, especially during the early days away when he had needed him, came rushing back.

He breathed deeply to compose himself and blew the air slowly out of his mouth. Tears pricked at the side of his eyes, but he was determined not to cry and thought of Quicksilver and how he would never let anything faze him. He knew he couldn't trust himself to speak. Toby had no such restraint. Remembering his father's voice, he squirmed out of Alfie's arms and jumped down, then flashed a look at him.

'Wait here, you'll see him in a minute.' He turned his little brother around to face him. 'Don't you do anything daft, Toby, remember what Aphrodite said. You listening to me?'

Toby nodded and quickly turned around to face the door again. It opened and the vicar stepped in. Right behind was their father.

Toby ran to him and was swept up and crushed into his overcoat and scarf, his small arms wrapped tightly around his father's neck. Over his shoulder, Alfie could see his father's eyes squeezed shut. They opened and focused on him. For a couple of seconds, no one said a word. With Toby still sticking to him like a limpet, Peter Lovett came and sat down next to his eldest son. Alfie was suddenly shocked to realise that he had never known what his father looked like, not really, not all the little features that he was seeing now; the shape of his eyebrows, dark stubble on his face, colour of his eyes. It was as if he was seeing him properly for the first time. His father reached over and gently took off Alfie's cap and studied it.

'Thought you didn't like caps. You hated your school one.'

Alfie remembered the moments of fuss so long ago.

'I forgot I still had it on.'

His father prised Toby from his neck and took his cap off too. He stuffed them both in his overcoat pocket.

'So, you've decided to come home and see us at last,' he said gently. He had composed himself on the way over and was recovered enough from the shock to appear as calm and normal as possible.

Alfie struggled. He knew it wouldn't be easy, but not as hard as this. He understood now why Anja hadn't come. He remembered what she'd told him. *No lies, Alfie, but remember, they won't understand, whatever you say. Just tell them what we agreed.*

'We went to get Toby, Daddy. It was a long way.' He felt himself filling up and stopped.

'Alfie, it's all right. All I care about is that you're back.'

He knew that it wouldn't be as simple as that; he could see by the look on the constable's face. They might leave it for now, but they would ask again. As if he had heard his thoughts, his father took his hand.

'The constable says that Anja isn't with you, that she's somewhere near.'

Alfie sighed. 'Anja is near, but somewhere else. She just couldn't come with us yet.'

'She *is* all right, though?'

They kept asking that. 'Yes, you should see her, Dad. She's so beautiful, isn't she, Toby?'

Toby's eyes grew wide. 'Anja's a beautiful princess.' Then he looked towards Alfie for reassurance, caution drilled into his little mind by Anja and Aphrodite.

'I know,' their father said, breathing deeply to control his own emotions, 'she's always been our princess.' He crouched down and drew Alfie to him. Alfie brushed his soft cheek against the familiar lines and stubble of his father's face, breathing his smell. Tears wet both their cheeks. He pulled away and wiped his eyes, flushing at this weakness.

Peter Lovett turned to the vicar. 'Right, I think I'll take them home now. Thank you for all that you've done. Their mother will be beside herself; she still doesn't believe it. I don't think I did until I saw them.'

'Can I have a word first, sir, in private,' said Constable Rose, 'just a quick one?' He opened the door to the kitchen.

Their father gave Alfie a reassuring wink before following him.

'I'll have to report that I found them in the morning. I mean, there was a huge hunt for them and all that. You'll probably get a few visitors over the next few days. It's all a bit unusual, you've only got to look at them.'

Peter was a big man and far fitter than the constable; his eyes grew narrow. 'You didn't find them, though, did you? You saw them on their way home. When was the last time any of you went looking for them? I'm quite capable of asking them what happened and I don't want anyone bothering them before I do. With all due respect, I know that you mean well, but I don't trust the "authorities" to have my family's wellbeing their priority.'

'Well, it won't be my decision, I'm afraid, and perhaps not yours either. After all, there's your daughter still missing, and I'm convinced that they've been with someone. The boy has almost said as much.'

'You don't seem keen to mention your predecessor,' Peter said, his tone cementing the look in his eyes. 'Whoever's handling this can give me a call tomorrow. I'll also be getting legal advice in the morning.'

'Right you are then, Mr Lovett. I do understand your position, sir, but I have my job to do.'

They shook hands and Peter returned to his sons. Picking Toby up again, he took Alfie's hand and led them to the door. He politely thanked the vicar, and they left the cottage.

Now the really difficult bit, Alfie thought. *Mummy.*

That thought was being echoed by his father. They had kept up a semblance of living, working, following routines, anything to block the awful thoughts that crept into their minds when they let their guard down. Peter devoted himself to supporting his wife.

'If only,' she'd murmured recently, 'there was a way to say goodbye.' But there wasn't. Now, as suddenly as they'd gone, Alfie and Toby were back. Relief hadn't had time to develop.

Helen was waiting by the gate, wrapped in a dressing gown with a heavy coat thrown over it. She'd been there since her husband had left, blankly staring after him. As he reappeared down the lane with one child in his arm and another holding his hand, her mind spun and began to slide away. She leant on the gatepost for support and the moment passed. She should be running to meet them, but her feet remained stuck to the frozen ground.

Peter whispered something in the ear of the child in his arms and its head turned to her. There was a small shout, 'Mummy!' and her heart pounded, recognising his voice and his face at the same moment, familiarity she thought she would never hear again.

'Oh my God,' she murmured.

The next minutes were a blur and it was much later that reality hit them. The children's beds were there, but most of their clothes had gone to charity, and they hadn't had the courage to let things like favourite toys go. Practical issues took priority and a bizarre normality suddenly descended on the household: supper, making up their beds, saying goodnight… And then they were alone again, sitting looking at each other, as they had done almost fourteen years ago after bringing Anja home as a newborn baby and realising then that they were no longer just a couple. Helen broke the silence. 'Where on earth have they been?'

'I can't even guess.' She'd been too calm, Peter was glad to see concern on her face. 'But it *is* them.'

'I know, Peter, they're different.'

'Of course they're different. They've been gone for a year and a half.'

'A year and a half, almost to the day. But that's not what I mean. They've changed… not in the ways they should. Alfie should be almost ten, but he isn't. Toby should be four. He's not, but his speech is so good, and he used the toilet. And those clothes…'

'Yes, it's all very strange. No underclothes either.'

'They're both brown as berries, and that's not a tan that you can get here, even in the summer. And they smell strange, not dirty but unusual. Alfie's is exotic, sort of spicy, but Toby's is different, like a little animal. Why aren't they older, Peter?'

'I don't know, and it doesn't matter until we know more. Let's try to get some sleep and we'll talk with Alfie later. It's almost three and I need to get up early. I'll need to call work, and I don't want anyone bothering us.'

They went to bed and, despite what he had said, for the first time since the children had disappeared, Helen responded to his affection.

Alfie lay awake for some time, partly due to the

unexpected familiarity of his bed but mainly because he was worried what the morning would bring. In the end, he wrapped a blanket around himself and slept on the floor. Toby curled himself up into a ball in the middle of his old cot and dreamt of the river.

It had been light for a while when Peter and Helen crept to the boys' bedroom door but didn't go in. They could hear Alfie whispering to his brother; they listened for a few seconds but couldn't make out what he was saying. Content that it was still real, they went downstairs, and a little later called the boys down for breakfast.

Alfie asked if they had any honey. 'Toby loves bread and honey,' he explained.

'Doesn't he eat anything else? What about milk and other food?'

'Yes, anything, but he really likes bread and honey, and lots of fish.'

'Well, he looks a bit thin, as do you, young man. What have you been eating?'

Alfie shrugged. 'I eat anything, though I like honey cakes as well.'

As he ate, he could feel his father's eyes on him. He tried not to meet them and when he did, he quickly flicked his own back to his plate.

'We're going to have to talk, Alfie.'

Alfie nodded glumly. 'I know.'

'Will you tell me what happened?'

'You won't say that I'm telling fibs?' Alfie replied, thinking about the advice he'd been given again.

'No, but I want to know what happened.'

Toby seemed oblivious to the conversation, but Alfie knew he was taking in every word.

'Can we go into your room, just you and me?' Toby flashed a look at him but didn't protest.

His parents looked at one another and agreement silently passed between them.

'After breakfast,' his father said.

Alfie felt better, sitting with his father in the big old leather chair in the study. He told his father what had happened, pretty accurately up until they woke up in the Land. From there on, Alfie told his father the version that he and Anja had agreed. The general gist was that they had travelled a long way to find Toby by the ocean and then travelled back. He mentioned they'd been helped. He didn't describe or name anyone, nor did he mention anything dangerous.

His father considered this as he ran his fingers through Alfie's hair and traced the contours of his face. 'That's not much considering you've been away for a year and a half. You'll need to fill in the gaps, Alfie, a bit more detail... Where's Anja, Alfie?'

'She's not far away, Daddy. She's waiting.'

'Waiting? Is she frightened to come home, in case I tell her off?'

'She was, but I don't think she is now.'

'So, what's she waiting for?'

Alfie screwed up his face. 'Promise that you won't laugh or be angry with me.'

'I promise.'

'Well, it's different there, and we're different, all of us,

301

but mostly Anja.' He coloured at this. 'She's so beautiful now, Daddy, it makes you forget anything else. She is *so* beautiful.' He didn't know how else to describe how Anja was now.

'Why is she waiting, Alfie?'

'She is coming back, not yet, but she is and then you'll understand.'

Peter hugged his son; he did not want to push him. He would believe everything Alfie told him, no matter how far-fetched, and not show any disbelief, because it was all so improbable.

'We'll stop for now, Alfie. You do understand that the authorities will want to ask you what happened?'

'Can't I tell you and you tell them?'

'If I have my way, yes, let's wait and see.'

Alfie went off. Peter stayed in the chair, deep in thought. It was obvious that Alfie had skimmed over what had happened, but he hadn't lied, he was sure. If he was honest, he didn't really care. They were back and for now that was more important. But when the authorities saw and questioned them? Alfie hadn't mentioned the missing policeman, and he hadn't asked. But his going missing at the same time couldn't be a coincidence. He continued to sit, pondering.

Meanwhile, Toby was with his mother, sitting on her lap playing a favourite old game of theirs: "ride a cock horse". Alfie had joined them. Toby was cackling with laughter as he bumped high on his mother's knees, their eyes sparkling together. As the rhyme reached its climax, he threw back his head, giddy with happiness, singing with her, "*She shall have music, wherever she GOES!*" His bottom left his mother's knees, and, clasping her fingers for balance, he turned his head towards Alfie to see if he was watching all the fun. Alfie's laughter froze as he saw his little brother's ecstatic face, blotched with happiness, suddenly flicker.

'Toby!' he shouted, grabbing his brother and pulling him off his mother's lap. He shook Toby hard and locked eyes with him. Toby hardly reacted to the rough treatment and his colour returned to normal. He made a face, jumping back to the safety of his mother's lap.

Helen was stunned; she turned on him. 'Alfie! You don't treat your brother like that.'

'I'm sorry, Mummy. He was getting overexcited. It's not good for him after all he's been through, I didn't mean to be so rough.'

'I can see that we'll have to smooth out some edges, little man.'

Alfie wilted. This was not good.

In the early afternoon, the phone in the study began ringing. Alfie couldn't hear any of the conversations. He was mostly up in the bedroom, playing with Toby. He heard his father's deep, muffled voice and the door close. Then his mother joined his father. He sat at the top of the stairs trying to catch what his parents were saying but couldn't because they were whispering. Finally, his father called him down.

'If I said that we will believe everything you told us, no matter how silly it sounded, will you tell me everything that happened? Everything, Alfie.'

'Why, what's happened?'

'Your clothes, Alfie. And you look no older than the day you went, but you have matured so much in all other ways. You don't feel the cold either, do you?'

Alfie shook his head.

'And there's so much more we've noticed. So, we believe you're telling us the truth, but only the barest details. For us to protect you, we need to know everything. The vicar and Constable Rose also noticed, Alfie. People will be coming to see us, to see you. I tried but can't stop them. It will help me and Mummy decide how we're going to respond. What do you think?'

Alfie was relieved; things were not going well, he had to tell them more.

His father sat him on his lap and his mother drew close, sitting on the desk chair.

'You said Anja has changed a lot, Alfie, and you and Toby, how have you two changed?'

'Not like Anja.'

'How then?'

'Toby was ill when we found him, really, really ill, almost dead. So Aphr… this lady made him better. I don't really know what she did, but he's a bit different now.' Alfie didn't want to say any more about Toby.

'Okay, we'll leave Toby for the moment. What about you?'

'I had this friend. He helped us but got really hurt. It was before we rescued Toby. Anyway, I'm a bit like him now, and I can do some things.'

'What sort of things, Alfie?'

Alfie leant forward and put his hand on the study

desk. The varnish felt strange but then the wood beneath it began to react. The grain opened, and his fingers sank in. He had never done it anywhere except in the groves and was surprised to discover that the desk wood was not dead at all. Pictures began to form in his mind, memories of the massive oak it had once been. He gently removed his fingers, saddened by the brief interchange.

'Can you do that with anything?'

'No, just wood, I go into it. If I do it with a tree, I sort of mix with it. I mean… when I'm in it, I'm not solid anymore, I'm part of the tree.' He realised he'd said too much and stopped.

His parents stared at him. The desk still had four small discoloured marks where the varnish had not reappeared.

'Well,' his father said eventually, 'that *is* different; and it's not a little thing, Alfie. Where is this place?'

'I don't know, it's the Land, sort of another world. We got lost and were there. Everything is sort of different there. We wouldn't have lasted five minutes if we hadn't had help.'

'Who were these kind people who helped you, Alfie?' his mother asked. 'We have a lot to thank them for.'

'Don't laugh, because they're a bit different as well.'

'No, just tell the truth.'

'The first one is the Lord of the Great Forest. That's where we went from the wood by the churchyard. He's a bit funny-looking and I didn't like him at first, but now I think he's probably all right.'

'Funny-looking?

'Yes, he's got funny animal legs and horns on his head. He's called Pan.'

Alfie had expected a reaction from his parents; ridicule or disbelief, but their reaction instantly made him regret telling them, and he understood why he'd been warned not to.

His mother had her hand over her mouth and looked so shocked that he almost burst into tears. His father stopped the situation deteriorating.

'It's not a problem.' He took his wife's trembling hand. 'We asked him to tell us,' he said, looking into her eyes.

She nodded, but what had been said couldn't be undone. 'I'll go and make a cup of tea,' she whispered, and got up.

Peter Lovett was torn between his wife and his son, both in need of his support.

'Let me go and see if Mummy's all right and I'll come straight back.'

Alfie was glad; he made his mind up then that he wouldn't say any more. They didn't understand, just as he'd been told.

It was quite a while before his father returned. He had a cup of tea in his hand. Putting it down, he made out as if what had happened had been of little consequence.

'So where were we? You were telling us about the people who helped you.'

The look in Alfie's eyes and his expression told him that it wasn't going to be that easy.

'Come on, Alfie.'

Alfie looked down at the carpet, shaking his head.

'Alfie, this is all a bit of a shock to us. Mummy didn't mean to be like that.'

'Anja said that we shouldn't tell you. Not to lie or

anything, but because you wouldn't be able to… I can't remember the word she used. Can I go now?'

'Of course, but we will talk again later.'

As Alfie climbed the stairs, trying to think, he heard splashing in the bathroom. He raced towards the sound.

His mother's head came around the door as he got there. She seemed to have recovered from her reaction to his revelations.

'Oh, Alfie, good. Toby's in the bath. Can you look after him for a second while I get some more towels? He's like a little eel.'

Alfie pushed past her and slammed the door shut as she left. He was just in time. He grabbed Toby and lifted his head from under the water.

'Stop it, Toby, you remember what Aphrodite said.'

He was greeted by a stream of water in the face and had to muffle Toby's squeaks.

'Please, Toby, you promised Aphrodite.'

Toby's face was already changing back and his fur was disappearing. Just as they could hear their mother coming back, he regained his human form.

'I *want* to,' he protested.

'I know, but you mustn't. Mummy will have a fit.'

Their mother came back in.

'I might as well get in with Toby, Mummy,' said Alfie. 'No good wasting hot water.'

'Okay, but I think that I'll stay as well. Make sure that my little boys wash properly and dry everywhere.'

To Alfie's relief, Toby was good for the rest of the bath, but he kept close to him for the rest of the day, just in case.

26

Peter and Helen Lovett sat quietly together on the settee in front of the glowing fireplace.

'The authorities are coming.' Peter broke the silence.

'Can't they leave us alone, just for a while?'

'They already have, I might be able to put them off for another day, but no longer. If they'd come straight back here, it wouldn't have been so bad, but what with the vicar and the constable…' He paused. 'Even then, we couldn't have kept them hidden for long.'

Toby climbed out of his cot in the early hours and slipped under the covers that Alfie had pulled around himself on the floor as soon as he heard his parents close their bedroom door. The boys slept for a couple more hours before waking again, hours before the sky would lighten enough to draw freezing mists across the fields. Toby was curled tightly against his brother's lap, but Alfie knew he was awake.

'D'you want to see Anja?' he whispered.

Toby squirmed around, took his thumb out of his mouth and said, 'Yea, she coming?'

'She's in the forest. Do you want to go back and see her?'

'Now? I want to swim in the pool.'

'Not right now, but do you want to?'

Alfie felt Toby's agreement; it was a mixture of grunt and nod, with his thumb now firmly back in his mouth.

'Tomorrow night,' said Alfie, 'but you've got to be good and really loving for Mummy and Daddy today.'

The grunt was repeated. Alfie had never felt so sad, but he knew that they'd have to go back. He couldn't stay. He'd tried but didn't like it. Even if he could, Toby couldn't; he was too different. He felt torn: Mummy and Daddy?

*

In the forest, Anja smiled as she sat at the side of the waterfall pool, gently swishing the surface of the water with her bare feet. She soothed Alfie's worries as best she could and, closing her eyes, drew the memory of Toby's toddler scent into the back of her nostrils until it bathed her mind with pleasure. She slipped out of her dress and into the water.

Nearby, Aphrodite was watching from the cover of the bower. She sensed a tiny movement behind her.

'It's not over.'

'Hello, Maia, I didn't think it was.'

'Stay near and follow her.' The little fairy flew close, whispering gently in her ear, then was gone.

*

The next day passed slowly in the Lovetts' cottage; a day waiting for something to happen. Life ground to a halt. Peter hadn't returned to work, and no one went out. Helen did only basic chores, and the boys stayed close to their parents, or maybe it was the other way around. There were more phone calls and the vicar came to the door, to be politely but firmly turned away by Helen. The afternoon saw them all on the sofa, dozing in front of the fire, as if they hadn't slept the previous night, which all of them had, if fitfully.

No one noticed when afternoon became evening and they carried their sons up to bed, where they both slumped so deeply asleep that they could shower them with kisses without a stir from their angelic faces. Returning to the warmth of the sofa, they gently fell asleep in each other's arms.

*

When the church clock struck half past ten across the clear, freezing night, Anja and Pan reached the Great Forest side of the portal. Aphrodite followed at a distance and leant against a tree watching them. The portal was closed but waiting.

*

Alfie's eyes opened and he slid out of the bed he couldn't remember getting into. He quietly opened the drawer he knew his mother had put his clothes in and dressed. He took Toby's out and put them on the bed. Toby was watching him. Alfie beckoned him and within seconds his brother was pulling his on. They went downstairs without making a sound. A thin glow of light framed the closed lounge door. Alfie slowly opened it and peeked in. His parents were asleep on the sofa, the backs of their heads melded as one against the dull glow of the fading fire. He gently shut the door again.

'Can I give Mummy a kiss?' Toby asked. 'They won't know.'

Alfie nodded and opened the door just a few inches. A little dark shape squeezed through and a minute later slipped back out again. Opening the front door quietly took an age, but at last they stood on the threshold. Alfie put on the latch so that the door wouldn't slam and pulled it to. He took Toby's hand and they set off.

This time, there was no talk, but neither did they hurry. They weren't running away; they were going to meet Anja. Warily, they crept past the constable's small cottage and Alfie was so relieved when they had passed it that he forgot about the vicarage. And there, waiting for them by the small lynch gate, stood the vicar. He had slept badly since the return of the Lovett boys. He had been upstairs setting a small fire in his bedroom grate when something drew him to the window. Coming along the lane were the boys. Rushing downstairs and donning his overcoat, he was ready to intercept them.

'On our travels again?' said the vicar.

Alfie nodded.

'Isn't your brother cold, Alfie? You've both hardly anything on.'

311

'We don't get cold,' Alfie said, not caring anymore.

'Will you come in and talk with me first? If you do, I won't try to stop you,' the vicar lied. 'I need to understand.'

Alfie wanted to refuse, but the vicar was blocking their way and there was no hurry because it wasn't time anyway. The vicar herded them through the trellised gate, its frosted rose hibernating, dreaming of spring glory. They went inside and entered his cosy study through the first door on the left. The vicar sat in his chair and the boys stood. The small fire was dying, so he prodded it to life with a poker and added a couple of lumps of coke. He'd petitioned the diocese for central heating, but little ever changed in the village.

'So, where are you two going on such a frosty night? It's drawing close to midnight.'

Alfie was relaxed; everything was going to be fine.

'We have to go back.'

'Back where, Alfie? And why?'

'Because we have to.'

'To Anja?'

'Yes.'

'What is it like, Alfie, this other place? It is another place, isn't it? Is it like here?'

So Alfie told him: that it had no towns, no houses, and no roads; that it had vast forests and great never-ending downs and hills, rivers and oceans; that it was warm all the time in the forest and hot in the south, by the ocean.

The vicar listened in silence. When Alfie paused, he leant forward. 'How far away is it, Alfie?' he said.

Alfie grinned. 'We just have to go through the little wood by the churchyard, at the back, you know, where the fallow field is.'

The vicar's eyes widened with astonishment, as Alfie had hoped.

'Is Anja waiting for you?'

'She's there now.'

'On her own, in this other land?'

'Nothing can hurt Anja.' Alfie turned his head slightly, as if listening. 'Anyway, she's not on her own.'

'Someone's with her?' The vicar could not keep the excitement out of his voice.

'Who is it, Alfie, is it the policeman?'

Alfie looked at the vicar for a moment or two, deciding. Then he remembered his mother's reaction to the truth and grinned again, mischievously.

'What policeman? No, it's Pan.'

The vicar blanched, barely suppressing a groan.

'Do you know about him?' Alfie asked, gloating at the vicar's reaction. 'He's a bit scary, but he helped us. Anja loves him.'

The vicar's mind was spinning. He fought to collect his thoughts. He had asked and the child had told him. He wished with all his heart he hadn't brought them in, but it was too late.

The doorbell tinkled.

'Who could that be?' he exclaimed theatrically, grasping the sound like a lifebelt. 'I expect it's your father, looking for you.'

'No, it's not,' smiled Alfie. 'It's Anja.'

Toby clapped his hands.

Too late, the vicar remembered he had not closed the front door properly; he had just pushed it to. He stood up but couldn't gather his wits. Trepidation crawled up his spine, leaving a gnawing fear in his stomach. His knees were trembling, so he sat down again. They were all looking at the closed study door. He almost cried out when two light taps sounded.

Alfie looked at him. 'It's only Anja, she knows we're in here.'

The doorknob turned; the door opened.

Anja had decided to walk down to meet them, unsure of what exactly she was going to do. She'd asked Pan before she crossed the portal. He'd shaken his head and laughed. 'You'll know what to do,' was all he had said, walking away. 'I'll be at the camp.'

She passed through the portal just as the church clock struck, and looked back, smiling once, aware that her brothers had left the house.

Walking slowly across the field, her footsteps thawed the frosty grass and, reaching the vicarage gate, she sensed that they were inside. Her hand rested on the trellised arch, fingers brushing the cold entwining stems of rosewood. As she continued up the path, the frost melted from the thick stem and three small buds poked their heads out. By the time she reached the vicarage door, they'd blossomed and froze, grey-red in the moonlight.

Anja stood just inside the study. No one moved. She smiled and they all smiled back. She had decided to wear something special for the occasion; a gold-embroidered green dress and a thin circlet of gold studded with green emeralds shone against her dark tresses, the gold matching her eyes. The fire in the grate had begun to die down again; now its warmth was augmented by a gentle breeze and the subtle fragrances of summer. Her eyes met those of the vicar and her smile broadened.

'Hello, Vicar.'

The vicar couldn't reply. He whimpered and sank into his chair, unable to turn away from the golden eyes swallowing him. Everything faded and the room was gone. He was sitting facing her in the fallow field by the little wood behind the churchyard. Warm, dry grass tickled his legs and heavy bees droned by. The sun made him squint. He heard merry laughter, laughter that he knew well.

'Come on, Jones!' Someone was calling his name. Of course, his best pal Eames and the others, on their way to choir practice. Pulling up one constantly errant grey sock, he jumped up to join them. A forest fly tickled his nose. 'Come on, hurry up,' his friend repeated. 'Old Trembeth will be livid if we're late again.'

His sock slid slowly back down, and he ignored it. It was so hot. He wished he could run into the cool of the wood and climb his favourite tree. Lord, they were going to melt in those thick black cassocks. He paused for a moment. What was it he had been doing before Eames had called him? Yes, that was it, the girl. He didn't have much time for girls, but she'd been very pretty and he'd been about to ask her something, something very important, just on the edge of his memory.

'Vicar!' Alfie's voice was dragging him back. 'Vicar!'

He didn't want to listen; he'd be late for choir practice.

'Vicar, we're going now. Are you all right?'

The vicar's vacant eyes looked blearily around the room for support. He shook his head; the droning and faraway laughter was pulling him back. Then he saw what he'd been looking for: his bible in its usual place, secure, well thumbed in its soft black leather binding. He couldn't get his limbs to respond. Anja walked over to the desk, picked it up and placed it in his lap. He recoiled from her, trying to scream, and his mind withdrew to a place from which it would never return. Realising she had unwittingly done too much damage in the brief time she'd been there, she naïvely hoped that leaving might make things better.

As they left the study, Anja turned and softly called his name.

Deep inside his broken mind, the vicar clearly heard her. The horror and confusion faded. That girl didn't matter; they always unsettled him. His chums were still calling, and he could hear the choirmaster thumping away at the practice piano. Crikey! He was going to be late. Laughing, he tore up the path, the marbles he'd brought to win Eames' "trebbler" after choir practice glassily tinkling in his pocket. He stumbled and hopped as he tried to pull up his sock and avoid an old gravestone. Crumbs, it was *so* hot!

Anja retraced her steps back to the lane where her brothers were waiting.

'Is he all right?' Alfie asked.

'No, of course he's not. What did you have to go and tell him about Pan for?'

'It wasn't me. He was all right until you came in. One look at you and that was it.'

'I know, anyway, it's done now. Take Toby back to the forest. Wait by the portal, I'll be along later.'

Alfie was about to ask her why, but then he knew and for once did exactly as he was told without a murmur. Toby looked up at her with a sulky expression on his face.

She bent down and cuddled him, rubbing the tip of her nose against his.

'I won't be long. I think that I should see Mummy and Daddy, don't you?'

He brightened up. 'Can I come?'

'No, you've seen them, and I haven't. I won't be long.'

She watched as they walked off, before taking a deep breath and heading down the lane towards the house. As she walked, she thought about the disastrous visit to the vicarage. She'd discussed her intentions with Pan, and he'd warned her that she had very little control of her changes, and whilst her parents should be able to endure her presence, others would not.

'Hopefully, you will find it easier to control your mind when with them,' he reasoned, 'but I'm not sure, so be careful. Don't get angry or upset, keep composed.'

Now she understood, but when she thought about her parents, she could already feel emotion rising. She paused to compose herself. Approaching the little cottage, her throat tightened again. She opened the gate and waited for her breathing to slow, resting her hand on the frost-covered post, oblivious to the seasonal chaos her presence was causing.

She walked up the familiar path to the front door and was about to tap when she realised it wasn't closed, and pushed it open. As familiar smells she thought she'd forgotten hit her, she closed her eyes against the rush of memories welling up. Sensing her parents were in the lounge asleep, all doubt and apprehension dissipated.

Quietly, she entered the room. Her smile widened and she bit her lip as a tear trickled down her cheek. Her mother's head was snuggled into her father's shoulder. She stood in front of them, the dying fire behind her.

Peter Lovett woke but didn't open his eyes, smelling the warmth and closeness of Helen's face, not wanting to disturb the even, soft breathing that told him she was still asleep. He allowed himself to drift back into the warm world of memories of their early married life when Anja had still been a baby; pushing her proudly through the village in the new pram, with the flimsy shade up to protect her from the sun, knowing that as soon as he lowered it, her gaze would be constantly on him.

He felt his wife stir and kissed her on her brow, resting below his stubbly cheek. He still didn't want to open his eyes and murmured something unintelligible to her. She stretched slightly and turned her lips up to his. He sensed they were not alone and, without opening his eyes, whispered, 'I think Toby's crept down and is watching us.'

27

Peter slowly raised one eyelid. Helen felt his sudden start and she opened her eyes and gasped.

'Sorry, you look so lovely.' Anja couldn't stop the tears trickling down her cheeks.

They couldn't move. Peter recalled Alfie's words, '*You should see her, Daddy. She's so beautiful, like a forest princess,*' but nothing could have prepared him for the sight of his daughter standing there.

'Are you both all right, I mean, do you feel all right?'

'Oh, Anja, of course we do,' he said. 'We're so, so pleased to see you. Why did you wait? We've missed you so much. Oh God, come here and let me feel that it's really you.'

She perched primly on his knee, kissed her mother first and then her father, laughing with happiness.

'Where did you get those clothes and things, Anja?' her mother asked, finding her voice at last. 'That's real gold.'

'I've got lots of wonderful things. Alfie is always

bringing me more, and P… some of the others give me beautiful things as well.'

'I can't believe it, Anja,' her father said. 'I can hardly think straight, my mind is spinning, and I'm so warm, it's so hot.'

'That's me, Daddy. It's why I didn't come before.' Anja caught herself lying a little. 'If it starts to affect you too much, I'll have to go, but I'm trying not to make it happen.'

'No, don't, it's all right. We understand, don't we?' He turned to his wife for support.

'No we don't really understand, Anja,' she said. 'Not yet, but it doesn't matter, nothing matters except that you're here.'

Her mother brushed her hand against Anja's cheek. Then she slid her hands down her daughter's body to make sure she was real.

'Is this all that you're wearing? You'll freeze.' Her hands slid down over her hips. 'Just that dress? Oh, Anja!'

Anja giggled involuntarily. It was almost as if she hadn't been away; it was so lovely to hear her mother chide her, especially like that.

'It's really warm where we live now, it's always summer, and I don't feel the cold here. None of us do.'

The fire was almost dead in the grate, yet the room was comfortably warm and smelt of fragrant woods and shaded leaf mould, dry seeding grass and bracken humming with insects. They were hot and drowsy. Anja stood up and walked back towards the fireplace.

'Is that better?' she asked. 'I'm really trying to control myself.'

'You *are* real, Anja, aren't you, you really are here?' said Peter. 'This feels dreamlike.'

'I'm doing that, Daddy. I'm a bit changed, we all are. Otherwise, we wouldn't have survived. It's so wonderful there, but it's different, we all had to change a bit.'

'A bit?'

'We had to become part of it, it's not like here. Everything is sort of more alive. Alfie is… well, he's changed in another way.'

'And Toby, too?' her mother asked.

'Yes, that's why we went, to find Toby. We fell asleep and when we woke up, he was gone. The front door was open. We followed him and then we were there, in the other place. It took us such a long time to find him and we travelled hundreds and hundreds of miles, and when we did, he was really ill. Aphrodite saved him, but she had to change him a little bit, to save him.'

Again, her mother emphasised the question. 'Just a little bit?'

'What do you mean?' Peter wondered why she was being so insistent.

'I *know*, Anja, I'm his mummy. He can't hide anything from me, he's too young. I saw him in the bath. Alfie tried to hide it from me, bless him.'

'It was the only way, Mummy. He was dying, you should have seen him.'

Peter felt his daughter's anxiety rising and his head began to spin.

'Anja, it's all right, but whatever it is you're doing, please stop or I won't be able to think,' he said.

321

Anja winced and took a second or so to calm herself. 'I'm sorry, is that better?'

Her father smiled and nodded.

'It isn't a problem, Anja,' he said. 'Whatever happened has happened, and we have to accept it. You, Alfie and Toby being alive is all that matters. We thought we'd lost all of you. If you had to change to stay alive, well, we must accept that, mustn't we?'

He gave his wife a "drop the subject" look.

Anja took a deep breath. 'We can't stay here, Daddy.'

'We know, Anja.'

'Don't you want us to?'

'More than anything, darling. But anyone can see that Alfie and Toby are different, they can't hide it. We've already made excuses and people want to come, government people, and they'll take you all away from us.'

Anja shook her head. 'I could stop them, Daddy. They couldn't do anything if I didn't want them to.'

'Anja, it wouldn't work, would it? We *do* understand.'

'Alfie and Toby have already gone.'

At once, she regretted being so abrupt, seeing disappointment cloud their faces.

'We'd have liked to have said goodbye, Anja.'

'I'm sorry, I didn't mean it to sound like that. Alfie didn't know what else to do, then I just wanted to see you again. I've missed you so much, and it was all my fault. I lost Toby.'

'No.' Her father reached his hand out to touch hers. 'If it's anyone's fault, it's ours. We left you alone, Anja, *we left you alone.* It's not your fault and never will be, do you understand?'

Anja didn't get the chance to reply. Her mother had picked up on something Anja had said. 'Who's Aphrodite, Anja?' Her father sighed.

How do I get out of this one? Anja thought. 'She's someone who helped us find and rescue Toby,' she said. 'She lives by a great river.'

'Did she make Toby like that?'

'She had to, she's very powerful. She looks after the rivers and all the creatures that live in them. She can change as well.'

'I do recognise her name, Anja. I think almost everyone would, from ancient times. It's the name of a Greek goddess.'

'That's who she is, Mummy, but she isn't a god. People just thought they were, a long time ago. They didn't belong here and left. The Land, where we…' she didn't want to say live '…it changes you. It's what's happened to me, and Alfie and Toby.'

'And what's the name of the other one that helped you? Alfie let it slip out.'

'Pan. I suppose you've heard of him as well?'

'Yes, of course I have. And who do you stay with?'

'Pan mostly, he looks after the forests. He helped us when we first got there. But I sometimes stay with Aphrodite as well. She has a real home.'

'Did he change you, Anja?'

'No, the Land changed me. Alfie and Toby were changed by others, but I was changed by the Land. That's why I am… well, like this.'

323

'Your Pan has a reputation, you know, Anja. There are lots of myths about him and the sort of creature he is. I hope that he is proper, Anja.'

Anja shrugged and her brow creased. 'Proper?'

'You know what I mean, young lady,' her mother said. 'Does Alfie stay with him as well?'

'Sometimes, but Alfie wanders on his own mostly. He's happier in the groves on the Downs or just walking in the woods. He's not so close to Pan.'

Her parents were looking at her sceptically.

'It's different, Daddy, it's not the same as here. Anyway, it happened, and we've tried coming back, but it hasn't worked.'

Her parents exchanged a look, an unfathomably sad look. Her father swallowed and smiled. 'Sit between us for a moment, Anja,' he said, 'just so that we can share you for a little while.'

Anja squeezed in between them. Initially, her nearness threatened to overpower their senses, but after a second or so they both leant against her and her mother kissed her cheek, and her father kissed the top of her head. She turned from one to the other and kissed them both lightly on their cheeks. All three cuddled together. Anja could never remember this ever happening before. Her father had always been kind but rather strict. As she'd begun to grow up, she realised that he showed affection with his eyes rather than words, but she could only remember kissing him, not him kissing her.

'We lost you all, Anja,' he whispered, 'all at once. Can you imagine how that was? We didn't know what had happened to you. A young policeman disappeared at the same time and he was blamed. We had nothing left, me and Mummy just going through the motions of living. Then, you all come back, and now you're all leaving again.'

Her mother kissed her again. 'It's wonderful, Anja, just to know that you're all alive and well, just to see all of your beautiful faces again, but it's so cruel. We do understand that you can't stay, but it's like you don't belong to us anymore.'

'We do, you're still our mummy and daddy. Pan and Aphrodite and everything, they are part of something else. You're still my parents, I love you more than anything. We will come and see you again.'

A distant look came into her eyes; both parents noticed it.

'I have to go now.'

'Can we come with you, Anja?'

She shrugged. 'I don't think so. The Land isn't like that, it doesn't really like humans. It accepted us because of me, it wanted me. That's what Aphrodite thinks. I daren't just take you. I don't know what will happen.'

She rose, facing them.

'I *will* come and see you, I promise, and Alfie and Toby will, too.'

They shared a long, silent moment after her hollow assurance. She turned and went to the door.

'Bye,' she said, unable to think what else to do as she desperately tried to control the emotions threatening to engulf her. They didn't hear the front door close.

Peter and Helen hadn't left the settee since the moment they'd woke to find her there. It had all been too quick and like a dream. Helen's head fell into her hands. 'I can't go through it again,' she said quietly.

Peter tried to comfort her, but he felt the same. She looked tearfully up at him. 'What are we going to do?' she asked, and saw the answer deep in his eyes. Time no longer registered as they silently comforted each other.

A firm knock echoed from the front door, then two more. They exchanged startled looks, for a second; *had the children come back?* No, more likely the authorities had decided to not wait until the morning. Sometimes, things were better conducted in the dark, quiet hours, away from public scrutiny. Had they caught Anja?

A single knock again. Peter stood up and walked firmly to answer it. Helen followed. The door, still on the latch, had been pushed open. The chill suddenly hit them.

A woman stood on the doorstep, her face shrouded in the deep hood of a cloak. Without waiting to be invited, she stepped forward, eased them to one side and entered. As she brushed past them and went into the living room, she pushed the hood back and it fell to her shoulders. She stood by the now dead fire, in the same spot Anja had so recently vacated, and waited as they entered and sat back on the settee.

Peter and Helen looked at the young woman. Her face was mesmerisingly beautiful, her eyes gorgeous pools of turquoise.

'I haven't been back for a long time,' she said breezily. 'I promised myself not to return openly, but I have, for Anja.'

The woman's presence was overpowering, more so than they'd felt when Anja had been there, and they knew that she was controlling its effect on them. They also realised who she must be.

She looked at Helen. 'She is *so* like you, I would have known immediately. You're quite as beautiful.'

'Why are you here?' Helen asked calmly. 'Our children have gone.'

'Yes, I waited until Anja left. I didn't want her to see or sense me. I am Aphrodite, I have tried to help and support your children.'

'Yes, Anja mentioned.'

'This land still stirs powerful memories within me.'

'What do you want?' Peter asked, his voice not cold, but weary.

'I've come for you. There's nothing left here, is there? You may come and take your chance in the Land, but we must go now.'

'Anja said we couldn't. Why you and not her, will we be with them?'

'You'll be in the Land, which is where they are, and not here, where they're not. I am not here to answer all your questions. Either you come or don't.'

'She said your land doesn't like humans'

Aphrodite sighed. 'If you wish to come, it must be now. No matter what Anja promised, they can never be here with you. But you know that, and there is nothing left for you here.'

Helen began to protest, but Peter shushed her.

'All right, we'll come. You knew what we were thinking?'

Aphrodite nodded. 'Anja would sense if anything happened and never forgive herself.'

'We can't just leave like this, we have to pack,' Helen protested.

'There's no need, is there?' Peter said.

'No, you need nothing.' Then Aphrodite turned, expecting them to follow.

'Wait, it's so cold, we need our coats,' said Helen.

Peter took her hand. 'Come on, we don't need anything.'

The small group walked up the path, leaving the door gaping wide, and turned through the gate and on up the lane, towards the church. As they passed the vicarage, they briefly noticed the light still on in the study where the vicar sat, rocking mindlessly in front of the dead fire. He was hot from the summer sun and filled with the limitless energy a small boy has playing happily in the wood behind the churchyard.

Back at the little house, a chill began to creep into the corners of every room, the fire a warm memory. A grey moonlit silence that would never lift settled behind the sad windows that would always look for its family, the six lives that had left it forever.

THE LAND
BOOK TWO

'That which cleans man's dirty slate'

The story continues…

No species shall destroy the balance.

For the first time in my eternal existence a particle of me has developed empathy; a fondness. Soon the girl must take on the task. I am not concerned for her, she survived the creature, although it was merely a symptom of the problem. However her power, despite already beyond anything I intended, is still nascent. She lacks control, and is not ready, but the threat is imminent. Now that everyone she loves is with me she will take on the task with the single-mindedness of a child, and holding the unswerving belief that what she is doing is right, will not be deterred by consequences. She must go to her birth land and restore the balance. My other servants can help but must not influence or impede her intention; they harbour too much remorse, too many memories. She has been tested. She *will* do what must be done.

Adore her; her beauty, charm, her innocence, but always, always, fear her.

This book is printed on paper from sustainable sources managed under the Forest Stewardship Council (FSC) scheme.

It has been printed in the UK to reduce transportation miles and their impact upon the environment.

For every new title that Matador publishes, we plant a tree to offset CO_2, partnering with the More Trees scheme.

For more about how Matador offsets its environmental impact, see www.troubador.co.uk/about/